SECURITY CONSULTANTS INTERNATIONAL *— 'The Workshop', as it is known-offers to provide 'highly trained personnel for the performance of any security, investigatory or quazi-military task' that its employers might require.*

The brain child of Victor Kaplan — a retired S.A.S. major — the Workshop's duties over the past 10 years have ranged from supplying bodyguards for African Heads of State to recruiting mercenaries for South American republics. All its 'operatives' work free-lance. They are usually ex-army: hard men playing a dangerous game; soldiers of fortune, unable to settle into civilian life after their military experiences. They are assisted by the Workshop's worldwide network of contacts, by its extensive system of records and by the infallible memory of Cpl. Smedley, Kaplan's only full-time assistant.

Only the fact that the Government knows S.C.I. will not undertake assignments to British interests allows the Workshop to continue its operations, from an unprepossessing office off Railston Road in Brixton, London. There have even been occasions when the Government itself has found it useful to use S.C.I. instead of its usual security units.

Passport Thrillers *will document some of the Workshop's more unusual assignments, and each title in the series will be located in a different holiday resort.*

DEATH ON DELIVERY

"Funny it should have happened there — a place like Torremolinos. Sun, sea and sangria; the clink of raised glasses over the murmur of holiday laughter; the evening breeze coming off the sea, warm with the memory of Africa. But for a few weeks last summer it showed another face: an evil face...a killing face. I know. I was part of it."

The task is simply to deliver a sealed brief-case to a retired rock-star in Torremolinos, but even before Frank Rogers sets out things start to go wrong...

Lord knows what's inside the damned case, but whatever it is there's a lot of people interested; and interested enough to stop at nothing to find out.

Death on Delivery

by E.L. Sloan

Messenger Books Passport Series

First published in Great Britain in 1984
by MESSENGER BOOKS LIMITED,
19 Silver Street, Bury, Lancashire.

Edited by Maclean Dubois (Writers & Agents)
10 Rutland Square, Edinburgh.

Printed in Great Britain

ISBN 0 947651 20 9

PART ONE: THE WORKSHOP

PART TWO: A TANGLED WEB

PART THREE: PORTIONS AND PARCELS

PART FOUR: THROUGH A GLASS DARKLY

PART ONE: THE WORKSHOP

"AN ART CAN ONLY BE LEARNED IN THE WORKSHOP OF THOSE WHO ARE WINNING THEIR BREAD BY IT"

Samuel Butler: "Erewhon"

FUNNY it should have happened there — a place like Torremolinos. Sun, sea and sangria; the clink of raised glasses over the murmur of holiday laughter; the evening breeze coming off the sea, warm with the memory of Africa. But for a few weeks last summer it showed another face: an evil face . . . a killing face. I know. I was there. I was part of it.

It would be easy, Kaplan said. A simple job lasting two or three days at most. When he told me what it was, I was forced to agree. Deliver a package to Spain, make the most of whatever time and expense money I had left, then catch a flight home. As he said, easy. A month later I was still there, playing pig-in-the-middle with the Mafia, the KGB and various other interested parties, reliving the best forgotten nightmares of another time and another place, up to my sunburned neck in betrayal and blackmail . . . and dead bodies. Yes, indeed: there was an embarrassing amount of those. Even now it's all over I don't fully understand where all the characters fitted into the drama. Perhaps telling the story will help . . .

But we must start at the beginning. The name's Rogers: Frank Rogers. 'Ginger' to my friends. A somewhat obvious nickname, but I'd probably have got stuck with it even if my surname had been Smith or Jones. I could always have dyed my hair black, I suppose . . . or green, or purple, as seems to be the fashion nowadays . . . but I've become quite attached to my mop of red curls over the past thirty-two years and whatever I do to the barnet cannot disguise the freckles that came in the same package.

I'm a Bermondsey boy, myself. First outpost of civilisation south of the river — or *sarfaleriva* as they say in my neck of the woods. I never knew my dad. 'Killed in the war he was, dear', my old mum used to say. Exactly which war she never did specify, but I grew up under the assumption that it must have been the last big one. By the time I was old enough to realise that this would have involved a gestation period of some seven years, I was also old enough to know that to dig any further would be unwise and probably pointless.

We had a picture of him, though. A gilt framed photograph, up on the mantelpiece. Dark good looks, a moustache on his lip, a medal on his chest and three stripes on his arm. Maybe it was that old photograph that first encouraged me to think seriously about a military career for myself; keeping up the family tradition, as it were. Joining up seemed the natural thing to do at the time and, once I was in, I loved it. Every minute of it. I've got no regrets even now; a year after they kicked me out.

It was my fault, so I can't bear any grudges. I served twelve years in all, going up and down the minor ranks like a yo-yo until settling on Sergeant for the best part of the last three. I realise I could have done better, but I've always had a problem with my size ten mouth. 'Incurably insubordinate' was how my CO described me, and I guess that just about says it all.

He was a decent bloke, though, Colonel Howard. Laying out the Sergeant-Major at a Regimental knees-up turned out to be the last straw as far as the Army was concerned, but the Colonel made my going as painless as possible. Even took the trouble of looking me up a few months ago and put me in touch with Major Kaplan. That's where this story really begins. That's how I got involved with The Workshop; *Security Cosultants International'* as it says on the brass plate outside Kaplan's office. The job he offered me sounded a good deal more stimulating than fitting exhaust pipes at my local garage so, quite naturally, I jumped at it.

He's not a bad bloke, either. Major Kaplan, that is. A bit crusty at times, but who wouldn't be with the likes of me on the payroll?

He knows his business inside out, too, and always plays it fair and square. You have to respect a bloke like that. I call him 'Chief', which he pretends not to like. His reactions vary between amused tolerance and the blankest stare, and they're a good indication of the mood he's in. Useful that, sometimes.

And he certainly appeared to be in the very best of spirits when I reported to the office, as ordered, at nine o'clock that Tuesday morning. The same good humour appeared to have drifted through to the outer office and even ex-corporal Smedley smiled as he saw me coming out of the lift. At least he did his best, a sort of twitch near the corners of his mouth.

"Morning, Sergeant" he said chirpily. "Lovely day, isn't it? The Major's expecting you. Go right in."

All this left me somewhat nonplussed, as all I usually get from Smedley is an irritated grunt and a finger pointing to one of the hard, upright chairs in the Workshop's outer office. It was not long, however, before I realised what lay behind this uncustomary bonhomie: the imminent departure of the Chief for the first holiday he had allowed himself in years. This was going to be a totally new experience for Smedley too, and he was looking forward to being in temporary control with obvious relish.

Still, it made a nice change, whatever the reason. And I must own up to feeling pretty good that morning myself, the July sunshine thawing me out after a week under canvas in Iceland testing a new material for thermal underwear which didn't work.

Kaplan had promised me variety in this job and, although I'd been with The Workshop for little over a month, he'd certainly proved a man of his word. Most of my first week had been spent shadowing Harry Sanders around Benidorm*, the second watching my bodily extremities turn blue in the full fury of an Arctic wind. And, as I strolled along Railton Road on my way to the office that morning, I couldn't help wondering, perhaps a trifle warily, what he could possibly have up his sleeve for the third.

The beauty of working for an outfit like The Workshop was that

* See Messenger Books 'Prodigal Gun' by E.L. Sloane.

anything could happen and, if my limited experience of the set-up so far was anything to go by, usually did. Kaplan had made it very clear when I joined that Security Consultants International would never take on an operation that was downright illegal but, as he so succinctly put it,". . . there are an awful lot of grey areas in between, old man!" Providing I could keep myself all in one piece, the job certainly had plenty to offer — reasonable money, the chance for a bit of adventure, foreign assignments taking me to sunnier climes and, remembering the last few days stranded in the Arctic wastes, the occasional wintry one as well. So, with not the foggiest notion of what could be in store for me this time, I knocked on the boss's door.

I did not have to wait long to find out. He was standing in front of his desk as I entered his office, a floppy canvas hat pulled low over his eyes, a sleeveless anorak zipped up to his chin, his legs disappearing into a pair of thigh-length rubber waders.

"See what I mean, George?' he said to the no less startlingly attired man who was sipping coffee in an easy chair on the far side of the room." Once mastered, never forgotten. Keep the elbow locked and give it a flick of the wrist as it comes down . . ."

Now, I've never been a great one for fishing myself, but even I could see he'd got it all wrong. His casting arm certainly wasn't what it was, assuming it had ever been anything in the first place. His action reminded me not so much of Walton's *Compleat Angler* as Walt Disney's *Return of Zorro*. Not my place to say anything, though. Especially with the rod still quivering in his hand, rapidly taking on the aspect of a potentially lethal weapon.

Like many officer types of what I like to think of as the 'old school' Kaplan cultivated a somewhat aloof and distracted air, and very much enjoyed playing the role of a benevolent despot; a military edition of the mythical 'tart with a heart', if you get my drift. One of his most infuriating little ploys was to totally ignore you when you first came into a room. You could enter on the back of a roaring bull elephant and the Chief would do more than raise a practised eyebrow before returning to whatever he had been doing and keep you waiting for the moment he considered most propitious to formally acknowledge your prescence. Irritating rather than downright rude. I had become well accustomed to such mannerisms after twelve years of Army life in the lower ranks, and I now accepted these little peculiarities as pretty much par for the course.

"Ah . . . there you are, Rogers," he said at last, laying the fishing rod across his desk. He inclined his head towards his guest and continued: "I'd like you to meet Sir George Lorimer. George . . .? This is the chap I was telling you about. Frank Rogers . . . one of my most reliable and experienced men!"

I tried to appear flattered rather than flabbergasted, and I must have made a pretty good job of it as Sir George did no more than grunt a greeting and return to his coffee. With a surreptitious wink in my direction, Kaplan motioned me to a chair and resumed: "We're off to the Highlands for a few days' break. Fishing holiday actually . . ."

Oh, really? I thought. I'd never have guessed . . .

". . . and Sir George has been kind enough to pass a little business our way which should keep you out of mischief during my absence. A simple little courier's job, collecting a package from London Airport and delivering it to an address near Torremolinos. Two or three days work at the most. It all sounded pretty straightforward when Sir George explained what was involved, so I immediately thought of you . . ."

"Thanks, Chief," I replied with a neutral smile, not quite sure how I should take that last remark. "It certainly sounds a lot more inviting than another week in Iceland!"

I knew straightaway I'd said the wrong thing. Kaplan's face darkened and he sighed heavily. "Hmm . . . yes. Iceland. I'd almost forgotten about that. I've been reading your report and . . . well, there's a couple of points I'd like a word with you about before I leave . . ."

Right on cue, Sir George rose from his chair and coughed pointedly.

"I'll leave you to it, Victor," he said, exchanging his waders for a pair of canvas casuals and gathering together their anglers' accoutrements as he moved towards the door. "I'll get these loaded in the car and meet you outside in ten minutes."

"Nice meeting you . . . er . . ."

"Rogers," I reminded him.

"Yes . . . quite. Ten minutes then, Victor. The sooner we're on the road the better!"

The dying remnants of Kaplan's good mood lingered on after Sir George had left, which was just as well as he was about to give me a rocket. He leafed through the report I'd handed in on my return from Iceland and a series of questionnaires I'd been obliged to fill in on the effectiveness of what our clients had termed: 'A Revolution in Attitude towards Thermal Underwear,' then threw them back on his desk with ill-disguised disgust.

"In view of the fee we received for this assignment, Rogers, I think you could have done better than this!"

"I answered all their questions!" I pointed out in defence.

"You answered *some* of their questions, to be strictly accurate. The reports for the first four days are alright, but I really do think you'd have done better on the last three to have ticked the box marked 'Inadequate', rather than putting a line through each page and writing 'BLOODY USELESS!' all over it!"

"If you wish to continue your career with us, Rogers," he continued in his best Commanding Officer's voice, "you'd be well advised to remember that we have a certain reputation to maintain. And that, without putting too fine a point on it, is for thorough professionalism in everything we do!

"Now you've already proved yourself to be more than effective in a tight corner, pulling Harry Sanders out of that rather ugly business in Benidorm, but I run a tight ship here and procedure must be followed to the letter. That's why we've managed to succeed in a very competitive business, and without it we'd soon find ourselves in Dicky's Meadow and you'd be back selling double glazing or whatever you were doing before you joined us.

"Not a very appealing thought, is it?"

He had a point, and one I was not slow to acknowledge with a hang-dog expression and a carefully constructed smile of apology. In my defence, I thought it only fair to point out that when you're fighting off the ravages of frostbite and hypothermia on top of a mountain in the Arctic Circle, the term 'Inadequate' doesn't exactly come off the page as a reasonable response. This he accepted, albeit grudingly, then issued a final warning to watch my 'P's' and 'Q's' in the future before hurrying on to the business at hand.

"The package in question will be coming in via bank courier, on a flight from Zurich to Heathrow this afternoon," he informed me, taking a foolscap envelope from the top drawer of his desk and passing it across." You'll find the flight details and courier's name in there. Also your tickets to Malaga. They're open ended, just in case you experience any difficuly making delivery . . . though what could get in the way of a simple little job like this, I can't begin to imagine!

"The recipient's name and address in Torremolinos are in the envelope too. And remember this, Rogers. You're to deliver this package in person, to him . . . . and him only! Those are our instructions and I want them carried out to the letter. Clear?"

With a nod, I confirmed that indeed it was, then asked: "Seems a bit strange to fly it into London first, don't you think? I mean, why doesn't the courier take it direct to Spain himself?"

"Haven't the foggiest," Kaplan replied with a shrug of the shoulders. "But ours is not to reason why, and all that. It's none of our business."

"Any idea what's in the package?"

"As I've just said, Rogers, it's not our business to know. But it won't be anything . . . how can I put it? . . . *shady*, if that's what you're worried about. Not with Sir George involved . . ."

"Of course not!" I gushed in agreement. "Perish the thought!"

A scowl began to form on his face but got no further than a shadow as his attention was diverted by the impatient blast of a car horn, directly below the window. Collecting what was left of the luggage, he paused in the doorway to add: "You can collect your expenses from Smedley. I'm giving you five hundred, just in case . . . but I expect receipts for every single penny, and at least four hundred of that back! And Rogers . . .?"

"Yes, Chief?"

"Don't cock it up, there's a good chap!"

I feigned a cough, rushing a hand to my mouth to cover the involuntary grin which sprang immediately to my lips. Whatever I'd been expecting in the form of a 'play up and play the game' speech to send me on my way, I couldn't help feeling that 'don't cock it up' lacked that certain something in terms of morale boosting, positive encouragement. Still, if the job was as straightforward as the Chief had made out, then there seemed little possibility of anything getting in the way of my fulfilling his finial order to the letter — no matter how negative the phase he had employed to issue it.

On my first little sortie to Spain, I discovered that I really quite liked the place. The operation itself had been a bit of a nightmare, with the new boy Frank Rogers having to baby sit another operative who had gone off the deep end trying to settle an old score with a particularly unsavoury Turk. But that's another story...

I was there for less than a week but, even in that short time, I could see that Spain as a holiday haven had a hell of a lot going for it and why the millions continue to flock there, year after year , in search of the sun; perfect weather, ridiculously cheap booze, an endless parade of long legged lovelies baring all but the merest fraction of their deeply tanned bodies and, despite popular myth, not a single bar anywhere which sold Watney's Red Barrel. All that considered, it was perfectly understandable that Burton should have chosen the Costa del Sol to establish his retirement retreat. But what a pompous old codger like Sir George Lorimer could possibly have to do this former wild man of rock I couldn't even begin to imagine.

I watched him drive away in Sir George's BMW, then helped myself to a glass of his best whisky and settled down to examine the contents of the envelope. When I saw who I was to deliver this mysterious package to, I almost took a bite out of the glass. Mikki Burton . . . well, just fancy that! It had to be THE Mikki Burton, not any old run-of-the-mill M. Burton Esq., the spelling of his first name gave that much away. Lead singer with The Rats, and a face that decorated many a teenager's bedroom wall through the sixties and early seventies. Including mine, I have to admit. This looked like it was going to be fun . . .

And then the penny dropped. The connection was made. There had been something familiar about the name Lorimer, although I hadn't been able to quite put my finger on it. Not universally recognised for his prowess with a fishing rod, he was better known as the chairman of BMI, Britain's foremost electronics and leisure conglomerate, a division of which included Mammoth Records. And, if my memory of the hairy elephant logo spinning round on my turnable served me correctly, that had been . . . and still was, as far as I knew . . . The Rats' record label. Not that there was a band called The Rats anymore. Everyone knew that. John, Freddy and Boz . . . all dead. Rock n' roll casualties, I think the phrase is. There was just Burton left now: the sole survivor . . .

I polished off the whisky with a flourish, eagerly looking forward to the next few days, all memories of Iceland quickly forgotten. Carefully wiping the glass, I replaced it on its exact spot in Kaplan's cocktail cabinet. No point in taking any chances, even when the boss was away. I didn't bother to alter the mark on the whisky bottle, though. I was sure Smedley would be helping himself with the Chief away, so I thought it better to leave the execution of that little deception to him.

Returning to the outer office, I collected my expenses from Smedley, and signed my name (in triplicate, of course), in his legendary 'Book of Chits'. Smedley set great store by this, regarding the signatures therein with much the same nostalgic longing other people reserve for the autographs of movie stars. The running joke around the office was that it would go with him to the grave, his mortal remains duly despatched with the name of the undertaker scrawled across the final page.

"Off to Spain then, are we?" he grinned, carefully perusing my signature before locking the book away in a drawer of his desk.

"Well, I am, Corp.. Don't know about you . . ."

He chuckled, quite unnecessarily and far too long. Smedley wasn't very good at that sort of thing and the strain was beginning to show. If he carried on smiling like that, I reasoned, he'd probably end up with lockjaw, so I decided to do us both a favour and left.

* * *

Heathrow Airport was like Piccadilly Underground on a Friday evening; very hot, very crowded, and not a smile to be found anywhere. All was chaos and confusion: happy holidaymakers barged, pushed and elbowed their way into check-in queues, wielding their baggage like battering rams and hurling abuse at anyone within earshot wearing a uniform; bawling kids squatted on suitcases, unappeased by parents' promises of imminent departure or yet another packet of crisps.

To make matters worse, I was nearly half an hour late. The motorway had been solid from Chiswick to Heston and, not over fond of traffic jams, my old Mini had decided to take this one personally. Steam spouted from either side of the bonnet and the dashboard was studded with angry flashing lights. I had no choice but to pull over and let it cool down, and since the temperature outside was well into the eighties I knew that would take time.

As I sat there, staring impotently at the traffic plodding past me, I made yet another solemn promise to get myself a more reliable form of transport. The Mini and I had fallen out before — many, many times before — and this was the final straw. As if possessed of a mind of its own, it always contrived to pick the worst possible moment to go sulky on me; a heavy date, a job interview I couldn't afford to miss, an urgent appointment with a bank courier from Switzerland on a limited stop-over at Heathrow. With its rust nibbled bonnet, its buckled bumpers and a sticker in the back window which looked forward to the World Cup Championship of 1966, this clapped out old Mini of mine would just have to go.

Perhaps when this job was over — if it ever got started, that is I might twist Kaplan's arm into advancing me a grand or two to purchase something more suited to a man in my peculiar position; a James Bond DB-5 with machine guns in its wheels, a Churchill tank. . .anything!

But the minutes ticked inexorably away, and by the time the engine was rested enough to start again I had began to panic. The traffic alongside was now at a complete standstill, so there was nothing else for it but to set off at speed along the emergency lane, returning the sneers of the stationary drivers on my right with a regal wave.

As luck would have it, every other car on the road that day must have been in a vastly superior condition to mine as there was no sign of any other breakdowns blocking the hard shoulder, enabling me to exit at the next junction and make rapid progress along the more minor roads.

Having finally left the Mini on the top level of the airport multi-storey car park, I followed the signposts to Terminal II and pushed my way through the wall-to-wall bodies in the general direction of the Information Desk. He was already there, standing out like a shoulder of ham at a Bar-Mitzvah with his heavy raincoat, his Alpine hat and a briefcase cuffed securely to his wrist.

"Herr Grüber?" I checked, introducing myself and extending my hand.

He accepted it and shook it firmly, brushing all apologies for my late arrival aside with a generous smile that was prompted more by relief, I suspected, than courtesy. His practised eyes darted quickly over the relevant parts of my I.D. and then, apparently satisfied, he said: "I am glad to meet with you, Herr Rogers. My return flight, she has already been called."

"Is that it?" I asked, indicating the briefcase and wasting no further time on an explanation of the mechanical shortcomings of a twelve year old Mini.

"Ja! Ja!" he answered, freeing the case and handing it across.

It had been Customs sealed, I noticed, as was the envelope

containing the accompanying documentation, duly addressed to the receiving authority at my point of entry in Spain. Grüber further pointed out that it was combination locked, the pre-set sequence of digits required to release the tumblers having already been relayed to Burton himself.

"Do *you* know what's in it, Herr Grüber" I ventured, giving the briefcase an exploratory shake like a curious child investigating an intriguing package at Christmas.

Gruber flashed me the look of an irate bank clerk who had just been asked for fifty pounds worth of halfpenny pieces. Everything about him spoke of the precision and minute detail that had elevated the Swiss to the position of bankers to the rest of the world. Nothing wrong with that, of course: seeing how well they've done by it, we could well do with a bit more of that kind of attitude over here.

I shook the case again, then looked up to plead: "Come on, Gruber — you must have some idea what's in it! Cocaine, perhaps? Explosives? Feeelthy pictures. . .?"

"No, my friend," he replied with a wry grin. "And I would not tell you if I did. We Swiss have a tradition in such things.

"Also I ask you not to have such curiosity. And please! .. . do not shake it so. We are using this type of case since many years now. My Bank had it specially made by Hofstedder of Zurich. It has been fitted with . . ."

He broke off, his sales pitch interrupted by the sound of his name being broadcast over the public address system, together with the urgent plea that he report immediately to the departure gate where his flight was about to leave.

"I must go, Herr Rogers," he said, pumping my hand furiously.

"What was that you were saying about the case?" I asked, scampering after him as he jostled through the crowd.

"Nothing," he called back over his shoulder, "It is nothing, It will not concern you . . ." And then I lost sight of him, swallowed up by the hordes of travellers folding back across his wake..

If there's one thing guaranteed to get the Rogers' nose

twitching, it's being told that this, that or the other 'doesn't concern me'! As if the contents of the case were not mystery enough, it appeared that there was some extraordinary quality possessed by the case itself. Nothing I could do about it now, though. Not with Grüber already on his way back to Zurich. He had said it wouldn't be a problem, and I had to take him at his word. Annoying, though; not knowing. I gave the case a final once over and could find nothing the least bit odd, so I shrugged my shoulders and headed back to the car.

Outside the air smelled sweet after the air conditioned fug of the Terminal building, filled though it was with the roar of taxi-ing jets and the smell of car exhausts. I strolled back towards the car park, enjoying the sunshine, whistling cheerfully, the briefcase swinging in my hand with its open hand-cuff clattering merrily against its side.

So far, so good, I concluded. Very little do do now but decide what colour of swimming trunks I'd take to Torremolinos, and how best to conduct myself in the presence of the legend I was so shortly to meet. For a fleeting moment, I even considered taking along a couple of my old Rats' albums for him to sign. After all, I could always say they were for my kid sister. . .no; far too corny, and any sister old enough to have bought their albums would be on the wrong side of thirty by now. Or my Auntie Rita in Newport Pagnell? No; far too insulting. Perhaps I should own up and admit that they were really for me? Oh no — definitely not! Far too uncool! Nothing else for it then, but to hope for an autographed polaroid of me and the great man shaking hands to impress the regulars at my local pub. Maybe not, thinking it over: as far as they were concerned, I made my pennies as a diving equipment consultant, and explaining away the presence of a retired rock n' roll singer on an oil platform in the middle of the North Sea could well turn out to be a little on the tricky side . . .

It was then that things started to go wrong. As I reached the second level of the car park, I heard footsteps behind me, clicking rapidly in an effort to catch me up. The look was unmistakeably

American: trousers terminating just above the ankles, heavy Brogue shoes, a thick bull neck and sagging jowls below a service-order crew-cut which would have done credit to the Lawn Keeper at Kew Gardens. He was in his late fifties, I estimated as he drew nearer, his hands stuffed deep in the pockets of a crumpled, lightweight jacket.

" 'Scuse me, buddy," he said through lips that were clamped tightly around an unlit cigarette. "You gotta light?"

I smiled and nodded, fumbling in the breast pocket of my shirt for my matches. The next thing I knew was his knee in my stomach and a vice-like grip on my wrist, twisting my arm behind my back as he pushed me, face down, across the bonnet of a nearby car.

He snatched the briefcase and increased the pressure on my arm, bringing his face down level with mine: "Gimme the keys! Gimme the keys, Goddammit, or I'll break your fucking arm!"

"I haven't got them!" I croaked back, my mouth squashed flat against the bonnet of the car.

"What'sat? Whad'ya say?"

"I said I haven't got them, for Crissakes! There aren't any! It's a combination . . ."

He slammed the case down hard on the bonnet, just inches from my face, then reached inside his jacket with his free hand.

"OK, bud! One chance . . . and one chance only! What is it!"

The gun barrel felt cold and clammy against my cheek. Or maybe it was the other way round. Not being a great one for heroics, I decided the best policy was to tell the truth.

"I don't know," I gasped. "I swear. On my life . . ."

"You said it, fella!" he replied, cocking the hammer.

I had to tell him something. Anything to buy more time. Numbers raced through my brain but something . . . call it blind panic if you like . . . prevented me from putting them together. And then, for the first time in my life, I remembered the area code number of my bank.

"Alright! You win! It's . . . 20-31-40 . . ."

He eased back the hammer and directed his attention to the

briefcase, the tumblers clicking round as he lined up the sequence I had just given him on the three combination locks. Then he reached for the catch . . .

I can't remember what came first; the wailing siren, the purple smoke or the telescopic aluminium arms, four of them in all, shooting out of the side of the case at right angles to each other, a good three feet in every direction. What I do remember is one of these arms homing in on his crotch, the pain on impact doubling him up and knocking him to his knees.

The instinctive reaction to cup both his hands around the offended area also demanded, I'm glad to say, the simultaneous release of my arm. Wedging myself between its extended arms, I grabbed the case and swung round, aiming a kick at his jaw with my right foot. Tennis shoes are not designed for that sort of thing and I can't say who it hurt more, him or me, but he was still rolling around on the cement floor as I hobbled away in a shroud of purple smoke, carrying the case as best I could.

It was slow going, what with the smoke in my eyes and one of the arms wedged tight between my legs. As I climbed the final ramp and spotted my car, I could hear the echo of his footsteps,
It was slow going, what with the smoke in my eyes and one of the arms wedged tight between my legs. As I climbed the final ramp and spotted my car, I could hear the echo of his footsteps,
slow at first then gradually picking up speed, two floors below.

There was no way the case was going to go through the doors of the Mini, so I didn't waste valuable time trying. He was getting nearer by the second, and the only important thing was to find some cover before he reached the top level. Out in the open, I would have been a sitting duck.

This was the sort of emergency that twelve years of army exercises getting a platoon of men across a swollen river with no more than an oil drum, a lenth of rope and an implement for getting nails out of Boy Scouts' hooves should have prepared me for. It obviously hadn't, for I was beginning to panic and found myself distinctly bereft of bright ideas. I couldn't get into the case to stop its wailing and smoking, nor could I retract the telescoped legs. Leaving it behind was totally out of the question: the threat of the dole queue implicity in Kaplan's warning about 'cocking things up' being all I needed to dissuade me from that. Worst of all, the American was closing with every passing second and it was he who had the gun . . .

And then it came to me. With no time to spare on inner debate, I reached into the car and unlatched the sun roof, rolling it back as far as it would go. It was a struggle, but I managed to squeeze two of the arms down through the aperture, leaving the other two thrusting skywards out of the roof of my car in the form of a gigantic 'V'. With purple smoke still billowing from its base, it looked like a backdrop to the final act of some German opera.

Not that I had the time to conjure up images like that. I could hear him below me, only yards away from the foot of the ramp. Getting myself into the Mini proved hardly less difficult than loading the briefcase had been, and I wasted valuable seconds avoiding the two telescopic arms that now took up most of the available space. Indeed, even once I had squeezed in, my mobility was restricted by the forward projecting arm making a diagonal across my chest and I was forced to hold my head slightly to one side to stop the bloody thing throttling me.

Still hot under the bonnet after its experience on the motorway, the carburettor flooded as soon as I turned the key. The only result was the familiar sound of the starter motor whirring round with nowhere to go, spelling out loud and clear that it wasn't going to start. There was nothing I could do, trapped as I was by the metal rod across my chest and the engine failure, so I eased my foot off the throttle, leaving the ignition on and switched on the demister fan to clear a hole in the clouds of purple smoke. The only thing left was to wait.

He appeared at the top of the ramp, a smile buckling his thin lips as he saw me sitting there, no more than twenty yards away. Holding the gun at arm's length and steadying it with both hands, he dropped on one knee and took aim.

Praying that enough time had elapsed for the carburettor to have cleared itself, I stabbed gently at the accelerator and turned the key. It fired immediately, but this was neither the time nor the place to start offering congratulations. Slamming it into reverse, I screamed out of the parking space just as he fired off the first round.

The bullet whistled past my windscreen, and shattered the side windows of the next five cars in line. His second took out one of my headlights as I spun the Mini to face the ramp. Foot flat on the floor I drove straight at him, leaving no time for him to adjust his aim.

He seemed to freeze as I closed on him, his eyes wide with horror, his feet rooted to the spot. But then, even as I was bracing myself against the impact, he regained his senses and vaulted clear over the low wall which skirted the ramp.

I did'nt hang around to find out if he'd landed safely. No need; the hail of bullets that peppered my tyre tracks as I raced towards the exit on the lower level proved that. Ignoring the yellow direction signs painted on the concrete floor, I took the shortest route to ground level, driving blind down the 'UP' ramps and blasting an urgent tattoo on the horn to clear a path through the procession of more orthodox motorists.

With the siren still wailing, the smoke still billowing out of the sun-roof and the two projecting arms converting the car into an obscene gesture on wheels, I hurtled down the final ramp and screeched to a halt just short of the exit barrier.

"Ticket?" the attendant drawled mechanically, his upturned palm reaching towards me through the open window of his booth.

"WHAT?" I shrieked back in total disbelief. "Are you blind? I've got to get out of here . . ."

"I can't help that, sir," he coughed and spluttered through the screen of purple smoke. "I need to see your ticket. The one you got on your way in . . ."

This can't be happening, I told myself; not in real-life. This was the stuff of Pythonesque farce, not real-life tragedy. And there was no doubt that 'tragedy' would be the word as soon as one demented American caught up with me.

A number of options raced through by brain, none of them immediately attractive: I could crash through the barrier, but it looked prohibitively solid from where I was sitting and I was behind the wheel of a clapped out old Mini, not an armoured car. Or I could get out and lift it. This didn't make any sense as I would probably have to flatten the attendant in the process and with the lunatic gunman not that far behind, I'd be shot full of holes long before I could squeeze myself back into the car.

And then I remembered something I'd read in *Readers' Digest*, the last time I visited the dentist: a psychological analysis of the two things guaranteed to frighten the living daylights out of just about everybody — including officious little jobsworths with a peaked cap to cover the gaping cavity where his brain should be: the open jaws of a Great White shark, and the immediate proximity of . . .

"A bomb!" I bellowed at him: "I've got a bomb in here . . .!"

With all that noise and smoke still coming from the interior of my car, he didn't take a lot of convincing and threw himself flat on the floor of his booth, obligingly pressing the button to raise the barrier on his way down.

A couple of minutes later, I was through the airport tunnel and joining the London bound carriageway of the M4 Motorway. Constantly checking my rear view mirror for signs of pursuit, I kept my foot down hard for the next two or three miles, and didn't ease up until the Chiswick flyover and the knowledge that I was in the clear.

By this time, the needle of the temperature gauge was again pushing ominously into the red. What with that, and the ever present possibility of being pulled over by a police patrol and asked questions to which I could not begin to supply sensible answers, I slowed to less than thirty miles per hour and insinuated myself between two lumbering lorries in the crawler lane, determined to remain as inconspicuous as possible. . .

So now I knew what Grüber had been trying to tell me at the airport; the secret of his exploding briefcase. *"It will not concern you . . ."* he had said and, under normal circumstances, I suppose he would have been right. This was meant to be a simple, straightforward job after all according to Kaplan. But, all of a sudden, the rules had been changed and I had found myself in another ball game entirely. Whatever was in the briefcase appeared to be worth killing for: or, to be more precise, killing *me* for.

Thinking about it, it occurred to me that I would be well within my rights to open it there and then and find out what all the fuss was about. Thinking about it further, I decided against this move: it could have been mistaken identity at the airport; the American may simply have got the wrong man or perhaps he was no more than an up-market mugger chancing his arm. And if I did force it open, and discovered nothing suspicious, Kaplan would certainly have my guts for garters and I would soon find myself shuffling in line at my local Employment Exchange.

It would have been useful if Kaplan had been behind a phone and not halfway to Scotland, swapping fishing stories with Sir George. There was always Smedley, of course, but I was reluctant to ruin his day. It had started so well, after all, and there was too little to go on to warrant his cancelling the job on his own authority. I knew already what his reaction would be: a predictable, but perhaps wise, "wait and see . . ."

One thing was certain, however: I couldn't go much further with the case in its current condition. So I pulled off the main road into a maze of secluded side streets and set about the task of returning it to normal. Fortunately, it had run out of smoke by this time and the batteries appeared to have given up on the siren, but I still had the problem of what to do with the protruding legs. I spent the next ten minutes trying to persuade them to retract all to no avail. I pushed and pulled and sweated and strained, but they stubbornly refused to budge. Eventually, I gave up what had long since proved a pointless exercise and slumped down on the bonnet of the car, collecting my thoughts over a nerve steadying cigarette.

There had to be a way. It had been designed, primarily, to startle, and very effective it had proved too; but cases like that wouldn't come cheap and would almost certainly possess a facility for re-use. I began working through the chain of events that had started it off in the first place: the American feeding in my phoney combination, activating the booby trap as he attempted to release the catch . . .

Oh well, I shrugged as I redirected my attention to the case; anything's worth a try. I returned the tumblers to their original setting, lining up a sequence of zeros across all three locks, then pressed down tentatively on the nearest arm. To my huge relief, it telescoped back and clicked into position with no trouble at all, as did the other three. The case looked as good as new.

One problem solved; countless others waiting in line. The first thing to decide was what to do with the bloody thing now. Kaplan hadn't specified what should happen to it in the interval between collection and delivery; understandable enough, as the question would have appeared superfluous at that stage. There was, after all, no way he could have foreseen third party interest in what purported to be a perfectly innocent package on its way back to its rightful owner.

Leaving it in the office safe was the obvious solution, but I decided against it for precisely that reason: it was *too* obvious. If the American kenw enough to be waiting for me at the airport, then it was odds-on he'd know all about The Workshop too, and there was no denying the possibility of safecracking as well as armed assault being listed amongst his nefarious talents. On top of that, there seemed little point in getting Smedley into a lather. Not yet, anyway. I might well need a favour from him later, if things continued as they had started.

No; Kaplan would have expected me to work this one out for myself. Using my initiative was what I was getting paid for, after all. So I left the car and caught a tube to Victoria Station, changing carriages every other stop to keep a check on whether I was being followed. By the time I reached my destination, I was satisfied that I was in the clear so I deposited the briefcase in a left luggage locker and booked a ticket for the Gatwick train the following morning.

Following the same procedure on the return trip, I collected my car and drove back to my flat in Ealing.I spent the rest of the afternoon working on the Mini, clearing out its badly corroded cooling system, then rewarded myself with a lengthy soak in a soothingly hot bath.

* * *

I had a heavy date lined up for that evening, and one I was extremely reluctant to break. We'd met only once before, and very briefly at that, the night before I flew off to Iceland. I'd been on a date earlier that same evening, but it hadn't worked out. Nobody's fault, really; just one of those things. Jayne turned out to be not my sort at all . . . or, perhaps more accurately, I turned out not to be hers. We came from different worlds: she was champagne and pate de fois gras; I was pie and mash smothered in green sauce. Smashing girl, though . . .

As was Sharon; a vision of loveliness glimpsed across the crowded, smoke filled bar of a late night drinking club in Soho. I had gone there to drown my sorrows and she appeared to be pretty much at a loose end herself, her escort having passed out across their table. I couldn't take my eyes off her, entranced by the natural grace with which she was bouncing peanuts off his head, and fell instantly in love.

Well nigh legless myself by this time, I staggered to her aid and suggested that her boyfriend might benefit from a breath of fresh air. She agreed, and followed me up the steps as I carried him outside. We hit it off straightaway, chatting easily between his bouts of vomiting in a nearby alleyway. Her job in Woolworth's provided little grist for lengthy conversation, but she seemed suitably impressed with my role as secret agent, flying off to beat back incursive Russkies in the frozen wastes of the Arctic Circle. Her boyfriend was beginning to show sounds of coming round, so we hurriedly fixed a date for the evening after I got back, blowing kisses to each other as I wobbled away in the general direction of Oxford Street to search for a cab.

As I drove towards Hammersmith that evening, I tried in vain to conjure up her face. I managed to get a hazy picture of the overall image . . .the ample chest, the skirt that came to an abrupt halt only six inches after it had begun, the legs that seemed to stretch all the way down to Australia . . . but the finer points continued to elude me. It had been dark in the club, after all, and even darker in the street outside. Moreover, I'd had other things on my mind during the past week, as anyone forced to spend seven days above the snow line in long-johns that wouldn't keep you warm on Midsummer's Day in Barbados, understandably would. No matter, though: I remained convinced that some part or other of her would strike a familiar chord when she eventually turned up.

It was now coming up to quarter past eight, and I'd been waiting outside the Odeon for the best part of half an hour. I didn't want to appear over keen, so I decided to give her another fifteen minutes before ringing the number she'd scribbled down on the back of a book of matches.

By half-past I was beginning to fear the worst. I crossed over the road to a phone box, fumbled the matches from my jacket pocket, and dialled the number. All I got was an answering machine, informing me that the Pregnancy Advisory Centre was closed and quoting an alternative number *to ring in case of emergencies. I didn't bother.*

All in all, this was turning into a day I wouldn't want to remember. The job that had all the makings of a cushy little number was rapidly turning into a right mess, my car had requested a transfer to the nearest scrap heap and, to finally put the cap on it, I had wasted half a bottle of *Eau Sauvage* and my last clean shirt on a girl who was even now, probably, opening another packet of peanuts to throw at her snoring Romeo's head. . .

As I drove back home, I suddenly remembered her face and took some measure of comfort in the thought that I hadn't missed out on much anyway. Still early by my standards, and in sore need of some company after the ups and downs — mostly downs — of the day, I decided to stop off at my local and have a couple of pints before turning in.

That was to prove a big mistake. Determined not to have a thick head the following morning, I ordered up my beer in half pint measures, drinking it slowly and making it last. But then I got embroiled in a marathon game of dominoes and, by closing time, I'd managed to get through two and a half pints and a double whisky nightcap. Not a lot, I grant you; but as events were about to prove, more than enough . . .

I hadn't driven to the pub as I live directly opposite, little more than a hundred yards away across a square of clumpy grass, known locally as The Green. I could see lights burning in my flat as I emerged from the pub, but there was nothing unusual in that: I was brought up in a basement flat, and never kicked the habit of flicking the switches everytime I enter a room and, much to my regret when the electricity bill comes in, I usually forget to turn them off on my way out. But then, about halfway across The Green, I happened to look up again and caught the faint silhouette of a figure against the drawn curtains, moving about my room.

I sprinted the remaining fifty yards to the front door, then tiptoed cautiously up the stairs. The door was slightly ajar, a thin sliver of light escaping into the darkened hall. I hovered outside for several seconds; listening, just listening. I could hear drawers being pulled open and slammed shut; the banging of cupboard doors; furniture scraping across wooden floors; the sound of footsteps hurrying from room to room.

I was unarmed, of course. No reason for it to have been otherwise, but a pity nevertheless. There was no way of knowing how many were in there; probably only one, but you can never be sure. I waited until the sounds moved through to my bedroom, then squeezed past the door into the lounge.

The room was a complete mess: chairs upturned, cupboards ransacked, records and books littered all over the floor. Keeping my back pressed against the wall, I inched towards the bedroom door and peered inside.

He was bent over a chest of drawers, muttering obscenities to himself as he rummaged through my clothes, slamming each drawer shut with disgust before moving on to the next. There was no need for him to turn round. I knew immediately who it was: the shoes, the trousers, the jacket; the occasional 'Goddammit!'. I crept up behind him, fists clenched and ready.

"Gotta light, buddy?" I said.

If it had been a movie, he would have straightened up and spun round, setting himself up for my right hook. But this one was a seasoned performer. He remained in a crouch and kicked back wildly, catching me just below the knee. It was only a glancing blow, but enough to push me off balance and send me reeling backwards across the room. He was on me before I knew it, two well aimed lefts to the stomach bringing me to my knees.

Before I could stagger to my feet again, he caught hold of the collar of my shirt and dragged me across the floor. With all the assurance of a man who thoroughly understood his business, he pinned my flailing arm with one heavy brogued foot while the other drove fiercely into my belly, pausing only for an instant before hammering back for seconds.

Doubled up and gasping for breath, I could do nothing as he sped past me, his running footsteps echoing along the hall and down the stairs. I struggled upright with the support of a nearby chair, still clutching my stomach as I set off after him, gulping air greedily back into my lungs.

I got outside in time to see him jump into his car and drive away, his tyres squealing as he swung round the bend at the far corner of The Green, speeding off in the direction of Ealing Broadway.

"Ohhhhhh . . . shit!" I spat through clenched teeth, pummeling my fist against the gate post in frustration; " .. . shit oh shit oh shit oh . . ." And then I saw him pull up sharply, blasting his horn as he found himself snarled up at the wrong end of a long queue of traffic, waiting for a red light to change.

I knew those lights from bitter experience; an infuriating

sequence of three, with less than fifty yards between each one. If he got through this one, and the next, he was certain to be pulled up again at the third. Moreover, once past that he had to turn left, with no escape from the one way system until the next intersection, the best part of a mile away.

I realised this was my chance. As the adrenalin began to flow and the pain disappeared, I raced to my own car and set off in pursuit, cutting across The Green to save precious seconds and nearly running over a couple of would-be lovers.

Bouncing back onto the road, I caught sight of him clearing the last set of lights and accelerating away along The Broadway, heading west. With my horn blaring and single headlight flashing, I kept my foot hard down and ran three red lights, emerging into the main road to see him swerving to overtake a bus about a quarter of a mile ahead.

Whatever advantage the extra horse power of his brand new Ford might have given him on the straight was more than matched by the manouevrability of my Mini as I kept the throttle wide open and zigzagged a path through the accompanying traffic, his tail lights coming closer with every yard.

I was almost on him when I was dazzled by a pair of headlights in my rear view mirror. Simultaneously the familiar wail of a police siren started up and a hand ordered me into the kerb.

I could have wept. The American was already out of sight, swallowed up in the anonymous flow of London bound traffic, just another face behind the wheel of yet another Ford. But there was nothing I could do about it. It appeared I had more pressing problems to contend with: the driver and his colleague were getting out of their car and striding towards me, caps set squarely on their heads in a daunting, business-like kind of way, an unmistakeable gleam of professional anticipation in their eyes.

They appeared to have their routine off pat, one of them scribbling in his notebook as he checked the car over for minor infringements, the other one encouraging me to open my window so he could read me a list of the major ones.

" 'Evening, Stirling . . .," he sneered sarcastically; "Brands Hatch closed tonight, is it?"

I looked up at him and smiled, somewhat stupidly. I hadn't expected much in return and I was not disappointed. Instead, he opened my door and, with clinical politeness, suggested that I should step outside.

He took down my particulars, then advised me of my rights before reeling off the catalogue of offences I was about to be charged with; speeding, reckless driving, ignoring a stop light (I didn't tell him about the other two), a dodgy back tyre and a broken front headlight. I didn't want to get into a lengthy expanation of how *that* had happened as he was too busy preparing himself for . . . the BIG one!

"Would you blow into this, sir?" he asked, thrusting a bag under my nose. I followed his instructions and fully inflated the bag, handing it back with a sense of impending doom.

"Oh dear!" he muttered as he examined the colour of the crystals under the glare of a street lamp; "Oh dear, oh dear, oh dear!!"

"Down the station then, is it?" I prompted, helpfully.

"If you'd be so kind," he answered, pointing to the waiting car.

* * *

THEY kept me at Ealing nick for nearly three hours, waiting for the doctor to come and confirm the findings of the breathalyser with a blood test. The delay was due to a multiple accident on the North Circular which was tying up the quacks for miles around; unlucky for some but, as the cheery sergeant behind the desk kept informing me at regular intervals, extremely fortunate for me. And so it proved, for as soon as the doctor had taken his sample and left, I was asked to blow into the bag again to see if I was in a fit condition to drive my car home. This time the crystals remained clear, and I was handed back my belongings and instructed to 'Bugger off!'

I arrived home shortly after 2:00 a.m. Ignoring the mess the American had made of my flat, I poured myself a stiff drink, then cleared the sofa of debris and sat down to think. I hadn't offered up the events of the day in mitigation at the police station. I couldn't: Kaplan would have been furious. Breaking clients' confidentiality, and all that. But I knew now that it hadn't been mere coincidence at the airport. It was also pretty clear that I could expect more of the same until I got shot of the case!

Not that seeing it delivered safely into the hands of its rightful owner would solve anything. Not for me, at any rate. It was no longer as simple as "*. . . here you are, Mikki Burton — This Is Your Case! Sign here and thankyou very much . . .*" No; it had already gone way past that. I didn't have to be told what Kaplan's advice would be: get rid of it and get out . . . it's none of our business. I could see his point, but that didn't automatically mean I had to agree with it.

Whatever was in that case was obviously something my airport Yank wanted very, very badly; probably something unique, something that couldn't be replaced. It wasn't money, I was already convinced of that. The case was too light for one thing, and anyone reckless enough to start a shoot out in a public place like a multi-storey car park wouldn't think twice about making a really worthwhile job of it and robbing a bank. No; to take those kind of risks, he would either have to be stupid, which I doubted having witnessed the efficient work he'd put in on me and my flat; very highly paid, which I also doubted judging by the cut of his clothes or, the obvious front runner, very, very desperate. . .

What was really bugging me was how he had found out where I lived. A spy in The Workshop, perhaps? No; that was ridiculous. Kaplan and Smedley were above suspicion, and agents were never told about each other's assignments. From what I'd been able to make out, it had been a rush job arranged between Sir George and Kaplan himself. So that one was clearly out the window; there had to be some other way.

I poured myself a refill and worked steadily through the possibilities, and as the clock on the mantlepiece struck three I had an inspiration. I thumbed through my ancient, dog-eared diary and returned to the phone, dialling a once familiar number.

It rang for what seemed like forever, and then I heard a click and a sleepy voice mumbling incoherently at the other end of the line.

"Hello? Ted? Is that you . . ."

"Hello? Hello? who is this . . .?"

"Ted? It's Frank. Frank Rogers."

There was a pause, and then: "Who? Who did you say?"

"It's Ginger, mate. Long time, no . . ."

"Ginger? What the . . . do you know what time it is?"

He ranted on for several seconds while I absorbed the insults and waited for a convenient pause.

"Listen, Ted. I'm sorry for disturbing you so late but . . . yes . . .

yes, I realise I woke you up . . . Ted . . . please . . . WILL YOU JUST LISTEN FOR A MINUTE?? . . . Yes, that's right . . . and I AM sorry for ringing at this hour of the morning, believe me, but I really need your help."

"Alright, Ginger. I'm awake now. But I must say you've got a bloody nerve! You don't show your face around here for . . .what is it now? . . . three years? . . . and then you ring me up in the middle of the bloody night and ask for my help?"

I didn't answer. There was nothing more I could say. He was right, after all.

"So what is it?" he said at last to break the silence, sighing heavily.

"Are you still on the force?"

"Yes" he replied, "but I'm not at Bermondsey anymore. I'm C.I.D. now, working in the City. Why do you ask?"

"I need a favour, Ted, and you were the only person I could think of. For old time's sake, eh?"

He sighed again. "Depends what it is?"

"I need some info from the Police computer, and I need it fast!"

"As I've already said, it depends what it is . . ."

I hesitated, not sure how much to tell him. Ted and I had been through school together, the best of mates until I enlisted with Her Majesty's and he went off to Hendon as a police cadet. But, as he had so rightly pointed out, it *had* been more than three years since I'd been back to the old stamping ground, and you know what they say about policemen . . .?; once a copper, always a . . .

I decided to tell him as little as possible. "I don't want to make this official, Ted. Strictly off the record between you and me, OK?"

"For the third — and last — time, Ginger . . . it all depends on what you want! You must realise the position I'm in. Ask away . . . I can only say 'no'!"

That was as much as he was going to give, so I took the chance. "Alright, Ted. This is what I want you to do. Find out if there's been any enquiries made about me in the past twenty four hours.

Especially my car number. I need to know if anyone's been trying to trace my address through that and, if so, . . . who, where and when.

"Could you do that?"

"Sounds simple enough. But what's all this about?"

"I wish I could tell you, Ted, but I can't. Honestly. But take it from me, it's important. A matter of life and death, as they'd say in the movies. MY life and death, to be precise.! So what do you say?"

"Alright. I'll do it. Give me the particulars and I'll get back to you tomorrow afternoon."

"No good, Ted, I'm afraid. I'll only be here till about ten at the latest, and I've got to know before then . . ."

I could hear a sleepy woman's voice in the background, imploring him to turn the sodding light off and get back into bed. He muttered something back, indecipherable through the hand cupped around the receiver, then came back on the line to say: "OK, Ginger. I'm on early shift tomorrow — or should I say today? — so I should be able to ring you about eight, providing I don't meet any hitches with C.R.O.

"Give me the details, and I'll get back to you first thing . . ."

I gave him everything he might need, then rang off with: "Thanks, Ted. I owe you one!"

"Damn right you do! And Ginger? Don't make a habit of this. I might have to say no next time, and I wouldn't want to do that. Not to a mate. Not even when that so called 'friend' can't be bothered to get off his arse and send a card at Christmas, but doesn't think twice about ringing up at three o'clock in the morning to ask a favour. Not 'hello Ted, how's the wife and kids?' but 'Ted, I want you to do something for me'! Even policemen have feelings, Ginger. It might pay you to remember that next time you . . . oh, bugger it! I'll ring you in the morning!"

And, with that, the line went dead.

He was right, of course. All in all, this hadn't been one of my better days: beaten up, shot at, burgled, arrested and, to round it off nicely, I'd ended up insulting an old friend.

Suddenly, I felt very, very tired. The chaos in my room swam hazily before my eyes and the glass felt heavy in my hand. I replaced it on the coffee table, still half finished, and staggered off towards my bedroom, not even bothering to undress as I stretched out on the bed and fell instantly asleep.

The phone woke me, just after eight.

"Morning, Ginger! You were a busy boy yesterday, weren't you?"

The intervening few hours had certainly influenced Ted's mood for the better. His early morning chirpiness was in direct contrast to my own bleary eyed, bad humour. The sight of the damage done the night before didn't help much either.

He told me about the enquiries from the Ealing police, but then I already knew about those, and then came something I hadn't been expecting.

". . . and the other one was from the American Embassy!"

Not exactly the kind of news for such a delicate hour of the morning. Nor was it an acceptable time to polish off the remnants of the Scotch, but that was exactly what I did. Understandably, my first thoughts were of the CIA, but then Ted went on to explain: "It turned out to be a perfectly routine enquiry . . . much to my disappointment! It seems you smashed into a tourist's car yesterday afternoon, and didn't bother to stop. Apparently, he didn't want to make what they call a 'federal case' out of it, so he contacted the Embassy and asked for help in tracing your address, so that he could sort out the insurance position with you direct. As I said, perfectly routine."

I'd guessed right; he *had* traced me through my registration number. I had to hand it to him, though: he must have more bottle than Watney's to chance showing his hand on a bluff like that. Just as he was able to get a line on me, he must have realised that I would be able to backtrack and find out about him. Assuming I was still alive and kicking, that is. Whoever he was, he knew what he was doing. He was a *professional*, and would have made contingency plans either way: if he'd got the case, he'd probably have got out of the country as fast as possible; since I still had it, his only option was to stick on my tail and wait for the chance to make it third time lucky . . .

"Ginger? You still there?"

"Sorry, Ted. A couple of dozen nasty thoughts just occurred to me . . . Did you get a name out of all this?"

"His name's Bryant. Harry T."

I reached for a scrap of paper and scribbled it down.

"Anything else? I asked.

"The address he gave the Embassy was a small hotel in Earl's Court. And, before you ask, I've already phoned them . . ."

"And?"

"No go there, I'm afraid. He left yesterday afternoon."

"Shit! I don't suppose he was thoughtful enough to leave a forwarding address?"

" 'Fraid not. Just a box number in Los Angeles, that's all."

I swore again. The chances of that being genuine were about as remote as me winning Miss World. Probably less. I said as much to Ted and he agreed. But then he continued: "One piece of info I got from the desk clerk might be of interest. It appears our Mr. Bryant is a cop. Or was. The clerk had a dekko at his passport when he checked in, and remembered that the picture inside was of him as a much younger man, wearing a khaki shirt with insignia on the sleeves and a badge pinned to the front.

"That's all I've got, Ginger. Any help?"

"Could be Ted; could be. I can't thank you enough . . ."

"No need," he interrupted, kindly. "Just don't be a stranger, that's all. And Ginger? Perhaps you'll tell me what this is all about someday?"

"That I will, Ted. I promise you. If I'm still around to tell the tale, nothing'll give me greater pleasure . . ."

I rang off, checking my watch. I didn't like what I saw; a million and three things still to do, and less than an hour and a half before I had to leave for Victoria to collect the case and catch the train to

Gatwick. My flat looked like it had just spilled out of a tumble dryer, I hadn't even begun to think about what to pack for the trip, and my stomach was as empty as my refrigerator. But all that would have to wait; there were other things on my mind ., . .

Smedley sounded as depressingly cheerful as he had the day before. He explained that the Chief had called already that morning to say he would be unavailable for the rest of the day, promising to check in again around supper time. I could have done without that; I needed Kaplan's help, and I needed it urgently. I had no other choice but to rely on Smedley, an expedient no less distressing for him than it was for me. I could sense his mood darkening by degrees on the other end of the line as I chronicled the events of the past twenty four hours.

" . . . so what I want you to do," I told him in conclusion, "is to get the Chief to check this Bryant out with his American contacts. I realise there's not a lot to go on, but if he can't do it, nobody can. I have to know who this guy is. Maybe then I might get some idea of what all this is about . . ."

"The Major's not going to like this, you know," Smedley pointed out in that irritating Florence Nightingale way of his. "Having his holiday disturbed like this."

"Well, that's just tough as far as I'm concerned, Corp!" I sneered in return. "I haven't exactly been having much of a time of it myself, lately! Just relay the message, and the Major can give me a bollocking when I get back. IF I get back, that is!"

There was a pause, and then Smedley asked: "So what are you going to do now?"

"What *can* I do?" I replied. "The Chief's not around to give the whole assignment the elbow, so I can only go ahead as planned and see what happens. Get rid of the bloody case, and hop on the first available flight home.

"Any better ideas?"

"Not really, no . . ." he admitted, somewhat sheepishly.

"Right! That's settled, then. I'll check in with you as soon as I get to Torremolinos That should be about six or seven o'clock, with a bit of luck.

"And if you *don't* hear from me . . . I'd appreciate it if you'd put whatever wages I've got owing towards an obituary in *The Times*!"

* * *

I took a more circuitous route to Victoria than the day before, changing trains four times and more than doubling my normal journey time. Precaution or paranoia, call it what you will, but after all that had happened since receiving delivery of the case at the airport, I was determined to leave nothing to chance.

What I did choose to leave, however, was the mess in my flat. I had to; if I was going to spend an hour and a half in the Underground, there simply wasn't time to clear it up. "I'll do it when I get back", I muttered to myself as I took a last look at the wreckage, and in that, found an unexpected crumb of consolation. I now had another reason for coming out of this unscathed: after all, I didn't fancy being remembered as 'a pretty decent bloke, but a real slut when it came to housework!'.

Another pleasure I had to forego was breakfast. By the time I collected the case from the left luggage locker I had hired at Vicoria Station, my stomach had begun to grumble. With twenty minutes to spare before the train left, I settled myself down in the buffet and ordered up a round of British Rail cheese and tomato sandwiches and a mug of tea. It would have been cheaper, and probably a good deal more nutritious, to have bought a newspaper and eaten that, but it was between increasingly reluctant bites that I looked up and first noticed the American.

He was wiry without being thin, and in his late thirties, I guessed, judging by the peppering of grey at the temples of his immaculately groomed hair. In his Brooks Brothers' suit and wire rimmed dark glasses, the image was of the classic American

WASP, and that's what puzzled me: as he sipped his black, unsweetened coffee, he appeared engrossed in the sports page of one of our stuffier daily newspapers. Nothing too unusual about that, I grant you, but why would an American be so interested in a preview of the Test match that was due to start the following day?

Basic insecurity was perhaps playing tricks with my imagination, but I couldn't quite put the two together. After all, wasn't that what the War of Independence was really about? Cricket? There were explanations, of course: maybe he had lived over here for a number of years and had become converted to the finer points of our national game; or perhaps he was a chronic insomniac who made the pilgrimage across the pond every summer in search of a cure? Lord's rather than Lourdes, as it were. But, if so, why did he look as if he had just stepped off the plane from Washington? For that was his appearance; Secret Service, CIA, something like that. And as cool as a dry Martini on the rocks; unruffled in raincoat, mohair suit and high necked collar and tie, and me sweating like a pig in the oppressive heat in T-shirt, lightweight strides and tennis shoes.

It didn't pay to dwell on it, though. Not even when he boarded the train for Gatwick and then turned up in the departure lounge waiting for the same Malaga flight. Whether the eyes behind those dark glasses were studying me I couldn't tell, but if he *was* following me he was doing it in a very subtle way.

The departure lounge at Gatwick was a place to see and be seen. Clearly, this American was playing things cucumber cool and as he wasn't bothering to play hide and seek behind any fibreglass tubs of tropical greenery I didn't see why I should. Instead, I decided to belt back a few scotches as the best way to kill the time before the flight was called.

Having installed myself at the bar and ordered a large one, I found that I could still see Mr. Ivy League who was now immersed in a copy of the *International Herald Tribune.* I had a bad feeling about him; irrational perhaps, but I couldn't deny the tell-tale tightness across my gut nor, for that matter, the well proven proficiency of my nose. The former could have easily been put down to the revenge of those British rail sandwiches, but the renowned Rogers' proboscis was now twitching like crazy and I knew instictively that getting to know him better could well prove prejudicial to my health.

Although I hadn't been with The Workshop long, I'd had plenty of experience with queer customers like this one, sidling up to you in bars or standing behind you at bus stops, outwardly as respectable as church on Sunday, but smelling of trouble. Funnily enough, the really unpleasant types never have the zipper head, bolt through the neck looks you would expect. Nor any tattoos. They're usually cold fish, often teetotal, frequently immaculately dressed but possessing an air that tells you they'd put a bottle into a kid's face if the money was right.

Of course, I could have been wrong. Maybe the job was getting to me already, making me overreact, but somehow I couldn't figure this character for your average holidaymaker. You didn't have to be Sherlock Holmes to see that he stuck out like a stand-up comic at an undertakers' convention, and the more crowded the lounge got the more like a fish out of water he became.

The public address system was crackling away like crazy, most of it completely unintelligible, and the atmosphere, while you could hardly call it electric, was heavy with anticipation. As I watched hen-pecked husbands make efforts to control increasingly boisterous children, I offered a silent prayer that I wouldn't find myself stuck next to a bloody kid on the plane. Nothing against them as individuals you understand but, taken as a breed, children and I just don't get on. And Corporal Smedley, spiteful little runt as he can be at times, seems to have an uncanny knack of booking me on to planes full of school kids.

On that last mission, for example, the fiasco with the thermal underwear in Iceland, I had found myself on a flight of Reykjavic that was entirely filled with nauseating children on geology field trips, all screaming about lava flows and gushing geysers, their faces resembling the landscape they were getting so excited about, mountainous with erupting spots. To make matters worse and add insult to frostbitten injury, after a week of abject misery at twenty below I got the same crowd on the plane coming back.

I had just ordered my third large Bell's and reluctantly broken into another of Kaplan's fivers, when I detected a mass migration from the lounge. I cupped my hand to my ear to help decipher the gabble of the loudspeaker, but it was only when I looked up to check the information screen that I knew for certain that my flight had been called. Suddenly, it was as if someone had shouted 'Fire!' at a school open day, my fellow passengers rising like one and hauling their little 'dears' by the scruff of the neck towards Gate No. 5. Even the American looked more than a little ruffled as his attaché case received a sound trampling under the stampede. Serves you right, Flash Harry, I thought, knocking back the remnants of the scotch and picking up the box of tricks I was to deliver to Mikki Burton.

After another ten minutes of patient queuing, we were finally allowed to board the plane. Unlike policemen, I thought, air stewardesses appeared to be getting older. The one who directed me to my seat had attempted to prove the maxim that life begins at forty and had failed miserably. Her uniform skirt was cut far too short and her face was hidden by enough make-up to grease down a battleship.

By the time I had settled down in my seat, deep in the fuggy heart of the smoker's section, I had begun to discover what 'no frills' flying was all about. Squeezed between two stout, elderly matrons, I quickly found that I could hardly breathe, let alone move my arms enough to light a match. I spotted my friend with the dark glasses slotting himself into a place further down the plane and silently sympathised as two brutish looking pubescents, complete with Sony Walkmans, wedged themselves in beside him.

After listening with half an ear to the stewardess instructing us on the workings of the emergency oxygen supply, the location of life rafts and why we shouldn't panic if the plane takes a sudden nose-dive at thirty thousand feet, I listened to the idle chatter of the old biddies on either side for a while, read the instructions on the sickness bag stowed in the string rack by my knees, then closed my heavy lidded eyes and dropped off, gratefully, to sleep.

As I awoke, I felt as if I had gone fifteen rounds with a heavyweight contender. My head hurt, my back ached and my tongue felt like a solid, fur-upholstered brick.

"'Ad a nice sleep then, 'ave you, dear?" chirruped the kindly old Gorgon on my left.

I replied with a non-committal grunt, purposefully intended to dissuade her from any further chit-chat.

"We're nearly there, you know?" the thickly accented Birmingham granny on my right added in a voice that could have splintered firewood. I managed to mutter 'Thank God for that . . .' under my breath before closing my eyes again, hoping against hope that this would prove enough to put them off the scent.

Fortunately it worked and I was free to concentrate on just how bad I was feeling and wondering why I had never persisted with that course of Canadian Airforce calistherics. For a supposedly crack operative, I was in pretty poor shape.

On arrival at Malaga, I was feeling worse than ever as I shuffled listlessly out of our flying sardine can. My pet WASP didn't cast so much as a sideways glance at me as we filed off the plane — perhaps I had been wrong about him all along. Somehow, I didn't think so.

I struggled across the baking tarmac to the relative cool of the two-storey terminal building in time to see him waltz through the customs gate with an attaché case as his only luggage, then climb into the back of a waiting limousine and drive away.

Alright for some, I thought, as I prepared to battle my way through the crowd thronging three deep around the baggage carousel. I scanned the huge electronic signboard above for notification of my flight. Sure enough, 'Gatwick' was illuminated; also Glasgow, Birmingham, Frankfurt, Vienna, and about five or six others as well. Consequently, there was no way of identifying the nationality of the luggage choking the conveyor belt at any given moment. My concern appeared to be shared by those around me, especially as one suitcase gets to look very much the same as another after the first twenty minutes or so. I have no such problem with mine: with its scratches, scuff marks and rope handles, it stands out like a sore thumb.

It was nearly three quarters of an hour before it made its appearance, lying almost apologetically beneath a set of extremely expensive looking golf clubs. I grabbed it and joined the queue for the Customs desk, handing over the transit documents for the briefcase to a stone faced official who read them through without emotion before ushering me through with a condescending nod of his head.

PART TWO: A TANGLED WEB

"O, WHAT A TANGLED WEB WE WEAVE,
WHEN FIRST WE PRACTICE TO DECEIVE"

Sir Walter Scott: "Marmion"

SHE WAS the first thing I saw as I emerged into the lobby and set foot on Spanish soil proper. As the song says, I would be as corny as Kansas in August if I were to say she took my breath away, but that's exactly what happened. Tall and deeply tanned, with long blonde hair cascading in loose curls across her shoulders and ending in perfect symmetry just above each nipple. Even at a distance of some thirty feet, I could see they were in exactly the right place as they strained against an indecently tight T-shirt. Her legs were as long and as shapely as Shergar's, and moved with much the same rhythm and grace as she set off across the lobby in my direction.

I looked behind me to see if I could spot the lucky guy,then turned round to discover it was me.

"Hi," she drawled in a neutral American slur, not smiling: "You the messsenger from London?"

"Could be," I replied with a non-committal shrug, keen to prolong this ecstatic moment for as long as possible.

"For Mikki?"

I nodded.

"Well, I'm Linda Love!" she announced with well deserved pride.

"And I'm Frank . . . darling!"

I smiled. She didn't.

"No, no, no . . ." she rejoined, not the least bit amused and sighing impatiently. "That's my name. Linda Love. Didn't your people tell you about me?"

I shook my head. "*Warn* me might have been a better way of putting it., But no, they didn't . . ."

She fixed me with a glare that would normally have been reserved for a disagreeable substance discovered on the sole of a shoe, then continued in a voice to match: "Cut out the smart-ass shmaltz, man! I had better things to do with my time today than run errands for Mikki, so I'm already up to here with it . . . right? Just give me the case, and you can fuck off back to London on the next plane - OK?"

I must say I preferred her before she opened her mouth. I do with most women, come to think of it. The suggestion was an inviting one though, even if it might have been better phrased. There was nothing I would have liked more than to have dumped the case there and then, and finally frustrate any further desires of that crazy Yank who kept trying to fill me full of holes. But my instructions had been to deliver it to Burton himself, and orders is orders. I told her as much and she appeared none too pleased.

"WHAT?!"

"I said I'm sorry Linda, but I have to deliver the case to Mikki himself."

"Do you want his autograph, then? Is that it?" she tried, spitefully.

Despite this chick's blatent charms, she was now beginning to get right up my nose. I narrowed my eyes and flashed her a look which was every bit as accomplished as the one she was giving me, and replied: "No! It isn't! I've been sent here to do a job, and that's precisely what I'm going to do! I don't know you from Adam . . . or Eve, come to that . . . and after all I've been through since I took possession of this sodding briefcase, I'm not about to give it away to any Tom, Dick or Harriet who taps me on the shoulder and asks for it. And none too politely at that, if I may say so . . ."

"But . . . but you don't understand! I'm Linda Love! Mikki's old lady, for Chrissakes! He's in Cannes on business for a few days and told me to come here and get it! And what do you mean, '. . . all I've been through . . .'?"

I waved the question aside. I had already said too much. "Er . . . nothing. Figure of speech, that's all. And if Mikki's away like you say, I'm afraid the case will just have to stay with me until he gets back!"

With a look that could have dissolved an oil slick, she spun on her heel and stormed off, muttering 'Asshole!' under her breath.

I chased after her, calling: "Linda? What should I do in the meantime? Till Mikki gets back . . .?"

She stopped, turned, and squeezed through suddenly pencil thin lips: "Listen, man — let's get one thing straight. The hired help around here calls me *Miss* Love. Not Linda. And it's *Mister* Burton when you meet him. OK? Do you think you can remember that?"

I gulped and nodded a meek confirmation, her venomous tone leaving me stranded and somewhat at a loss. After all, we'd been getting along so well. "And? Until then . . .?"

"Here," she said, taking a notepad from her shoulder bag and scribbling furiously, "this is our number. Find a hotel in town, then call me. I'll let you know when Mikki gets back."

She tore the sheet from the pad and passed it across before stomping off towards the exit door.

"Not much chance of a lift into town then?" I called after her.

I'd assumed correctly. She turned, halfway through the door, jerking her thumb over her shoulder as she replied: "Take a bus! You can wait for it out there!".

The back view of her proved almost as satisfying as the front as I followed her progress towards the car park, the poetic syncopation of her gait perhaps exaggerated by her furious mood. Without looking back, she deposited that magnificently rounded rear end on the driving seat of an open topped Stingray, the wind blowing her golden mane behind her as she roared away and disappeared from sight.

*

THAT, then was my first encounter with the girl who called herself Linda Love. I already doubted if that was her real name; the alliteration seemed somehow too perfect, too contrived. Not that there aren't quite a few 'Loves' around: I had one as an English teacher at school, but his first name was Cecil. No; this one was much more likely to have been born a Frykowski, a Cruddup, or a Glump. Nothing wrong with that, of course, but there aren't many Glumps in showbusiness.

Linda Love. . .Linda Love: the name was so calculatingly provocative it just had to be the brainchild of a Morty Silverstein or a Lou Kahn, a small time tinsel-town agent determined to forge a career for his latest 'hot property', launching her into the ranks of peroxide haired starlets who fought in the mud with each other for bit parts in daytime soap operas, as hostess in game shows or, when the going got really tough, the occasional few minutes of simulated passion in a low-budget porno flick. I could just see Morty or Lou or whatever his name was, mentally juggling with combinations of ludicrous monikers until he dreamt up the suitably preposterous Linda Love.

However, there was no time to waste in idle speculation. It was now late afternoon, and I still had to find somewhere to stay. Ignoring Miss Love's advice, I by passed the bus queue and the taxi rank and made straight for one of the many car hire offices that flanked the terminal building.

It was like an oven outside the terminal. The heat bounced off the surrounding tarmac and concrete, sucking the air dry. I felt like a piece of new bread that has just been popped into a toaster.

I ducked into the first office I came to and was so grateful for the cool blast of air conditioning on my face that I would have gladly hired a three ton truck if that was all they had. Luckily, they offered a rather more manageable Fiat or 'Seat' as they are called in Spain, so I took that.

Although the scenery around me was constantly changing — from traffic choked motorway out by the airport, to leafy avenues for the final approach to the centre of Torremolinos — the image in my rear view mirror remained the same; a large black Mercedes, the identity of its occupants concealed behind a windscreen of tinted glass.

I thought nothing of it at first. Why should I? It was the end of a working day, and I wasn't the only freshly arrived foreigner about to plunge himself into the delights of the Costa del Sol. It was only much later that I began to realise that the game had taken on a new, unexpected and even more sinister aspect.

All I was concerned with at that moment however, was finding somewhere to lay my head for the night, and trying to make sense of the infuriatingly complex one-way systems that snaked in every conceivable direction through the heart of Torremolinos. Driving around the urbanised areas or Spain requires intense concentration if you're not used to it: the road signs are indecipherable and written exceedingly small; traffic lights hover twenty feet above your head; illuminated arrows guide you through arse-about-face junctions whose design is anything but logical. Hammersmith roundabout is a walkover compared to any Spanish city.

I consider myself an experienced driver: advanced training in the forces on every type of vehicle this side of a tank, Army rally team through two successive seasons, etcetera, etcetera. But even I was confused by the traffic conditions in Torremolinos that particular evening. Of course, I hadn't the slightest notion of which way I should be heading; stop lights passed me by unnoticed as I scanned the skyline for likely looking hotels; streets narrowed without warning, leading nowhere. In the end I decided to park, lock my old suitcase away in the car and, with Burton's briefcase tucked securely under my arm, do the round of hotels, *pensiones* and tavernas on foot.

The guide books will tell you that, in height-of-season Torremolinos, the population swells to an equivalent of four persons per square metre, but that evening I thought the figure somewhat on the conservative side. Progress in any direction slowed to a pace that would have shamed a one legged snail; the crowds choking the pavements along the main thoroughfares established a peculiar momentum of their own, like a continuous Conga line weaving in and out and turning back on itself, swaying rather than moving purposefully forward. It was much the same story in the attractively paved and tree-lined pedestrian precincts, the shops, bars and restaurants filled to overflowing, the ring of cash-registers complementing the occasional blast of taped music, or the biting, evocative wail of a *Malaguena*.

Nobody seemed to mind the crush, though: wherever I looked I was confronted by a sea of suntans and smiles. And quite right, too. It didn't take me long to realise that the apparent rush and bustle was merely illusory, and that the only person hurrying to get anywhere was me. Everything anyone could possibly want from a holiday like this was right there on hand wherever you decided to stop shuffling your feet; food, drink, postcards for Auntie Vi, genuine Andalucian lace for dear old mum. And I would have been right there with them, standing shoulder to shoulder and sharing the fun, if it hadn't been for the fact that they all had hotel rooms to go back to and I didn't.

And, in that regard, I was getting nowhere fast. What was really foxing me was the sheer size and disorientating geography of the place. As Benidorm and Torremolinos traditionally spring to mind as the twin sisters of Spanish mainland tourist resorts, I had expected one to be much like the other. I had found Benidorm to be small, flat and manageable, the main streets laid out in neat patterns running parallel to the sea, the hotels thrusting skywards within a few yards of each other.

Not so Torremolinos. The shorefront stretches for miles, extending practically all the way back to Malaga in one direction, and on towards Fuengirola in the other. And, above it is the town itself — built on terraced ridges hewn from the rocky slopes where the Sierra de Mijas end in a final, sudden plunge to the sea. Consequently, the hotels are thinly spread to take full advantage of the space available, and I was to discover this meant a good deal of legwork, mostly uphill to get from one to the other.

I began my search in the centre of town, in the Bajondillo quarter, overlooking the beach of the same name. I tried The Cervantes, The Flamingo and a host of others of various size and quality, but all to no avail. It soon became apparent that in high-season Torremolinos there was no room at the inn. Not for me, anyhow.

By now the evening was drawing on, and my thoughts turned to kipping down in the back of the Fiat. As a last chance I took a cab out to the Playamar district and tried my luck at the sea front hotels as I worked my way back towards town along the Maritime Promenade. I got the same, now familiar, Latin shrug of the shoulders and shake of the head at The Principe Sol, The Don Pedro and The Don Pablo; always scrupulously polite, but with perhaps the suggestion in the eyes that, considering the time of year and the lateness of the hour, I was being downright bloody stupid to even ask.

The way my luck had been going of late, I was not in the least surprised that I eventually found accommodation for the night at the very last hotel on the strip, no more than a couple of hundred yards below where I had given up over an hour and a half before. No complaints about that, though; all was forgotten and forgiven in a flood of relief.

I was obliged to pay for my room in advance. Whether or not that was normal practice on a short term booking at this hotel, I could not blame the receptionist for requiring it of me. For I had no luggage and must have looked in a sorry state in my sweat-stained T-shirt and dusty tennis shoes. I was also carrying the suspiciously elegant, leather breifcase under one arm. All in all, I looked the type you wouldn't trust further than you could spit.

I hired a safety deposit box for the case, then hurried to my room for a blissful ten minutes of damage repair beneath a deliciously cool shower. With the panic of finding somewhere to stay now behind me, I suddenly realised how hungry I was. I checked my watch: just coming up to half past ten. Still early by the standards of a resort like this. I noticed the bar downstairs in the hotel was advertising snacks, but the guests I had passed while I was checking in looked a bit up-market, and I wasn't sure how they would react to my travel-stained T-shirt and sneakers. What I really needed was a change of clothes from my suitcase, still locked away in the boot of the Fiat. So I decided that my best course of action would be to head back into town and collect it, grabbing something quick to eat on the way

The first thing to do, though, was ring Linda Love and tell her where I'd ended up. Whether she would appear the least bit interested or not remained to be seen, but I didn't hold out many hopes.

I listened to the ringing tone at the other end for an eternity and then, just as I was checking the sequence of digits she'd given me to see if I had dialled correctly, she answered in a sleepy drawl and recited the number back at me.

"Linda? Sorry . . . Miss Love, I meant to say. This is Frank Rogers. Remember? The guy with the case . . .?"

"Yeah, Frank. What's your problem?"

Good start, I thought. "You told me to ring you when I'd found a hotel . . ."

"Jesus Christ!" she interrupted icily. "Couldn't you have called before now, man? I was asleep!"

I held my watch to my ear. No; it hadn't stopped. The memory of how she had looked at the airport that afternoon was certainly the best advertisement for getting to bed early that I'd ever seen, and I would have gladly told her so if she hadn't already displayed a certain immunity to the old Rogers' charm. Nor did I think she would be that overwhelmed with a blow-by-blow account of my trek around Torremolinos looking for a room. So I bit my lip and apologised for waking her, then proceeded to give her details of m location, adding: ". . . but I'm only checked in till midday tomorrow. The hotel's full after that, so I'll have to ring you again when I've found somewhere else . . ."

"Er . . . no! Don't do that!" she broke in, somewhat mysteriously. "Mikki's scared about this phone being tapped. If you have to move, leave a note of your new address with the hotel you're in now, and I'll get it from them.

"And listen, I've spoken to Mikki and he's pretty uptight about the wayt you're playing this. Not letting me have the case at the airport and all. He's paying for this gig, remember?"

"Well, he shouuld have been there himself then, shouldn't he?" I snapped back. "Believe me, I don't want to spend a second longer here than I have to! As I've already tried to explain, I'm only following orders annd those were to . . ."

"OK, man . . ." she interrupted through a stifled yawn. "I *know* what you've been told, and I don't need to hear it all over again. It gives me a pain.

"Mikki'll be back in a coupla days. I'll get back to you then!"

"Bitch . . .!!" I breathed to the buzz of a disconnected line.

*

CLIMBING back into my crumpled clothes, I took the lift downstairs to reception and asked the quickest way back into town. I was directed towards a steep climb of irregular stone steps, cut into the cliff-face about fifty yards or so from the hotel. Although it was not yet completely dark, I missed my footing several times on the unlit steps, scuffing the knees of my trousers and givin myself a painful crack on the shin.

I was relieved to emerge eventually into a cluster of comparatively quiet streets. Bright neon signs revealed enough eating and drinking houses to keep me going for a week, let alone the couple of hours I'd planned to spend before turning in for a well earned night's rest.

The smells of cooking drifted past as I wandered around checking the menus displayed outside. They made me feel even more hungry. At times like those, one tends to get feverish and conjure up fantastic images of whole sides of beef, shoulders of lamb, fresh lobsters . . . I settled in the end for an attractively decorated and invitingly lit Pizzeria, reckoning that if one pizza wasn't enough I could always get another without making too large a hole in Kaplan's expenses.

I needn't have worried on either count. At the Pergola, I was presented with the largest and stiest seafood pizza I had ever come across. The prawns, shrimps and clams that sizzled on the top might have still been swimming around, they were so fresh.
Not surprising really, remembering that Torremolinos was no more than a sleepy little fishing village until about thirty years go, and the fact that a sizeable fleet still operates in the waters off this stretch of coast today.

The bill for the whole meal, including a couple of beers to wash it down, together with coffee and cognac chasers, came to less than a fiver. Go looking for value like that in London, and you'd be down with malnutrition in no time. More than satisfied with malnutrition in no time. More than satisfied with both the food and the price, I left an over-generous tip — a rash and untypical gesture which was to have serious consequences later.

Although the visitor to Torremolinos will find a welcome in any one of the hundreds of bars throughout the town, the influx is such that many are geared to cater for a particular nationality; German, Dutch, Scandanavian, and so on. I, quite naturally, gravitated towards the British end of the market, and soon discovered I was spoilt for choice: I found 'Rose and Crowns' and 'Red Lions' in abundance; also The Anchor, The Welcome Inn, The Duke of Wellington . . . the list goes on and on, and I indulged myself in a mini pub crawl before ending up at The Bar Kiko, otherwise known as *The 19th Hole*. I'd really had enough by that time and was on my way to retrieve the car, but the Beefeater sign hanging outside attracted my attention from the other side of the street

Why not, I thought; another one for the road can't do any harm . . . How wrong I was, as the course of events was destined to prove.

The friendliness of the place engulfed me as soon as I walked through the door. It was small, not that much larger than the sitting room of my flat, although a good deal tidier. The stained beams above the bar and horse brasses on the wall tried hard to give the feel of a 'local' at home. Everyone seemed to be on first name terms with everyone else: must be regulars rather than tourists, I thought.

I settled myself on a stool at the bar and ordered a beer. And then another. And then a nightcap to finish off. I was beginning to get double vision by this time, so I decided, reluctantly, that enough was enough. I nodded to Joan behind the bar and asked what the damage was.

The custom in Spain is not to pay for your drinks as you go along, but to settle up as you leave. Joan totted up my bill and I flicked open my wallet to count out the necessary. It was then I realised that I had run out of readies; *pesetaless* as it were.

"Oh dear! This is going to be somewhat embarrassing!" I squirmed as I leafed through the fivers, tenners and twenties I hadn't had the foresight to change before leaving the hotel. I explained my predicament to Joan, along with a potted history of my travels and travails since I arrived in Torremolinos. She listened and sympathised in her mumsy, Lancashire way, but I wasn't about to see her out of pocket.

"Tell you what I'll do," I suggested at last. "Here . . . take this tenner for now. That's more than enough to cover, and I'll be back with the negotiable tomorrow!"

"That's alright, luv," she replied, kindly. "We trust you."

"No, no, no . . ." I insisted, pushing the ten pound note across the bar. "Take it. Please. I'd feel better if you did . . ."

She still appeared reluctant, but eventually accepted with a smile and a shrug. Thanking her once again, I got up and went to find my car.

The streets were still crowded although it was already past 1:00 a.m., the people now mostly in their 'teens or early twenties as the

Discotheques opened their doors for another long night. If I hadn't been so tired and , frankly, drunk, I might well have joined in myself, but the only thing on my mind at the moment was stretching out between cool, crisp sheets and notching up a much needed eight hours: maybe tomorrow, I promised myself.

I wasn't fit to drive, but neither did I fancy the walk down those steps to my hotel. As my experience of traffic conditions in Spain was that most appeared to drive as if they were drunk anyway, I thought . . . 'what the hell? Who's going to notice another one?' It was only a short hop anyway, and I was certainly in need of my suitcase.

Ten minutes later, I was stripping off and taking a last look through my hotel window at the high tide lapping gently against the beach. And then I happened to look down at the car park in front of the hotel; there, in the space next to my car, was a large, black Mercedes with tinted windows, two cigarettes glowing in the front seats.

Coincidence, of course. Or that was what I thought at the time. Nevertheless, I put the chain across my door, just to be on the safe side. And if I was being followed, then whoever was doing the following would have a long night's wait. I wasn't planning on going on anywhere till morning.

* * *

THURSDAYS have always been bad for me. We all have them: certain days of the week which bring nothing but grief; the end of an especially torrid love affair, the death of a close relative, the perfunctory redundancy notice tucked into the weekly wage packet. Thursdays, as I've said, are mine. This one began promisingly enough but was to end in disaster for me, and a good deal worse than that for others.

My body clock woke me before seven. More than a decade of Army life had made me used to getting up around six, and I still regarded anything later as something of a lie-in. The hangover I'd been expecting hadn't arrived, so I sprung from my bed, then showered and dressed, feeling duly refreshed and eager for the day.

I had booked into this hotel on a 'room-only' basis, so the first thing on the agenda was a bite of breakfast. I changed some sterling at the reception desk, then went through the revolving doors of the hotel lobby into the glare of the early morning sun.

There was no sign of the Mercedes in the car park or in the street outside, and I was grateful for that: no point in *inventing* things to worry about when I had more than enough on my plate already. As I'd concluded the night before, it must have been a coincidence. Nothing more. And, from what I'd been able to gather from Linda Love, it appeared that the next twenty four hours would see the job completed and yours truly winging it homewards as fast as the first available 727 could carry him.

That was the theory, anyway.

I felt good that morning, strolling along the Maritime Promenade by the sea front, with the sun on my face and tangy, salt air filling my lungs. Dog walkers and joggers passed me by — the only other people up and about at such an early hour apart from the locals. I noticed a souvenir shop being unshuttered, so I ducked inside and bought a selection of local maps and guide books to study over breakfast.

Even before my eggs and bacon arrived, I had read enough to realise that I had been looking for a hotel in completely the wrong part of town. It was now apparent that Torremolinos consisted of two main areas; Bajondillo where I was at the moment, and the districts of Calihuela and Benalmadena further to the west. Most of the big hotels appeared to be clustered around the latter, so it was there that I decided to begin my search later that morning.

I was in the Lido Mar, a pleasant and friendly little Spanish cafe, just off the front. As I was the only customer, it seemed natural to swap small talk with the proprietor, whose English proved good enough for us to enjoy a reasonably intelligent conversation. I told him of my predicament and he confirmed that I would, indeed, be better off in La Calihuela, even offering to check out possible availabilities with his nephew, a bar tender at one of the area's largest hotels. He wasn't exactly rushed off his feet at that particular moment, and I think he was glad of something to do. He brushed my protestations aside, saying: "*De nada! De nada!* No problem!" as he lifted the receiver of the wall phone and dialled.

The ensuing conversation seemed to last forever, interspersed with long silences throughout which he tapped his foot impatiently and flashed me the occasional gummy grin. At last, he was able to call over to me: "Sẽnor? My nephew, he says the hotel has empty rooms but you must be quick or . . . or . . .," he paused and shrugged, searching for the right words.

"Or I'll miss the bus?" I put in, helpfully. This only confused him further, so I tried again.

"I have to reserve a room now or it might be too late. Is that right?"

"Si, Sēnor. Is correct!"

"Tell him to go ahead, then," I said, writing my name on a paper napkin and passing it across. I listened to him giving the required details of *Sēnor Rohhhhgers* to his nephew, then waited another ten minutes or so before I could thank him while he caught up on what I took to be the latest family chit-chat.

Finally replacing the receiver, he wrote down the name of the hotel for me and indicated its exact location on my street map. I thanked him once again and ordered another coffee: under the circumstances, it seemed the very least I could do.

With the sun streaming through the window and the air conditioning struggling to keep the heat at bay, I felt entitled to linger a little while longer and enjoy the sight of the tourists flooding past on their way to the beaches. I amused myself by picking out the different nationalities as they passed by the window: the British, lobster faced and beer-gutted, slouching by in nylon socks and plastic sandals; the Germans, immaculately overdressed; the Scandanavians, tanned and healthy and exhibiting as much of their bodies as public decency and the local by-laws would allow. And an American; *my American*; the one from Heathrow.

It didn't click at first. I mean, I hadn't been expecting it. Just the briefest glimpse of another face in the crowd. But then I caught sight of that crumpled linen jacket, the half-mast trousers, the heavy shoes. He had just emerged from a phone booth on the other side of the street and was looking around him, as if lost and wondering which way to go. By the time my brain had begun to adjust, catapulting me from my seat in the direction of the door, he had climbed into the back of a cab and was speeding away in the direction of town.

I made the token gesture of scampering after the retreating taxi, praying for a convenient stop light, but it was not long before I realised it was hopeless. I swore under my breath and returned to my seat in the cafe, switching from coffee to cognac. The sight of Bryant had given me a nasty shock, and I had some hard thinking ahead.

So he had followed me to Spain. Or, rather, he had followed the case, which was much more to the point. And only a few minutes earlier I'd been congratulating myself that the worst was behind me, and that all I had to do now was laze around and wait for Burton's return, then get myself back home in double quick time. All that had suddenly changed, and I realised I'd been fooling myself. He was here and he would be looking for me, remembering how adept he had already proved himself to be in that respect, I was convinced that it wouldn't take him very much longer to find me.

What made it even worse was that I still had not the slightest idea what was in the briefcase; what it was that could generate all this interest. In the heat of the moment, as I sipped my brandy and added another cigarette butt to the steadily growing pile in the ashtray before me, I resolved that I wasn't going to leave until I found out. And if Burton refused to tell me, then I would just have to keep possession of the bloody thing until somebody did!

I was determined, despite any objections that Kaplan might raise to the contrary. But then I kept remembering what he'd said, '. . .*it doesn't concern us; it's none of our business . . .*', and, once again, I realised that he was right. All I could do was seize the first possible opportunity to dump the case in Burton's lap and, in the meantime, stay very, very sharp. Keep my guard up at all times, and never take anything for granted. The only important outcome of all this, when all was said and done, had to be the continuing good health of one Frank Rogers esquire. Beside that, all else paled into total insignificance.

It would certainly make things easier for me, though, if I could speak to Kaplan direct. Communicating through Smedley was hardly the same thing. How watered down a version of my problems eventually reached his ears I had no way of knowing, nor how much the Major's instructions may have lost in the translation before they filtered through to mine. No; I was out on a limb, and the only counsel I could ultimately trust was my own. I would perform my duties, as ordered, and if somewhere along the line I could work out how to get to the bottom of this without making too many waves, then so much the better . . .

The first thing to do, though, was to check into my new hotel. And quickly. Whether or not the American had tracked my down remained to be see, but a change of address should help to slow him down a bit.

I paid the bill and thanked my host for his help yet again, then hurried back along the front to my hotel. The receptionist confirmed my fears with the news that an American of the same description had been enquiring after me no more than half an hour before. He had checked if I was staying there, then had asked for my room number and any indication as to my present whereabouts. The desk clerk could only tell him that I was out, and I offered up a silent prayer of thanks that I hadn't booked in for bed and breakfast. He had left no message: I would have been more than mildly surprised if he had.

My room had been made up by the chambermaid, but appeared otherwise untouched. With so little to pack, I was back at reception and settling my bill in five minutes flat. Collecting the case from the safe deposit box, I left details of my new location with strict instructions that it was to be divulged to nobody except a Miss Linda Love. And that included my American visitor . . . yes, indeed: *especially him!*

It was only a short drive, perhaps two miles if that, to my new hotel. The broad avenue that linked the two districts was lined with an uninterrupted parade of restaurants and bars, and a profusion of invitingly fronted discotheques which I promised myself I would investigate later . . . assuming, of course, that I was still around and in good health. I may have been joking at the time, but the events of the next few hours were to teach me never to tempt providence like that again.

I found the hotel without any great difficulty, and was relieved to find that the cafe owner's nephew had proved a man of his word and had reserved a room in my name. Just as before, I hired a safety deposit box for the briefcase after checking in, then ascended to the ninth floor in search of my room.

The first on the right as I emerged from the lift, it had been designed as a mini-suite, offering a small sitting room with a separate bedroom and bathroom off. There was also a bar, complete with stools and inset lighting, together with a well stacked refrigerator containing beers, miniatures of spirits and liqueurs, and every conceivable type of mixer.

Needless to say, the first thing I did was to pour myself a stiff one and adjourn to the balcony where I could enjoy it in the warmth of the midday sun. My eyes wandered appreciatively over the topless sun-bathers gathered around the pool, then swivelled to take in the column of skyscraper hotels lining the beach and stretching away into the distance, back towards the centre of town.

There was nothing to look at in the other direction save a pattern of access roads cut across a dry and dusty patch of waste ground. Nothing, that is, except an all too familiar black Mercedes, the sun glinting off its highly polished chrome and tinted windscreen.

"Oh shit!" I muttered under my breath; "Here we go again!"

There was no weighing up the pros and cons of coincidence this time. All such wishful thinking was behind me now. The question was . . . who was in there? The American perhaps? No; I doubted that. He struck me as very much the lone wolf, and I'd noticed two cigarettes burning behind the smoked glass as I looked down from my hotel window the night before. Besides, it was not the kind of car a visitor would be offered by a car-hire firm. It was too old for that anyway, I decided.

Whoever they were, there were no prizes being offered for guessing what they were after. But why? Trying to puzzle that out would inevitably lead me right back to where I'd started . . . precisely nowhere . . . so I didn't waste my time. Instead, I decided that it was high time I began to fight back, to take the initiative myself, and concentrated on laying plans of my own.

By the time I'd finished my drink, I'd assembled a mental list of all the things I had to do. Checking the items off one by one, I settled on the most logical running order and returned downstairs to make a start.

On my way in to the hotel, I had noticed an arcade of shops in one of the corridors off the main lobby. Sure enough,I managed to locate the leather goods shop I'd been hoping to find and purchased a briefcase of much the same design, size and colour as the one now locked away in the hotel strong room. Then I found a phone booth and put a call through to London.

"Corporal Smedley? It's Ginger. Any word from the Chief?"

The sound of him sucking air between his teeth came through the static, and I could picture him puffing himself up before replying: "Oh yes, Sergeant. There is indeed. And I can tell you he's none too pleased with you. Not very pleased at all! What with you interrupting this little holiday of his and all . . ."

"Does he think I'm making it all up then?" I interrupted, raising my voice perhaps more than I intended to.

"It's no good shouting at me like that, Sergeant!' Smedley snapped back. "I'm only passing on what the Major told me! All he said was . . . well, that you could be *exaggerating* things a bit. Getting it all a bit out of proportion . . ."

I bit my tongue and smothered my immediate response. It would do no good to antagonise Smedley at this stage. I let him prattle on a while longer, than asked: "Did he get that information I asked for? About Bryant?"

"Yes, he did," Smedley replied. "There's quite a bit . . ."

"Hang on a mo then, Corp.," I said, leaning out of the booth to ask for a pad and pencil from the switchboard operator alongside.

"Ready when you are," I announced, tucking the receiver under my chin, "Just give me the important stuff."

Smedley cleared his throat. "Bryant. Harry Thomas. Age fifty-seven. You were right about him having been a police officer, Sergeant. A County Sheriff, no less. Place called Buffalo Wells, South Dakota. It appears he opted for voluntary retirement about six years ago and hasn't been heard of since. Not so much as a parking ticket, according to this."

"Hmmm . . .," I said, taking it all down. "Nothing much to go on there. Any reason given for him quitting his job?"

"Nothing on record," Smedley replied. "But it appears he had some kind of family trouble a few years before. That could have something to do with it."

"What kind of trouble?"

"Well, from what I can make out, it seems his eldest daughter . . . er, Linda Bryant, that would be . . . went missing in the Los Angeles area in 1969, subsequently presumed dead. His son was found floating down the Hudson in New York with a couple of bullets in him a year later. After that, his wife was admitted to a mental institution, where she comitted suicide in '73."

I must admit to feeling momentarily sorry for the guy after hearing all that. Then I remembered the state of my flat, and the shots he had fired at the airport, and the moment passed. Pity didn't keep anyone alive.

"Anything else?" I asked.

"Not really. Only that his other daughter . . . what's her name, now? . . . ah, yes; here it is . . . Jennifer . . . did a disappearing act shortly before he did. Again, nothing known since."

"Thanks, Corp. . . Nothing much of any use there, I'm afraid. Not as far as I can see, anyhow. Still, at least now I know who I'm dealing with . . . Which is handy, because he's just turned up again. I saw him this morning . . ."

"Oh dear . . ." Smedley said.

"My sentiments exactly!" I agreed. "And you can tell Major Kaplan that I'm not imagining or exaggerating anything! I just happened to spot him in the street, but I found out he'd been making enquiries abut me at my hotel earlier. I've moved since, so that should keep him at bay for the time being, but I wouldn't want to lay odds on exactly how long!

"And that's not all . . ."

Smedley groaned.

"I'm being followed. A Mercedes has been on my tail ever since I left the airport. I wasn't sure at first, but it's out front now, waiting for me. I'm going to try and lose it this afternoon, but I've an awful feeling that if I do manage to get rid of this one, another one'll pop up immediately to take its place!"

"Who is it? Any ideas?"

"Not a sniff!" I admitted. "One thing's certain, though. It's the case they're after . . . or, rather, what's in it. I should have delivered it to Burton by this time tomorrow, but, if not, I'll need contingency plans from the Chief. The sooner I'm out of this town, the better I'll feel . . ."

I went on to give Smedley the details of my new hotel, with the request that he ask Kaplan to call me there as soon as possible so that I could explain the situation at first hand. Failing that, I promised to check in the following morning; or sooner, if events demanded it.

And, with that, I rang off. It was now almost one o'clock, and the lobby was beginning to fill with guests drifting towards the dining room for lunch. The food laid out on long tables at one end of the room looked appetising, but it would have to wait . I had work to do.

Leaving the hotel, I walked casually to my car, pausing occasionally to squint up at the sun and swinging the dummy briefcase jauntily as I went. I took my time unlocking the door, depositing the case on the roof in the meantime so it would be in full view.

Turning onto one of the access roads close to where the Mercedes was parked, I drew to a halt directly opposite, leaving about thirty yards or so between us. As much as I wanted to, I fought back the impulse to chance a look at the waiting car, making a great show instead of studying a map which I spread across the steering wheel.

I let the minutes tick by. Now was going to be the test. It had occurred to me that whoever was doing the following only seemed to show interest in me while I was in possession of the case; hence this whole charade of the fake briefcase and deliberate self-exposure. It was a risk, but one well worth the taking. I had to draw them out; sitting around waiting for a bullet in the head or a knife in the back made no sense at all. If I was right, then they would stay glued to my tail wherever I chose to lead them; and if I was wrong . . . well, at least I would be able to sleep that much sounder in my bed at night.

But I hadn't been wrong. As I joined the busy flow of traffic on the Avenida de Montemar, heading west towards Benalmadena, I checked my rear view mirror to see the Mercedes pulling out about twenty yards behind. And it was still there, a mile further on, when I swung off the main road and headed north, away from the coastline into the hills of the Sierra de Mijas.

Already the traffic was beginning to thin, the estates of white painted holiday villas now behind us as we approached the narrow streets of Benalmadena Puerto. Out in the open, the Mercedes had eased back, content to maintain a distance of about a quarter of a mile between us but keeping me in sight all the time and matching my speed exactly.

So I had proved my point; the only question remaining was what the hell to do now. The plan had always been to play it very much by ear, hoping the geography of the countryside would suggest this or that course of action. As yet, I had demonstrated no signs of panic or rush, so it seemed safe to assume that whoever was in the pursuing car would be still ignorant of the fact that I knew I was being followed. That was a big point in my favour, but there could be no turning back once I'd showed my hand. As soon as they realised the game was up, they'd be down on me like a ton of manure. A shoot-out was totally out of the question: not for them, perhaps, as they were probably carrying guns and I had nothing to defend myself with but my wits. No; I would have to dump them somewhere on the road, run them into a convenient tree or something like that. Exactly how or where I was to do this, however, remained anybody's guess.

As it turned out, the decision was made for me. Once through

Banelmadena Puerto we were on our own, with only the occasional goat foraging around amongst the stumpy vegetation of the surrounding hillsides for company. It was now they decided to make their move. The Mercedes suddenly increased its speed, the extra power beneath its bonnet closing the gap between us in a matter of seconds. One moment it was little more than a black speck in my mirror, the next it was drawing alongside, the passenger window winding down to reveal the glint of a gun.

With no time to think, what happened next was pure reflex. Instead of trying to accelerate away, I slammed down hard on the brakes and watched them speed on by, taken completely by surprise. The Mercedes skewered to a halt in a cloud of dust about forty feet further on and immediately began backing towards me. Now it was my turn to put the hammers down, hurtling past at full throttle and opening a gap the length of a football field before they realised what was happening.

I knew I didn't have the speed to maintain the advantage for very long, but I could do nothing more than make a dash for it and hope . . . no, pray . . . for the best. As I crested the next hill, I could see the bay of Fuengirola beneath me, a steep descent of about two miles along a narrow road hugging the sheer slopes of a cliff. That was my only chance; the alternative was to climb further into the hills, but I knew that big engine of theirs would be able to gobble up even the steepest of gradients, and my safest bet was to head for civilisation.

Nothing else for it, then, but to turn back towards the sea and make for Fuengirola. They were closing on me fast but I managed to keep the upper hand on the twisting road, the manoeuvreablility of my small Fiat giving me the edge on the hairpin bends which snaked back and forth down the almost sheer hill. The lumbering Mercedes in my mirror had a harder time of it. Its wheels slid perilously close to the edge as the softly sprung suspension took a hammering around the acutely angled bends.

My luck appeared to be holding as the road I had chosen turned out to be very much a minor one, hardly used and not marked on any map. It ran out in a quiet residential area at the northern tip of the town. Here the tangle of secondary streets again worked in my favour, giving the Mercedes no opportunity to overtake as I steered an erratic course in the general direction of the sea front, where I hoped to give it the slip, no matter how temporarily, in the heavy afternoon traffic.

The broad avenue of the Paseo Maritimo was indeed choked and almost at a standstill, the flow halted every fifty yards or so by sets of pedestrian lights allowing holiday-makers onto the beach. In these snarled up conditions, the Mercedes fell further and further behind as smaller cars took the opportunity to squeeze past it in the slow moving, horn blaring traffic. Then I got my chance. I cleared a stop light just as it was changing to red, leaving the Mercedes stranded about five or six car lengths behind. A signpost loomed up indicating the main road to Mijas, so I turned my back on the sea and headed towards the hills, picking up speed as I cleared the outskirts of town.

I have to admit to feeling pretty pleased with myself at the time. Admittedly I hadn't managed to get rid of them for good, but I was still very much alive and, no matter what the circumstances, there was nothing more important than that. Not to me, at any rate.

They'd still be looking for me, of course; I was under no illusions about that. As I saw it, my best chance would be to dump the car at the hotel, grab the case and go to ground somewhere else. Somewhere no-one could find me without a detailed street map and an engraved invitation; all in one piece behind locked doors and closed curtains. And if Burton wanted his case, then he would just have to come and get it himself. Let him get shot at for a change! I'd already had quite enough of that sort of thing, thanks very much! But, whatever course of action I eventually chose to take, at least I was in the clear for the time being. Or so I thought .

I had passed the Lew Hoad Tennis Ranch and was approaching Mijas when they caught up with me, angry headlights flashing as they bounced over the brow of a hill and appeared in my mirror. I was pushing seventy already and I doubted if I could squeeze much more than an extra ten or fifteen miles an hour out of my little car, while they were swallowing up the distance between us as if I were standing still. Only twenty yards behind me now, I could see a windswept face leaning out of the nearside window, the gun in his hand wedged into the crook of his other arm to steady his aim.

Zigzagging wildly, I offered no way past and not much of a target to shoot at, but I realised it was only a question of time before they could get themselves alongside and pick their moment to blow me away. Mijas was coming up fast; a pretty, white painted village, dozing peacefully in the afternoon sun in the shelter of gently folding, pine groved hills. We were about to wake it up . . .

The first thing I saw was a white helmeted policeman, blowing furiously on a whistle and waving his arms about in an effort to slow us down. I sped past him one way, the Mercedes the other, leaving him lost in a swirl of orange dust as we roared onwards towards the town. Tourists and natives alike scattered and pinned themselves flat against the walls of the whitewashed houses as the chase continued along streets hardly wide enough for a brace of cyclists, let alone two recklessly speeding cars.

They began shooting again; bullets richocheting off the cobbled walkways and smashing pots of flowers displayed proudly in the grilled windows of the tiny houses. Further and further into the older part of town we went, using the pavement when we ran out of road, horns blasting, lights flashing.

The streets were getting narrower now, and I realised to my horror that I was being driven inexorably towards a dead end. I could see the street petering out ahead of me, ending in a flight of steps which led down to a tiny courtyard with a long, low and windowless building beyond, its facade dotted intermittently with what appeared to be stable doors.

With nowhere else to go, I stabbed at the brake to check my speed and bounced down the steps towards the courtyard. On my right as I decended, and previously hidden from view, I could see the courtyard widening out to provide a 'taxi-rank' for the town's famous donkey-drawn carriages. Not that there would have been many left to transport tourists anywhere if I hadn't come to dead stop there and then. They were lined up in colourful profusion across the entire width of the courtyard, blocking my only exit — another flight of steps leading down to one of Mijas' main streets. The animals bucked and kicked and reared up in their harnesses with fright, their drivers rooted to the spot and staring at me, open-mouthed in astonishment..

And then I heard the crash. I swivelled in my seat to check behind me and could see at a glance what must have happened. The Mercedes had overshot the steps, the speed of its approach sending it hurtling through the air to crash into the stables beyond. It was lying on its side now, wheels still spinning furiously, two bodies hanging limp and bloodied through the shattered windscreen.

The donkeys were going crazy, scattering off in every direction with their handlers in hot pursuit, waving their sombreros and screaming; "*Burros! Burros! Burros! . . .*"

The steps were now clear, and I didn't waste any more time on my two pursuers. The police would soon be here and I wasn't going to get involved in any prison cell interrogation. I descended the second flight of steps rather more sedately than the first one and joined the main road out of town.

Following the signposts directing me towards Torremolinos, I was just emerging into open country again when I passed a parade of siren wailing police cars on their way in. I pulled over to let them by, acknowledging their nods of gratitude at my courteous gesture with a polite smile, just as any conscientious motorist would.

*

I had intended to go straight back to the hotel, but the events of the last hour began to hit me as I approached the outskirts of Benalmadena Puerto, so I pulled over and went looking for a bar where I could collect myself over a nerve steadying drink.

The shakes didn't fully subside until my third brandy, when I decided to switch to beer. I had succeeded in my original purpose, no matter how messily, but I knew this wouldn't be the end of it. As I'd already suggested to Smedley, there would be more black Mercedes types interested in me shortly, and the next lot would be really after my blood — especially after what had happened to their mates back in Mijas.

I would have to play it very, very carefully from now on, that was certain. Never take the car unless I had to; stay anonymous; lose myself in the crowd. And then I made a snap decision; according to the map, I was sitting in a bar no more than a mile from Burton's villa. Perhaps he had already returned, giving me the chance to get this business over and done with during the next few hours. If not, maybe Linda Love might take pity on me and offer me sanctuary — though I was certainly not going to take any bets on that! It could do no harm to check it out in any case; if the worst came to the worst, that might well be the only place I'd have left to run to, and it would be handy to have some idea of where I was supposed to be going.

So I finished my drink and returned to the car to study the map. It looked easy enough; turn back towards Mijas, take the first right and just follow the road. And so it proved. Within five minutes I was parked outside the villa's electronically controlled gates, stabbing at the button of the entryphone embedded in the wall alongside. There was a sign above which, even with my rusty Spanish, I understood as a catalogue of dire consequences likely to befall anyone foolish enough to enter without an offical invitation.

"*Si? Hola?* Who is it?" a female voice crackled through the intercom.

"Linda? Miss Love? It's Frank. Frank Rogers?"

There was a pause, then: "What the hell do *you* want?"

At least she was playing it true to form, a reassuring constant in a world suddenly full of unwanted surprises. "Er . . . I'm sorry to bother you again, but . . . well, can you let me in? I need to talk to you."

"Why? Have you brought the case?"

"No, I haven't, but . . ."

"Mikki's not back yet. Like I said, I'll call you when he shows. Jesus Christ! You've got a fucking nerve coming out here!"

"But you don't understand! I've been . . ."

"Shove it, creep! Get lost!"

Charming, I thought as the line clicked off. That's not exactly what I thought, but I'm not prepared to repeat words like that here. I was beginning to get really pissed off with this chick: I mean, REALLY pissed off! Standing there staring dumbly at the machine on the wall, I made a solenm vow to whoever up there might have been listening that those were the last civil words Linda Love was ever going to get out of me! What she needed was a crash course in manners, preferably across the backside and delivered in a language that would adequately match her own; something hard and spiky, like the sole of a running shoe . . .

As the chance of that happening in the next half hour or seemed somewhat remote, I decided I might as well try to get some idea of the layout of the villa's grounds. After all, I was as curious as the next bloke to see what kind of life millionaire rock stars like Mikki Burton chose to live in their retirement.

The estate was surrounded on three sides by hills, so I retrieved my binoculars from the boot of the car, then crossed the road and began to climb. I ran out of puff opposite a rocky ledge about halfway up, so I scrambled across and sat down, steadying the binoculars on my knees.

It was not as large as I had anticipated, but certainly large enough. There were four, maybe five acres of ground, completely encircled by a high stone wall, the electronic gates directly below me providing the only point of entry. The villa itself, painted white with a red tiled roof, was a one storey construction, built in the shape of a giant 'E' with three wings coming off at right angles to the main body of the house. The far wing resolved into an extravagantly arched and columned patio for half its length, the mosaic laid floor depicting what I immediately recognised as Burton's famous Golden Guitar, an Old English sheepdog stretched out asleep across its fretboard. The near side of the house was dominated by a circular extension of perhaps three storeys, its roof domed and equipped with movable panels like an observatory.

Impressive indeed; the more I looked, the more I liked. Especially when I focused on the swimming pool and got a very tantalising eyeful of Linda Love, completely naked and lying on a lounger alongside. It wasn't long before she flipped over to top up the tan on her back, but long enough for me to ascertain that she was certainly no natural blonde.

Reluctantly moving the binoculars about twenty feet to her right, I spied a strange figure swathed in orange robes, squatting on the lawn in a Lotus position, his eyes closed in spiritual contemplation. He was completely bald, his long, thin face painted with a single orange stripe which ran from his forehead to his chin. Apart from showing no interest whatsoever in the bountifully displayed charms of Miz Love, he had wrapped around his neck what appeared at first glance to be a brightly coloured scarf but which, when it started to move and slither across his shoulders and down the length of his arm, I realised with phobic horror was a snake. Ugh! I'm not overfond of snakes at the best of times; behind glass and fast asleep at London Zoo is how I best appreciate mine. But coiled around your neck and hissing sweet nothings in your ear? Oh, no; not for my money, thank you very much. That's . . .weird: really *weird*!

Linda Love's lounger appeared to have been vacated in the interim, so I decided I'd seen enough and lowered the binoculars. It was then that I caught a brief glimpse of something glinting in the sun behind a clump of bushes on an adjacent hillside. I raised the glasses to my eyes once again and homed in on another pair of binoculars looking at me!

That was enough after all I'd been through recently. I scurried down the hill and ran back to my car, determined not to stop until I was safely back inside my hotel.

* * *

Smedley seemed none too pleased with the account of my day when I reported in, shortly after returning to the hotel. I tried to explain that I was not altogether overjoyed myself but, by that time, he had decided to play the role of the third wise monkey and clammed up. However, he did promise to get Kaplan to call me direct if Burton still hadn't showed by noon the following day. Leaving him with the earnest hope that I would still be in a fit state to accept the call — that's to say, still *breathing* — I rang off.

The rest of the afternoon dragged by listlessly. I drifted down to the hotel bar but couldn't settle, now looking at every new face as if it belonged to a potential assassin. Reviewing the situation it made sense to abandon plans for a return to the centre of town that evening. Ten pounds seemed a small price to pay for my continuing good health.

But, when it came to it, I decided I was in sore need of some light relief and decided to go ahead with my original plan. The one concession to caution I did make, however, was to leave the car and make the journey by bus. There was a regular half-hourly service stopping just outside the hotel, so I hung around the lobby until I saw it arrive, waited until everybody else had climbed on board, then made a mad dash for it just as it was about to pull away.

I took the back seat to keep a look out for a possible tail, but all I saw of interest was a guy in a white suit running after it, waving his attache case in the air, as we moved off. "Tough luck, mate," I sympathised under my breath and thought nothing more of it.

Imagine my surprise then, when I looked up from my corner table at 'The 19th Hole' a half hour later to see the face poking out of that same white suit smiling down at me and saying: "Frank Rogers, is it? Mind if I join you?"

As he was already pulling out a chair and lowering himself down on it, his enquiry seemed somewhat superfluous. Nevertheless, I shrugged and replied, none too politely: "It's a free country!"

"Matter for debate that, old chap," he observed, then "Bottoms up!" as he raised his glass of beer to his lips.

"Ghastly stuff this, don't you think!" he continued. "I've been out here for more than a year now, and I still can't get used to it. A bit too chemical for my taste . . ."

"I rather like it" I interrupted, watching his every move and hardly daring to blink. The only reason I hadn't already bopped him and done a runner to be on the safe side was that I had always nurtured a preference towards eventually snuffing it at the hands of a fellow Brit, as opposed to any other less worthy nationality. So far, I had been chased, shot at and burgled by an American, and the nearest those two in the Mercedes had ever got to Blighty's shores was watching over-dubbed editions of *Coronation Street* on TV. This one was obviously as English as the Boat Race — but that still didn't mean I was automatically going to trust him.

There was a brief silence as we sized each other up, and then he said: "Perhaps I better introduce myself . . ."

"Perhaps you should," I agreed.

"Hamilton's the name. Toby Hamilton." He extended his hand. I ignored it.

He took another sip of his beer, studying me all the time over the rim of his glass. Then he pushed it aside and leant forward across the table.

"And you are Frank Rogers," he informed me. "Born Bermondsey, London, 1951. Nickname 'Ginger'. Twelve years' Army service, rising to the rank of sergeant. Thrown out September '82 for striking a senior NCO . . . among other things. Now employed by Security Consultants International and urrently on assignment to Spain as . . . Tell me, Frank — what *are* ou doing in Spain?"

"Depends on who's doing the asking." I replied, already nowing the answer to my own question.

"British Intelligence. Want to see my I.D.?"

"I didn't think your lot carried any. What's your interest in his?"

"In what, Frank?" he asked, retrieving his beer.

This was getting us nowhere. Stuff like this might make very ood reading in spy novels, but it can be a pain in the arse in real ife. They're all the same, these intelligence wallahs; couldn't give ou a straight answer if you asked them the time.

"Alright," I said at last. "You seem to know all about me, but I till know sweet F.A. about you, and I'm sure every British tourist o Torremolinos doesn't get this kind of personal attention. So vhy don't we start at the beginning and maybe I might be able to olve your problem . . . whatever it is!"

He laughed, and immediately seemed to drop his mask and elax. "Want a refill?" he asked, rising from his seat. I nodded and tudied him as he stood at the bar, ordering the drinks. He was bout my age, but baby faced and blessed with a shock of thick londe hair. His accent was pure Oxbridge, but I decided not to old that against him.

"Sorry about the third degree," he said on returning to the able. "To tell you the truth, I'm a bit out of practice with this sort of thing. This is my first time in the field since I got down here . . ."

"That's reassuring," I said, not meaning it to sound quite as unkind as it did.

He shrugged, almost apologetically, then took a deep breath before asking: "So what were you doing at Mikki Burton's villa today?"

"My business!" I replied. "Next question!"

He sighed heavily. "Don't be obstructive, Frank; there's a good chap. Look - cards on the table time, OK?"

I nodded.

He bent down to open his attache case, extracting a buff file i which he located a contact sheet of about twenty tiny photographs This he passed across, explaining: "About three weeks ago, m counterpart in the CIA turned up at our office in Madrid wit these. Er . . . do you recognise either of these men, by the way?'

I studied the photographs of two men; one about fortyish an quite good looking in a rugged, pugilistic sort of way, the othe much older and fatter, flat nosed and heavy lipped. They ha obviously been snapped surreptitiously through a telephoto lens at various locations but always huddled together in earnes conversation. Neither rang any bells with me, and I told him so as returned the sheet. He replaced in in the file and went on t further explain: "The younger one is Al Rossi, a particularly nast Mafioso from New York. The other is one Vladimir Ivanov officially a grain specialist attached to the Russian Trad Delegation in Barcelona, but better known to us as a colonel in th KGB. It appears they were seen spending time together here i Torremolinos. At that time Rossi became a regular visitor t Burton's estate. That's why the CIA passed the buck to us, Burto still being a British citizen — although he hasn't set foot in the ol country for the best part of ten years.

"I have to admit that we're completely at a loss as to what coul possibly be tying the three together, so when I saw you out ther this afternoon . . ."

"So it was you behind those binoculars, was it? " I interrupted.

He owned up with a nod and continued: " . . . I thought it bes to knock the ball into your court and see if you could throw an light on the matter."

"How did you find me?" I asked.

A smug smile twitched at the corners of his mouth as he replied "Oh, that was easy enough. I took a note of your car number an got your details from the hire company at the airport. The loca police ran through the lastest batch of hotel registrations for me and Bob's your uncle! I ran a check on you with London and when I found you were with The Workshop, it seemed safe enoug to approach you with this. After all, your organisation and mine, we . . . well, let's just say we have been known to rub each other's backs in the past, if you know what I mean.

"I came out to your hotel earlier this evening, just as you were leaving . . ."

"Yes, I saw you. But I'm afraid you've gone to a lot of trouble for nothing, Toby old son. I've no idea what the Mafia and the KGB are doing with Mikki Burton. I only wish I did . . ."

"Meaning what exactly?" he asked, rising to a bait I hadn't intended to offer.

"Meaning I can't help you."

"In other words, you could but you don't want to. Am I correct?"

I didn't answer.

"Look Frank," Hamilton resumed, "I can easily get clearance from your office, if that's what you're worried about. We could play it that way if you like, but that would only be a waste of time . . . mine *and* yours!

"Anything you can tell me now about what you're doing here, — and especially what that has to do with Mikki Burton — might take me that one step nearer to the bottom of all this. I didn't want this assignment, but I'm stuck with it and I've got a job to do, just like everybody elsse. I'm not asking you to get involved, just help me out with a little information, that's all."

I decided to tell him. Not through any great concern for the national interest, you understand; nor to help a fellow Englishman abroad out of a hole. No; my decision was entirely to do with my safety. As I saw it, the most important thing was to shift the attention of all interested parties from me to Mikki Burton, then get Torremolinos behind me for good. The last thing I wanted was Hamilton to go through with his threat to contact the office and make it official, possibly tying me up there for a further few days, maybe even weeks. So I told him all I knew about the briefcase, the mysterious Harry Bryant, the black Mercedes that I'd left as so much scrap metal in Mijas earlier that afternoon . . .

"So that little fracas was down to you, was it?" he interrupted, registering surprise.

"You know about that?" I responded with much the same emotion.

He nodded, and there was a faint smile on this face.

"Yes," he explained; "I was in the local police office . . . checking up on you, as a matter of fact . . . when the report of the incident came through. It caused quite a flap, I can tell you!"

"Any ideas who they were?" I asked. "The men in the car?"

"Just a couple of small time hoods from Seville, I understand. But they were known to have Mafia connections, so I wouldn't be the least bit surprised if they were following you on the orders of our friend, Mr. Rossi.

"They're both dead by the way . . .'

I shrugged. There was no point in going through the motions of regret; I had none to offer. After all, it could easily have been the other way round. Instead, I lit another cigarette and sipped my beer, saying nothing.

"So . . .", Hamilton said at last to break the silence; "Where's the case now?"

"Back at the hotel," I told him. "And the answer to your next question is 'No!' . . . so you might as well save your breath. I'm as interested as you to see what's inside . . . probably more so, seeing as how I seem to have been elected as target of the month . . . but you'll just have to wait until I've handed it over to Mikki Burton. Get your court orders or whatever then. While it's still my responsibility, that briefcase stays shut!"

"And that's your final word?"

"I'm afraid it is. It has to be. And please understand that I'm not just being bloody minded about it. I'd like to help you, God knows, but there's just no way. I've been given my orders and I intend to stick to them. Surprising as it may seem, I have a sense of duty too . . . No hard feelings, though . . . eh? Tell you what; why not join me for a slap-up meal tonight? On me . . . or, rather, on The Workshop . . . of course. What do you say?"

He smiled and shook his head. "I'm sorry, Frank. I would have enjoyed that, but I've . . . er, still got other things to do tonight. Another time, perhaps?

"By the way, before I go . . . " He reached back into his attache case and found a ten-by-eight blown-up photograph which he nudged across the table top towards me. "No reason why you should, but have you come across this little charmer on your travels?"

I recognised him instantly; the Ivy League suit, the glasses, the exquisitely cut hair. "Why, yes," I replied. "He was on my flight coming out. And before that, at Victoria, waiting for the airport train. Who is he?"

"Name of Curtis. Randall Curtis. He used to work for the dirty tricks department at the CIA, but went freelance about five years ago. A hired, gun and one of the best there is by all accounts . . ."

"So what's he doing here?" I asked. "Got something to do with this, has it?"

"Your guess is as good as mine!" Hamilton shrugged in reply. "All I know is that Rossi is here, Ivanov, Burton, you and that briefcase . . . and now Curtis. I know what you're doing here, but what about the others? Hardly the types to book a two week package tour to the sun, I'm sure you'll agree.

"And there's something else about Curtis. It may or may not be significant, but he's being driven around in a limousine registered to a local subsidiary of JGC Electronics. Mean anything to you?"

My face remained blank.

"No? There's no reason why it should." he resumed, "but the CIA are getting very jumpy about it. You see, JGC is currently under US Government contract to design and build the guidance system for the next generation of American long-range missiles. And with Ivanov sniffing around . . . "

"They think the two might be connected?"

"Could be. Nobody knows. It's making them very twitchy at any rate. And, to complicate matters even further, Calvin himself is due over here in a few weeks time to open another factory . . ."

"Calvin?" I interrupted, forgivably confused. "Who's he when he's at home?"

"Sorry, Frank; I should have explained. John G. Calvin III is the most recent embodiment of the American Dream; young good looking and very, very rich. He founded JGC while he was still a student at UCLA, building it up to multi-national status and a world leader in its field in the ten, eleven years or so since then. He's keeping a very high media profile in the States just now, some say as a first step towards a future Presidential nomination, probably in 1992. On paper, he would appear to be a very strong bet. And that would also make him the same age as Kennedy was when he took office. A somewhat obvious ploy, I would have thought; election by association, and all that. Still, that's America for you . . ."

I had to own up to being thoroughly confused. Hamilton agreed. Rossi, Ivanov, Mikki Burton; Bryant, a brace of dead bodies from Seville, Burton's briefcase and me; Calvin and Curtis, Old Uncle Tom Cobleigh and all. Thankfully, it appeared to be much more Hamilton's problem than mine. As far as I knew, whatever part I was supposed to be playing in all this was drawing to a close, and the next twenty four hours would, surely, see me safely back on British soil. How wrong can anyone be?

He gave me his card and I promised to be in touch as soon as I had delivered the case, or if anything else of significance happened in the meantime. Then he left, and I continued to mull things over in the company of another couple of beers. Getting nowhere, I said my farewells to Joan, Frank and Steve behind the bar — this time settling my bill in the proper currency — and went looking for something to eat.

I stayed in the Nogalera district, crossing the road from The 19th Hole to examine the display of menus outside the restuarants along the Calle Casablanca. I was sorely tempted to get my money's worth from *The Florida*, offering as much as I could eat for the sterling equivalent of three and a half quid; but, in the end and since this was supposed to be my last night in Torremolinos, I decided to go up-market and plumped for the Basque cooking of the *El Caballo Vasco*, just a few doors along.

The food was delicious and there was a lot of it: I emerged from the restaurant a couple of hours later feeling a good few inches wider around the waistline. It was still early, only about 11 o'clock so I decided to put my troubles aside for a few hours and visit some of the discos and bars along the Avenida de Montemar on a slow progress back to my hotel. After all, what's the point in having a job that gets me chased, shot at, burgled, arrested and insulted if I couldn't enjoy myself in the slack period in between? So I sweated off a few pounds on the dance floor at "Number One," then put them back on again with several beers at "Snoopy's" a so called Scottish bar, just along the street. Then on to "Gatsby's," packed to the rafters and buzzing with the accents of home, finishing up at "Cleopatra's" around 2 am. None of the young ladies I recruited as dance partners seemed that enthusiastic about the opportunity to share a nightcap with me back at the hotel, so I decided to call it a day about 3 o'clock and staggered off alone.

As I was picking up my key, the night duty receptionist informed me that I had had a visitor earlier that evening. "White suite, carrying a brief case?" I ventured.

"Si Señor."

That's alright, then," I confirmed with a smile. "I know about him."

If I hadn't been so...so...well, to put it quite bluntly, *drunk*... then I might have been able to put two and two together and come up with five, realising that the information I had just received from the receptionist didn't quite fit into the pattern off the evening's events as I understood them. I would have remembered that Toby Hamilton had followed my bus and had not gone into the hotel; not then anyway.

But, as I ascended to my top floor room, I was too busy humming the melody of a song I had particularly enjoyed dancing to at *Cleopatra's* earlier, jigging about to my own accompaniment in the cramped confines of the lift.

The light was on in my bedroom but, as I've previously explained, I'm the world's worst for that, especially in hotels where the price of a room remains constant no matter how frugal or extravagant a guest might be with the electricity. Thinking no more of it, I fixed myself a goodnight drink and settled down on the couch in the sitting room to smoke a last cigarette.

The evening's liquid refreshment had left me mellow but lucid, but when I glanced over towards the half-open bedroom door I sobered up instantly: lying on the floor I could see a polished black shoe and the bottom of a pair of neatly pressed white trousers . . .

* * *

I did not have to put a mirror to his lips or my ear to his chest to know that Toby Hamilton was dead: sightless eyes staring straight ahead; mouth open and twisted in a final paroxysm of pain; head lolling unnaturally to one side; his neck broken. The room was a shambles. Drawers hung half open, my belongings were scattered everywhere and the dummy briefcase lay open across the bed.

"You stupid bloody idiot!" I spat through clenched teeth, my reproaches falling on permanently unresponsive ears; "Why couldn't you have waited?"

"For what?!" a voice barked behind me as an arm clampled around my throat. "Waited — for what?"

The grip tightened, making it hard to breathe let alone reply. With a knee stabbing into the small of my back, my assailant marched me back into the sitting room and then out onto the balcony, doubling me up across the balustrade.

"So where is it?" he snarled.

"What?" I gasped back. "I don't know what you're talking about."

I soon realised that was not the answer he was looking for as he hoisted me over still further, forcing me look down with a grisly foretaste of what it would be to end my days as an untidy mess of blood and gristle, littering the concrete nine floors below.

"The case!" he tried again. "I want the case!"

I was right over the edge now, my arms paddling wildly through space. "Burton's got it!" I shouted back. "I delivered it this evening . . ."

I managed to clutch at the balcony railings a split second before he let go of my legs. Hanging on for all I was worth . . . quite literally . . ., I looked up and saw his face for the first time: Curtis; Randall Curtis. He took a step forward, crushing my fingers beneath his shoe.

"So Burton's got it, has he?" he asked, almost rhetorically, as he increased the pressure, making me cry out in pain.

"Yes! Yes, for Chrissakes . . .!"

"Then I won't be needing you anymore!" he sneered, unbuttoning his jacket and reaching inside. He was in no hurry, savouring every second as he screwed the silencer to the barrel of the gun and clipped home a fresh magazine. Slowly, and with the practised precision of a dedicated professional, he lowered the gun and steadied his aim . . .

With a life expectancy now hovering around zero, I had no other choice but to let go. Curtis panicked and let off a couple of wild rounds which hissed harmlessly into the deserted swimming pool below. Meanwhile, I was going down, down, down . . .

I made a desperate grab for the balustrade on the floor below, but only managed to hang there for a few brief seconds before losing my grip, my fingers clutching nothing but air as I plummeted down once more.

Suddenly I found myself participating in what can only be described as a miracle. Three storeys down, a sun shade canopy had been left unfurled across the balcony. The tightly stretched canvas cushioned my fall like a safety net before the entire structure collapsed under my weight, spilling me over the side once more.

But now I was falling in slow motion, with the time to get a proper grip on the railings as I toppled over. For a moment I hung there, swinging wildly, then I began gradually hoisting myself up, hand-over-hand, until I could clamber across the balustrade onto the balcony itself.

Badly bruised, but otherwise unhurt, I picked a path through the debris of the collapsed canopy and tried the door. It was locked. I considered knocking, but realised instantly how pointless that would be: if the occupants of the room had not been shaken out of their beds already, then they were either deaf, dead or — simply not there. So I climbed,to the neighbouring balcony, a simple manouevre after what I'd just been through, and tried my luck again. This time, the door slid open easily and I crept inside . .

Now I never knew you could do things like that with a bunch of grapes, especially such a *large, black* and *squelchy* bunch of grapes, but the couple on the bed seemed to know what they were up to and so engrossed were they that they didn't hear me tiptoe past their open bedroom door and make my way to the corridor outside. Under any other circumstances, I would have been tempted to linger a while longer and improve my education, but I did have a dead body in my own room to think about, not to mention a professional assassin itching to add mine to his list.

The room numbers told me I had ended up on the fifth floor, and the digital display above the lift shaft told me that someone was descending rapidly from the ninth. It was now close on four o'clock in the morning, a time for all right minded holidaymakers to be tucked up in their beds, (those without access to a bunch of grapes, that is), so I felt safe in assuming that the lift was being used by Curtis, either making his getaway or looking for me.

The lift didn't stop until it reached ground level, so I caught it on its way back up and returned to my room. The door was wide open, a situation I quickly rectified, locking it securely behind me. I had entered cautiously, prepared for the worst, but Curtis had disappeared. Unfortunately, he hadn't been considerate enough to take Hamilton with him: that little chore, it appeared, was now down to me.

But what to do with him? I could always call the police, of course. After all, it wasn't *me* who had killed him. Whether or not they would believe me was another matter. He had been making enquiries about me that very afternoon, and now he was lying dead in my room. Protestations of innocence would stand little chance when linked with circumstantial evidence like that. And even if they did believe me, other questions would inevitably be asked and there was no way I could even *begin* to answer those.

No; I would have to get rid of him. I had no other choice. Kaplan himself had told me as much in his briefing before my first assignment to Benidorm: . . .' . . . *we're not in the undertaking business, Rogers. If you come across any unwanted bodies along the way, just dump them. Understand? Forget about them* . . . . . .'

It wasn't as easy as the Chief had made out, though, when it came down to it. I had rather liked Hamilton and I couldn't help feeling in some way responsible for his death. If I hadn't gone back into Torremolinos to clear my bill at The 19th Hole, then he would have met up with me at the hotel and I could have shown him the case, safely locked away and beyond his reach. There would have been no need for him to break into my room and search for it himself; no need for him to die . . .

But all the regret in the world wouldn't solve the problem facing me at that precise moment. Dawn was not far away, and I would never be able to move him in daylight. I had to think fast.

There was a service lift at the end of the corridor and I decided to take him out that way. It ended in the basment, next to the kitchens and conveniently close to the parking area where I had left my car. Room service was shut down for the night and the cleaning staff, hopefully, would not be arriving much before six. I had to take the chance on that particular part of the hotel being deserted, and pray that there was no night security guard posted down there or any other member of staff using the facilities to fix himself a surreptitious snack.

My luck held. All was silence in the basement, the doors of the kitchens and utility rooms closed and padlocked, my way made easier by the occasional light left burning for the convenience of incoming staff. I propped Hamilton up in the back seat of my car and drove off into the night, still with no idea where I was taking him but steering a course away from the centre of town into the open country near Burton's villa.

The pattern of the roads and the geography of the surrounding countryside was still fresh in my mind from the previous afternoon and I soon found myself anticipating the landmarks over the brow of the next hill, or around the next bend. Sure enough, climbing out of Benalmadena Puerto, I remembered a pull-in about half a mile ahead, the lip of which overlooked a sheer drop into a deserted valley, overgrown with tall grasses and bushy trees.

As good a place as any, I decided: he wouldn't stay concealed there for very long, but with any luck, it would be long enough for me to have got well out of Torremolinos. And when he was eventually discovered, there was every possibility of the case being tidied up quickly with a verdict of accidental death.

I heaved him over the side then turned quickly away, sickened by the sound of his body thudding against the sides of the cliff on its way down. I was also pretty nauseated with myself: it seemed so callous, just tossing him aside like that, throwing him away, dumping him like so much unwanted garbage. A guy I'd been drinking with only a few hours before. But more than that: in his end, perhaps I glimpsed a reflection of my own.

I climbed back into my car and drove away at full speed towards the hotel, the half-light of dawn casting an eerie pallor over the retreating hills, the sea below me rippling blood red with the rising of the sun.

Returning to my room, I decided to leave the mess bequeathed me by Hamilton and Curtis. I had too much on my mind to bother about it there and then; there were questions to be asked, answers to be found, decisions to be made.

I pulled a chair up to the bureau in the sitting room, located pen and paper in the courtesy folder lying on top, and then, with a packet of cigarettes in front of me, I set to work.

Scribbling furiously, I chronicled the events of the past three days, together with a family tree of the characters involved, desperately searching for some kind of link. The obvious connection was the briefcase; or, to be more exact, what was in it. That particular problem had been plagueing me since the moment I picked it up, so I saw little point in wasting further time on it. I decided to work backwards, looking for less obvious relationships elsewhere.

I started with Bryant, scrawling his name in block letters across the top of a fresh page. Then I wrote 'MISSING DAUGHTER?' and 'MURDERED SON?' underneath, adding 'NEW YORK' alongside as I remembered what Smedley had told me about the circumstances of the latter's death. I thought it sounded like a professional job at the time, so there might be a connection there with Al Rossi. Maybe and maybe not, but worth bearing in mind . . .

But what about Curtis? Where did he fit in? He wanted the briefcase too, but for whom? Perhaps for himself, but I couldn't think why from the flimsy profile I'd received from Toby Hamilton. So who else? The obvious front runner was Calvin, the head of JGC Electronics, but I couldn't be sure. Still, it was all I had to go on, so I started another sheet headed with both their names, one on either side of the page.

I scribbled 'VICIOUS BASTARD!!!' beneath Curtis' name, but could get no further than that. So I concentrated on Calvin, and was immediately struck by an odd coincidence.

Hamilton had told me that Calvin's Presidential aspirations were levelled at 1992, making him the same age as Kennedy was in 1960 when he was elected. On a countback, that would make Calvin approximatley twenty one in 1969, and a student at the University of Southern California in Los Angeles. It crossed my mind that Bryant's daughter had disappeared the same year, from the same place . . . But this was clutching at straws: even a drifting lolly stick can look like a lifeline to a drowning man.

So far, so good: both Rossi and Calvin could be somehow linked with Bryant. But how? Why? Still no answers there. Hamilton had suggested that Ivanov's presence here could have something to do with Calvin and his involvement in the American missile programme. Since the CIA were involved, the obvious conclusion was that he was selling secrets to the Russians, with Rossi acting as a go-between. But that made no sense at all; a complete nonstarter. Firstly, Calvin certainly didn't appear to be short of a bob or two, so he wouldn't be doing it for the money. Secondly, the one thing Calvin *did* need was the love and respect of his fellow Americans, and he wouldn't get that by selling his country down the river. Thirdly, if he was going to deal with Ivanov, why did he need Rossi? As far as I knew, international espionage hadn't yet been added to the list of Mafia specialities. They were traditionalists — gambling, drugs, extortion, blackmail . . .

Now there was a thought! Blackmail! I quickly wrote that down beneath Calvin's name with the question: 'Rossi blackmailing Calvin for Ivanov re. rocket secrets???' A possibility, that. It would certainly explain Curtis' role in all this, assuming he had indeed been hired by Calvin. 'Bump off Rossi' I suggested beneath Curtis' name. That would have made sense of Curtis hadn't turned up in my room tonight, looking for the case . . .

So I had come full circle. I was back where I'd started, wondering what could possibly be hidden in Burton's case. And then I realised that, so far, I'd completely overlooked Mikki Burton. If there was a single linking element, then it had to be him. So I devoted another page exclusively to him, listing all the other protagonists below.

There was no apparent connection with Curtis or Calvin, none that I could see anyway, so I moved quickly on to Bryant. Nothing there either, except an overriding interest in the contents of the case. Rossi? Well he had been seen visiting Burton's villa on several occasions, so there was obviously something going between the two of them. I wrote that down, coming to another dead end with a heavily underlined 'WHY?'. And what the KGB could possibly want with a champion of western decadence like retired rock n' roller Mikki Burton I couldn't begin to imagine.

I stared at the sheet of paper for a long, long time, puffing away furiously at one cigarette after another as I tried to remember all I'd ever read about Mikki Burton's career with the Rats, hoping I'd find something there. It wasn't much: just the usual idolatry of the music press, and the scandalmongering of the tabloids. And then, quite out of the blue, another penny dropped. It was a wild hunch, but the more I thought about it the more it seemed to make sense.

If my memory served me correctly, The Rats had decided to call it a day around 1970, certainly no later than '71. Whatever the exact date, it was shortly after The Beatles had split; that much I did remember. And, being a fan, the memory of their retirement anouncement had stuck with me. It had meant a lot to the acned, star-struck teenager I was at the time: not only *how* it was made . . . and this is the important point . . . but *where!* Like so many other well heeled British groups at the height of their fame in the late sixties, The Rats were living in America. In Los Angeles, to be precise; the music capital of the world. So it was odds on that Burton would have been there in the summer of '69, along with Calvin and Bryant's mysteriously disappeared daughter . . .

The fact of twelve million or so other people having been there too didn't worry me in the slightest. I simply chose to ignore it. For I was really cooking now, my brain suddenly buzzing with unlikely possibilities, drawing conclusions from the flimsiest of evidence, finding confirmation in the slightest coincidence. Right or wrong, it was the closest I'd come yet to anything solid enough to hang a hat on.

LOS ANGELES. 1969. BURTON – CALVIN – LINDA LOVE . . . I realised my mistake even as I was writing it down, quickly scrubbing out LOVE and substituting BRYANT. Something could have happened out there involving the three of them, something which had now come home to roost in the none too savoury shape of Al Rossi, blackmailing Burton, or Calvin, or both. So what was in the briefcase? Money? To pay Rossi off? It did come from a Swiss bank after all, but the case felt too light to be carrying any great wad of notes. What else then?

I leaned back in my chair and lit my last cigarette. My head was swimming now, a vortex of assumptions, motives,wild guesses and conflicting evidence. I knew I could get no further; not until I found out what was in the case. I could work at it all day and come up with a plot as complicated as *The Big Sleep*, but it wouldn't take me any nearer the truth. I'd be stranded in a maze of false leads and reckless imaginings, with no map or compass to guide me.

And I was exhausted. I hadn't slept for the best part of twenty four hours and I suddenly felt knackered. I hauled myself into the bedroom, stretched out amongst the litter of crumpled clothes across my bed, and fell instantly asleep.

* * *

I must have been too sound asleep to hear the maid's knock, and she must have been scared out of her wits by the sight that greeted her when she came to tidy the room at nine-thirty. Tidy the room! Might as well heave the whole contents over the balcony and start again. The place looked as if a very large and very vicious animal had been imprisoned in it for a week without food or water. Or perhaps two very large and frantic creatures. Everything that could have been broken was broken; the mirror, the bedside lamp, the chair in the corner — even the door of the wardrobe was hanging by one hinge. The fridge was on its side, its contents flung everywhere, a sizeable puddle of water saturating the carpet in the middle of the room amid a stack of hotel notepaper and shredded magazines. My few possessions mingled with the broken glass of two or three bottles and a dozen tumblers.

My guess is that the hotel manager, fetched immediately by the chambermaid, had been rendered speechless when he first entered the room. He probably thought I had been murdered as well, spreadeagled as I was, fully clothed on the unmade bed. The moment I stirred he found his voice. "What is the meaning of this?" He was a small, tidy man, accustomed, no doubt, to tourists having a wild time, but mortified that such wanton destruction had been visited on one of his own rooms.

"What *has* been going on?" He tried again. He looked dangerously flustered and my first thought, as I sat up and swung my legs onto the floor, was that I was in the wrong room — his room — and that poor Hamilton's corpse was still hanging halfway out of the bathroom.

"I can explain everything..." I stammered, the events of only a couple of hours ago now coming back to me."... you see, there was a party."

"A party! You call this a party! *Madre di Dio,* this is...it is an earthquake! You ruin my hotel. And I have people booked into this room as soon as you leave. You ruin me..."

He was working himself into more and more of a rage, pacing about the room picking up bits of clothing and broken ends of bottle and then dropping them again.

"I will call the police! I will have you deported! You are an animal... a...hooligan!" He strode over to the window and hoisted the Venetian blind with an angry jerk, revealing a broken pane of glass. White light flooded into the room, making it look, if anything, worse.

"Senor, let me explain." I began in my best pidgin English, my mind racing at Mach 8. "I do not know who used my room for a party last night. It was not me. I arrived back late — maybe 4 o'clock. Just ask the night porter.

"Somebody has obviously played a trick on me. They get drunk and then invite all their friends to my room. And then they break everything and throw all my cloths around the place..."

I must have looked the picture of wronged innocence, the very model of righteous indignation, my little speech quite taking the wind out of his sails. He stood there gaping for a moment or two, ıen said: "But this is terrible. You have more enemies on your ɔur, yes?" I hid the smile that twitched at the corners of my ıouth, then said: "I suppose I must have done, though I don't now who it might be."

"We must speak to your tour guide," he decides. "She must find ›ut who it was that did this. I will throw them out of my hotel. I vill make them pay. I will..."

He was working himself into one of his frenzies again and had ;ompletely forgotten that I was there on my own and not with a ›our. It was time to placate him.

"Yes that is a good idea I will find the tour operator mmediately and demand that she sorts everything out.

"Don't worry Senor, by lunchtime you will be paid in full. What you must do now is make out a bill for all the damage. And make it a big bill. We'll teach these hooligans not to spoil your hotel."

At last I managed to get him out, still without having to divulge which tour I was supposd to be travelling with. I showered and shaved, pulled on a pair of dark blue cotton trousers and a denim, loaded my back pocket with pesetas from the Workshop's generous allowance and set off in search of a tour guide.

Yesterday I had noticed a pretty, fair haired girl from Newcastle collecting together a group of tourists from a bus trip: she would be the one to help me, I thought, and it was important that I find her before the hotel manager started making wild allegations about her flock. Mercifully I had little difficulty in tracking her down: she was sitting at a table in a corner of the terrace, adding up columns of figures and checking names off a list. She looked somewhat flustered, and clearly she was in no mood to be interrupted by strangers. But she looked up and said 'hello' as I approached, and when I said I had something urgent to discuss with her, reluctantly invited me to sit down.

"You are shortly going to be handed a hefty bill by the manager of the hotel, for damage to my bedroom" I began: no point in beating about the bush.

"Oh God. That's all I need. How do you know it was one of my crowd? You're not with us anyway, are you?"

"No I'm not with Skyways. I'm here on my own. The fact is tha it wasn't one of your party that damaged the room. In fact, i wasn't anybody staying in the hotel...."

She was looking at me candidly, listening patiently as if she wa used to coping with problems like this every day.

"Well, Mr., er..."

"Rogers. Frank Rogers."

"Well, Mr Rogers, if the culprit wasn't with Skyways, then th damage has nothing to do with me, has it?"

"I haven't made myself very clear, have I?" I found her eye disconcerting. She was rather like an indulgent primary-schoo teacher. "You see, I'm here on a job. I work as a sort of 'special courier' and I have to deliver something very important tc someone in Torremolinos, something so important that othe people want to get their hands on it before I hand it over. It was this that whoever it was who turned over my room was looking for..."

"Why don't you call the police?" she said.

"Out of the question, I'm afraid. The delivery is top secret... Is it too much to ask you to help me settle the business with the hotel manager quickly and simply? What I would like you to do is to accept the bill from the manager and pay it without question." Here I pulled out my wad of notes.

She seemed to be intriqued by the project, and slightly amused. "Mr Rogers, I don't believe a word of this 'special delivery' story, and I don't see why Skyways should spoil its good relations with this hotel by shouldering the responsibility for something that has nothing to do with us."

"Unfortunately, the die has already been case," I shrugged. "I'm afraid I've already laid the blame at your door. I could think of no other excuse when the manager woke me and hour ago.

"Look at it this way. Far from spoiling your relations with the hotel, you could enhance your reputation with the manager by paying his exhorbitant bill — and it will be exhorbitant, I'm sure of that. I should think he'll be asking for enough to refurbish at least three rooms — promptly and without question."

She realised she was in a cleft-stick. Her company was now involved whether she liked it or not and if she denied everything the manager would surely call the police and there would be an ugly and time consuming witch-hunt. And, I suspected, there was also something about this Frank Rogers she rather liked.

"You really give me very little alternative," she said.

I was more relieved that I cared to admit. If she hadn't agreed to connive in my deceit I would be up the proverbial creek. My relief must have showed on my face as I thanked her.

"I tell you what," I said as I handed over a bunch of 5000 peseta notes, "why don't I employ you as my guide to the best restaurant in Torremolinos this evening? You must be able to take some time off from chaperoning tourists? I'll pick up my change then and we'll spend it on supper."

"That would be very nice," she replied, a slight smile hovering around her lips.

"But I don't know how busy I'll be this evening. I must organise a bus trip to Mijas this afternoon, and I may be late back."

"No problem! I'll stick around and wait for you," I said as I got up to go. Little did I realise how impossible that was going to be...

***

I was as hungry as a horse. The sun was high in the sky and they had stopped serving breakfast hours ago. The manager was, thankfully, nowhere to be seen. As I left my room-key at reception I told them that I was expecting an urgent telephone call, and they were to take any messages and say that I would be back about one o'clock. Then I strolled out of the hotel into the sweltering midday sun and walked over to the Angel Bar, just across the road. With great relief, I noticed no sign of a black Mercedes waiting for me at the front of the hotel.

I had noticed the Angel yesterday afternoon. It had a large terrace covered with tables and chairs and vibrant with coloured tee-shirts and frocks. There was plenty of noise and activity on the terrace as I approached it now, all smiles and laughter as a tall thin waiter rushing about between the tables with trays of tapas and chips, wine and beer.

I was far safer in crowds. Curtis would not risk attacking me with other people around. Also the place had a pleasant, holiday atmosphere very far removed from the dire business that this trip was turning out to be for me. I didn't want to advertise my presence at the Angel to anybody who might be interested so I opted to sit inside. It was, anyway, cooler in the small bar than out on the blazing terrace. I drained my first San Miguel almost in one and, while I was ordering the next, struck up conversation with Pepe, the barman. His English was just about as good as my Spanish, which means pretty poor, but we were getting on fine and he had advised me to eat 'Antonio's burger and fries' for my breakfast/lunch rather than any of the complicated Spanish dishes that were also on the menu.

"Antonio, he make real hamburgers, like in America, fresh every morning. Plenty meat.'

I had just asked him what the ingredients of an *'espignada'* were when we were interrupted.

"Hey, Jimmy. Where'sa John?"

Pepe greeted the burly customer who had lurched up beside me with a look of blank incomprehension.

"Where's a pisser, pal? Where can ah go make pee-pee?"

Both parties looked at me helplessly.

"Se peuda visitar la toilette?" I seemed to remember the phrase from my guide book, but it achieved the desired result and Pepe directed the Scotsman towards the lavatories with complicated gesticulations.

By the time he returned I was sitting at a table parallel with the bar and tucking into Antonio's excellent burger. He sat down at the table next to mine, beside a badly sunburned girl in shorts and two other guys, and as soon as he had gulped down the remains of his beer he leaned over to thank me for helping him find the way to the gents.

"See that guy," he said to his friends in a loud voice, "he speaks the lingo like a native. Is that no' right, pal? Beautiful speaker. He's probably bi-lingual, you know or somethin'...Hey Jimmy, gie's some mair o' these Marks an' Sparks...'Saint Michael', y' ken: 'San Miguel'..." His friends started to laugh, and the laughter possessed them. Until the arrival of the beers they were convulsed in a sobbing, giggling huddle.

By this time I had finished my lunch and had ordered my third beer. The tall, thin waiter whom I had noticed as I came in to the bar brought it, and he had no sooner set it down than there were further cries from the next door table: "Here, Jimmy, I'll pay for that: yon big gingery boy's ma pal."

It turned out that the waiter really was called 'Jimmy' — or rather Jimi — and spoke far better English than the Scots did. This was an excuse for more drinks, and then it was my turn to buy a round back, and before long we were talking and laughing as if we had been friends all our lives.

Kenny — the boy in search of the gents —, Tommy, Hugh (known as 'Shug') and Margot were from Motherwell, near Glasgow. They were all in their early twenties and none of them had been abroad before. In the three days that they had been in Torremolinos they had ventured little further than the Angel, the beach, and the swimming pool at their hotel, but today was going to be different. They had hired a car and were going to spend the afternoon at Tivoli World, a gigantic funfair on the road to

Burton's villa.

"The lassie in charge of our tour says its great: 'Torremolinos' answer to Disneyland' and a' that," said Shug. "Why don't you chum along, Frank?" "Aye, come on Frank," the others chorused. "We need someone who can speak the lingo. It'll be a good laugh.

Their openness and warmth was a tonic after the pressure of the last few days, but I explained that I had to see someone that afternoon and couldn't make it. I suddenly remembered the telephone call and looked at my watch: 1.30. I got up and paid my bill and made plans to meet up with 'the team frae Motherwell' in the Angel sometime over the next few days, then dashed out and returned to the hotel.

There was a message waiting for me, and I felt a tremendous surge of relief as I took it from the receptionist. Burton was back; I would hand over the bloody case and get out on the next possible flight. I had had enough of this job, and of Torremolinos for that matter. But I was to be disappointed. When I tore open the envelope it simply said: "Await instructions at 5.00pm. LL"

I cursed aloud; I was already imagining myself back in London that night. Still, I reflected that — though it would be tomorrow night rather than tonight — I would soon be done with the whole messy business. But what to do between now and 5.00? I was still concerned about Curtis. He had tried hard to kill me only a few hours ago, and it was almost certain that he would try again. In the hotel I was a sitting duck, but roaming the streets of Torremolinos or hiding in a darkened bar was not much safer. I remembered the cheery Scots crowd and their plan to go to a fun-fair, and concluded I'd be safer in a crowd. Curtis would never risk attacking me there, and their company would certainly be welcome.

I walked quickly back to the Angel. They were just leaving to go, and welcomed me like a lost friend, delighted that I was coming with them.

We were crammed into their hired Fiat Uno, Kenny at the wheel, Margot in the front seat navigating from a tiny map; Tommy, Shug and I in the back singing 'I belong tae Glasgow' at the top of our voices. Early in the journey we had got lost and then trapped in a one-way systeem that led us to the 'Pink Elephant'. Kenny didn't even have to ask his passengers: he pulled over and we all went in for a 'pinta larger'.

Then we hit a section of the town that didn't seem marked on the map. "We're in the Lost Quarter, boys. A No Man's Land where tourists go to die" siad Tommy dramatically. "Ah think that calls for another pint. Ah could do wi' a piss, anyway."

This time it was 'The Anchor', and after that we stopped at 'El Sombrero' before reaching the outskirts of the town. Torremolinos' answer to Disneyland was, apparently, only a couple of miles away. I felt more secure than I had done since arriving in Spain: surrounded by my mates with a bellyfull of beer and 'Yellow Submarine' thundering from my lips.

At last we were there. The place looked enormous, a massive fun-fair with stalls casinos, 'pubs' and cafes; endless banks of electronic games, pin-ball tables, roundabouts, and the whole thing dominated by a collosal Ferris Wheel. I had been a great devotee of Battersea fun-fair as a kid, but this made Battersea look provincial.

We headed straight for a brightly lit 'Amusement Arcade', packed with tourists in beach-wear and young Spaniards trying to pick up fair-skinned girls. Margot and Kenny quickly won a pile of pesetas and the rest of us had difficulty dragging them out. They were keen to go on to the Casino, but Tommy had his eye on the Ferris Wheel and persuaded them to head off in that direction.

Thinking back over that fateful afternoon, I would like to think that even then, on the way to the Ferris Wheel, I had an intimation of foreboding. A slight chill in the blazing hot summer sun, pehaps; a sudden glimpse of the transience of youth as we stopped for hot-dogs. But there was none. We were on holiday, flushed with sun and drink, as happy as could be. The Scots kids kept up

an uninterrupted patter of wise-cracks and dry comments abou
everything we saw. I had banished all fears and worries from m
mind and, in a rash moment, even considered staying on for
couple of days more in Torremolinos once I had dumped the case
We all laughed a lot.

Margot refused to go on the Wheel when we finally reached it
and Shug happily volunteered to keep her company. Kenny
Tommy and I paid our entry money and climbed the four broa
steps to the landing stage. From here the Wheel seemed to towe
into the clouds and, a kid again, I was looking forward to seein
the view from the top. They were loading as we approached, th
Wheel moving slowly to allow the previous passengers t
disembark on the other side in a giggling, sqealing gaggle, and t
allow us to board the tiny, bucket-seated gondolas. When our tur
came we all three piled into one, although they were reall
designed for four chldren or two adults.

The Wheel began to revolve, and we began to climb — in slow
stages at first, until all the previous passengers had disembarked.
The gondolas ahead and behind were full of children, squealing in
anticipation and clinging on for dear life. Kenny was pointing out
this and that to me as we climbed and Tommy kept moaning that
he was going to be sick.

Then we were off. The Wheel began to gather momentum about the time we reached the top, and as we plummeted earthwards, all three of us, grown men though we were, uttered a groan of excitement. By the time we had reached the summit and were plunging down again, the Wheel had really begun to motor. Kenny was leaning against me and Tommy had his mouth open in a long cry, clutching either side of the gondola with whitened knuckles.

Round and round we went. At first you are utterly disorientated by the motion, unable to take in anything but a blur of rushing colours against a backgrond of grinding machinery, screams and battering hot air. But after a while the mind adjusts to the experience. You settle in your seat more comfortably. You force yourself to concentrate on one subject, and before long you are riding the carousel like a professional.

This didn't seem to be the case with my friends. Kenny was clearly loving it, but he looked completely out of control: he had flung his head back and was looking at everything upside down. And Tommy's mouth was a rictus of horror, looking as if he might vomit at any moment. I leant back like Kenny as the Wheel began to slow into its final few revolutions.

The instant Kenny slumped against me I knew what had happened, but my mind refused to take it in, refused to believe that he hadn't just fallen asleep. I jerked myself upright as we began to climb, slowly, into the final revoltuon. Keny's head lolled further over, his eyes staring sightlessly, and then I saw the neat hole below his ear on the side furthest from me.

I immediately leaned over the edge of the gondola and looked below at the crowd standing around the landing stage in time to see a tall fair-haired man hurrying away towards the hamburger stands and amusement arcades. Curtis.

Why had I been so stupid? Why hadn't I realised that having tried to kill me once he would stop at nothing to finish me off? I was not jeopardising his whole plan; I was a risk that had to be eliminated at all costs. And I had been stupid enough to involve other people; to think that I would be shielded by the crowd. Well, I certainly had been shielded, and the young, happy, generous individual who had shielded me now lay in my arms with his life's blood pouring out of his ears. I felt disgusted with myself, and I felt a great hatred for the man who had done it.

Tommy took a few moments to realise what had happened. At first he thought his friend had been struck by something — a stone or a coin dropped from above — and knocked out. But as the pool of blood began to spread over the orange plastic seat the truth seeped though to him. He began to shout, grabbing his friend and cradling his head, sobbing and repeating his name: "Kenny, lad, Kenny. Dear God, Why? Who would do this?"

I had to grab him roughly and shake him to make him understand.

"Tommy, the bullet was meant for me. I know the man who fired it, and I've just seen him leave the crowd. I'm going to jump off the Wheel and chase him as soon as we get close enough to the ground. You'll have to handle the authorities yourself. I'll see you later. Do you understand me?"

Every phrase had to be repeated two or three times, but by the time we were again approaching the landing stage I think he understood what I was going to do.

I stood up in the gondola when it was about twenty feet from the ground and, putting my foot on the edge of the car, sprang to the ground, landing with a parachute roll.

There was no sign of Margot and Shug as I sprinted for the exit, and there was no indication of anybody having noticed that one of the passengers on the Ferris Wheel had been shot. Curtis must have been on the boarding platform, and he must have fired at point-blank range as the gondola swung by. I barged my way through the crowds of tourists, deaf to their cries of outrage, conscious only of the blood banging in my temples and of a consuming hatred for the man who had killed Kenny.

I have no idea what I thought I would do if I caught up with Curtis. He was armed and mobile: I was unarmed and car-less. My only advantgage was that he thought he had killed me: I suppose I reckoned I could surprise him before he started shooting.

In the end it never came to that. I never caught up with him: he had vanished into the crowd. At the front gates I slowed my pace to a walk and thought about my next move. I was inclined to go back to the Ferris Wheel and explain what had happened to Kenny's friends, and to comfort them as much as I could. But this would necessarily involve a run in with the police, something I simply couldn't afford at the moment. Also it was 4.40: I had to be back at the hotel by 5.00 if I was to collect my instructions and get rid of the bloody case.

I reasoned that I could catch up with the kids from Motherwell once I had completed the job, hailed a taxi and was driven back to the hotel.

I was showering when Linda Love phoned about 5.45. When she was put through all she said was:

"Mikki's back and he wants you. Grab the case, check out of the hotel and get your ass over here. And he means pronto, man. Like...NOW!"

***

PART THREE: PORTIONS AND PARCELS

"ALL THINGS ARE TAKEN FROM US AND BECOME PORTIONS AND PARCELS OF THE DREADFUL PAST"

Alfred, Lord Tennyson: "The Lotus Eaters"

SO I was going home. It was over. My tiredness evaporated as I converted the mess in my bedroom to a mess in my suitcase. I had checked out and was on the road to Burton's estate within half an hour of Linda Love's call.

As I drove, I resolved to let the whole thing go; to make no waves, to ask no awkward questions. Just dump the case and go away. I would camp at Malaga Airport, for days if necessary, waiting for a flight home. I just didn't care anymore, my earlier resolve to get to the bottom of things now vanished with the anticipation of this godawful assignment coming to an end. I had come out of it alive, and that was more than enough for me. The pressure was on Burton now, or shortly would be. How right Kaplan was and how presumptuous I had been to assume otherwise: it was none of my business; it was not my concern . . .

I took a longer route to the villa, approaching it from the opposite direction to avoid passing the site of Toby Hamilton's temporary grave. It would have cast a shadow on my day, to say the least. I couldn't help thinking about him though: I managed to convince myself that I was not to blame, that he had simply paid the price for getting himself involved in such a shitty business in the first place. After all, there had to be easier ways of collecting a Civil Service pension. I could only hope that his body would be found soon, before the sun and the flies did too much damage.

I arrived at the villa and the electronic gates swished open the moment I identified myself over the entryphone. I was met at the end of the drive by a uniformed servant, (if you could call swimming trunks, flying helmet and a smile as wide as the Straits of Gibraltar a uniform), who introduced himself as José and informed me that Señor Burton was awaiting me in his study.

"Lead on, MacDuff . . ." I muttered as he escorted me towards the circular annexe I'd spotted from my hillside vantage point the day before. He indicated a pair of ornately carved double doors and then left. My knock was answered by the sound of a buzzer and the metallic click of the automatic lock springing open. I pushed the door to and stepped inside.

It was an impressive room: the walls were lined with bookshelves displaying everything from heavily bound first editions to a vast collection of modern paperbacks; a glittering accumulation of gold discs and other music industry awards occupied the wall-space in between, together with a wealth of twentieth century art from Ernst and Utrillo to Hockney and Warhol.

At the far end of the room, on a raised dais and seated behind the largest desk I had ever seen, sat Mikki Burton. He was swinging to and fro in his chair, eyes closed, his tented fingers tapping thoughtfully at the bridge of his nose. It was like having an audience with the Queen. I approached the dais and coughed.

There was no immediate reaction, not even so much as a change of rhythm to the drum pattern he continued to beat out on his hawk like nose. The reports I'd read in the papers about pop singers suffering premature deafness due to the incredibly high decibel levels of their amplification equipment appeared, for once, to have some basis in fact. I took a deep breath and coughed again.

He opened his eyes, looking me up and down but still saying nothing. Rising from his chair, he appeared much shorter than I had previously imagined, not more than five foot five at the most; he was painfully thin and his face was lined with the evidence of every one of his forty two years. Dressed entirely in black, a collarless shirt inlaid with thin gold braid and studded with pearls tucked into high waisted flared trousers, he could have won an award for the best dressed man of 1967.

He descended the dais, ignoring my extended hand and demanding the briefcase I held in the other with an impatient snapping of his fingers.

"That it?" he asked.

Stupid question; but, as Linda Love had so succinctly pointed out, he *was* paying the bills.

"Yes; yes, it is," I confirmed, handing it over. "I'm Frank Rogers, by the way, and . . ."

"I *know* what your name is, man!" he interrupted. "And there's something you better get straight, right from the off. When you're working for me, you do as you're sodding well told! Got it? I sent Linda to get this, two days ago. I needed it here, locked away in the safe, not out on the streets and up for grabs in the hands of a fucking messenger boy!

"Jeeessusss . . . I go away to take care of business for a coupla days and the whole frigging world falls apart . . .!"

It was plain to see where Linda Love had learned her manners. Is that all these people do, I wondered; scream abuse at each other all day long?

He ranted on, but my thoughts were elsewhere: I couldn't help thinking how much money I'd wasted on buying his records, if all those hard earned pennies had found their way into the pocket of this ignorant little shit. The records would all go straight in the bin when I got home, that was for sure; better still, I'd immerse them in boiling water and make ashtrays out of them so that every time I stubbed out a cigarette . . .

"Finished?" I said as the storm subsided, adding: "It doesn't really matter a toss either way, 'cos I'm off! My orders were to deliver the case to you, — *and only you* — and that's exactly what I've done. So enjoy it, whatever it is. As for me, I'm going home!"

I spun on my heel and stormed off towards the door. He let me get halfway across the room before calling after me: "No you're not, man!"

I turned to see him back on the dais, standing by his desk and waving a sheet of yellow paper in his hand.

"Here . . ." he said, his thin mouth curling up at the edges in parody of a smile; ". . . read this!"

"What's that?" I asked. Whatever it was, I had a funny feeling wasn't going to like it.

He didn't reply, just held the paper out towards me and waved i some more. I returned to the foot of the dias and snatched it out o his hand. It was a telegram, addressed to Burton and dated th previous evening. I couldn't believe my eyes as I read: CONFIRMATION ROGERS ASSIGNED TO YOU AS SECURITY CONSULTANT UNTIL FURTHER NOTICE STOP CONTRACT TERMS AGREED LORIMER - MAMMOTH STOP REGARDS KAPLAN

*

So there was I, feet back firmly on the ground with no prospec of escaping from this nightmare '*until further notice*'!.

I can't describe how I felt; the anger, the sense of betrayal, the despair. I tossed the telegram onto Burton's desk and slumped down dejectedly into the nearest chair.

"Feel free to sit down if you want to!" Burton sneered after a prolonged silence.

"Cheers!" I hissed in return. "I will".

Again his face cracked into a grin, the laugh of boyish glee which lurked behind his tightly drawn lips manifesting itself in the gleam of triumph which illuminated his heavy lidded, red rimmed eyes. I had to look away, muttering obscenities under my breath as I busied myself with a prolonged and totally unnecessary study of my shoes.

On top of everything else, there was another aspect to all this that had really got under my skin. So I asked: "How did you do it?

Get hold of my boss like that?" I had, after all, been trying to contact Kaplan myself for the past three days.

Burton shrugged. "Easy. I didn't. I tracked down Sir George instead. Or, rather my record company did. All they had to do was call the phone in his car.

"What's the matter, Frank? You don't seem that knocked out with our little arrangement . . ."

"Damn right, I'm not!" I snapped back. "Have you any idea what I've been through with that bloody case of yours? Well? Have you? I've been chased, shot at and thrown out of a ninth storey window! There's a good man lying dead at the bottom of a cliff not three miles from here, and the best part of another two splattered across a stable yard in Mijas . . . "

"That's rock n' roll . . ." he interrupted, hunching his shoulders.

"Is that all you've got to say? Just shrug it off like that? Don't you . . . don't you care?"

"Oh yes, I *care*," he replied as he returned to his chair, putting his feet up on the desk. "I care about Mikki Burton! Number one! I learned very early on that if you want to stay on top in a business like mine, then you've got to be hard. Look after yourself, 'cos nobody else will. That's what I care about . . .

"Why do you think you're here? Why do you think I'm keeping you with me for another month?"

A month? An involuntary groan escaped my lips. Why not make it another year? Why not a lifetime?

"You seem to be driving this bus," I shrugged; "You tell me!"

"Protection, man; I need protection. What you've got to understand is I'm into a really big deal here . . . and I mean BIG!! That briefcase you've been carrying means five million dollars to me, and your job is to make sure I'm still around in four weeks' time to collect."

Five million dollars! No wonder everybody had been so keen to get their hands on that case. What on earth could be worth that amount of money? I decided against pressing the point; he wouldn't have told me anyway, and I had a whole month to find out. Instead, I asked: "Why me? I'm just a messenger boy, remember?"

He threw his head back and laughed. "Nice going, Frank. Y'know, I think we're going to get along fine . . . just fine! You've done a good job looking after my investment over there. I hope you'll be just as careful with me."

"What if I refuse?"

He pointed to the telegram, now crushed beneath the heel of his boot. "That piece of paper says you won't. Your boss thought you'd be the best man for the job . . ."

I bet he did, I thought; save the price of another set of air fares, at least . . .

" . . . and so do I. You know how to stick up for yourself and you don't take any shit — I like that. And I hear the employment situation in the old country ain't too hot just now . . ."

So that was it; he had me against the ropes and he knew it. I could have walked out on the job, but Kaplan would never give me another chance after that. Nor had he promised an easy ride when he recruited me. Like it or not, my orders had been changed and I had no other choice but to carry them through, whatever the consequences.

Resigned, I sighed heavily and said: "OK — you win. What do you want me to do?"

"I've already told you, man. Stick to me like glue for the next month until I've finished my little bit of business with the contents of that case. There are some people around who are . . . well, let's just say they ain't too happy about the way I've decided to handle things. They might take it into their heads to conclude the transaction themselves . . . if you get my drift?"

Indeed I did. "Like who?" I asked.

Burton shook his head. "That's not for you to know. Just assume that anyone within a fifty mile radius could be gunning for me, and you won't go far wrong"

I wasn't about to let him off as lightly as that, and I had nothing to lose by revealing a little of what I had found out.

"I know about Rossi and Calvin," I told him.

His expression soured but he covered up quickly, his brows knitting in a puzzled frown as he replied: "Who? I know a guy called Al Rossi, an old buddy of mine from New York. He's . . . um . . . over here at the moment, as a matter of fact; taking care of a bit of business along the coast. But the other one . . . what did you say his name was again?"

"Calvin. John G. Calvin."

He repeated the name over and over again in a distracted sort of way, staring into space and drumming his fingers thoughtfully on the top of the desk.

"Sorry, Frank. Never heard of him. Now," he began, changing the subject a little too hurriedly; "how's your passport?"

"Much the same as everybody else's, I imagine," I answered, mystified. "Blue cover with my name on it, picture inside . . ."

He was not amused. "What I meant was, is there any place you're not welcome? Anywhere in Europe you've been kicked out of, arrested, anything like that?"

I shook my head.

"Good! 'cos we're going just about everywhere there is to go over the next few weeks. You'll get our itinerary from the Tour Manager later, so I won't bother about that now.

"Did you see the helicopter on the lawn on your way in?"

"Couldn't miss it!" I confirmed.

"We'll be taking off for Malaga in about half an hour, and from there we'll be flying to Cannes. Leave José the keys to your car and he'll see it's returned.

"And. . . Frank?"

"Yes, Mister Burton?" I responded mechanically, not really caring anymore.

He rose from his chair and walked towards me, grabbing the briefcase on the way. "Look after this, will you? We're taking it with us!"

*

The reason for the delay in boarding the chopper, I soon discovered, was Burton's insistence on taking his morning dip in the pool. Apparently, this was how he started each and every day, a ritual he shared with his Old English sheepdog, Trigger. Sitting by the pool in protective attendcance, I tucked into some fresh fruit and cream, delivered to me on a trolley by José. It was just what I needed after my hectic and sleepless night. This was followed by a seemingly bottomless pot of tea which Burton shared as he towelled himself dry.

The dog, however, preferred to shake the excess moisture from its shaggy coat, most of it ending up over me. This procedure was repeated several times, much to Burton's amusement and leaving me little alternative but to make a pretence of sharing the joke and curb my natural instincts to encourage it on its way with a well aimed kick to its backside. Eventually, Trigger padded off under her own steam to stretch out on the lawn, seemingly content to let the sun's rays finish the job off for her. Burton returned to a vigorous towelling down of his back, his hips swaying rythmically to the pumping of his arms like a belly dancer with a fearsome itch.

As he did this, he explained that we were about to embark on his come-back tour of Europe, subsidised by Mammoth Records to coincide with the release of his first new album in years, recorded in America the previous winter. The tour was scheduled to climax in a month's time with a special concert at the bullring in Malaga, staged to offset several years' worth of unpaid Spanish taxes. The authorities would commandeer ninety per cent of the takings in final settlement.

We were kicking off the tour in Cannes, he informed me, to capitalise on a convention being held in the town, attended by representatives of record companies and music publishers from all over the world. An offshoot of their traditional January bash, the Midem Festival, this provided another chance for record executives to laze about in the sun all day, giving 'definite maybe's' to each other on deals which would probably still be hanging in the air when they re-convened, six months later.

And Cannes was also home base for 'The Sonic Special ', the ustom-built train that was to provide both transport and ccommodation for the duration of the tour. Of pre-war vintage, it ad been converted by a team of enterprising Frenchies with the ock tour market in mind, minimising the astronomical hotel bills nd travel expenses which might otherwise prove prohibitive on a uge tour like ours. It had certainly made sense for Mammoth Records to charter it for this tour, what with Mikki Burton's ntourage, the five other supporting acts, the ancillary crews and ll the sound and lighting equipment that appears necessary these ays before any performer will consider setting foot on a stage.

"But I get train sick!" I owned up, somewhat sheepishly.

Burton said nothing, no doubt assuming this to be another ttempt on my part to cry off the job, and, as such, not worth the assle of a response. This was bad news for me, as I'd actually een telling the truth. I hadn't expected him to let me off with: '… orry to hear 'bout that, Frank. Under the cirumstances, why don't e just drop you off at Malaga so you can get the next flight ome", but, unhappy as I already was with the prospect of the oming month, I certainly didn't fancy spending it adorning the ailway tracks of Europe with the memory of every breakfast, unch and high tea I would be obliged to eat along the way.

At last, we appeared to be just about ready. My scratched and string-bound suitcase looked a trifle lost beside its snakeskin and crocodile hide counterparts as the luggage was loaded onto the helicopter, but no more so than its owner when, just before boarding, I was introduced to Mahavishnu Deva Ram. Still kitted out in the ensemble of orange robes, matching make-up and wrap-around snake he'd selected for his meditations on the lawn the day before, he placed his palms together in front of his nose and bowed his head as I rather foolishly held out my hand.

Plunged into embarrassed confusion, I forgot all about my extended hand, leaving it dangling indecisively in front of me. This was a big mistake. The python began to uncoil itself from his

master's neck and make for my outstretched arm. I hopped out o
range as if a hot brick had been dropped down my trousers, muc
to the amusement of Burton, José and the waiting pilot.

There was no change of expression on the face of Deva Ram however, as he retrieved his snake and stroked its head tenderl before delivering it into the care of José, its keeper for the ne month.

"Deva Ram's on a vow of silence this month . . ." Burto explained.

Very considerate of him, I thought.

" . . . meaning he speaks to no one but me. He advises me on a spiritual and business matters, so when we're in conference I wa you to make damn sure that we're not interrupted. OK, Frank? I that clear? Let nobody in . . . and that includes Linda; *especiall* Linda!"

From that, I could only assume that Linda Love and Burton' personal guru didn't get on too well. I could sympathise with bot points of view.

"Yes, Mr. Burton." I replied with a nod.

"And you can cut this 'Mr Burton' crap out. Call me Mikki . . ."

"Yes, Mr Burton," I said again, smiling.

He grunted and flashed me a look of considerable animosit before climbing into the helicopter behind Deva Ram. Passenge accommodation inside was for four. Burton and Deva Ram too the front two seats while I strapped myself in behind and waite with some apprehension for Linda Love to arrive.

The minutes ticked by, treading water. The pilot was getting anxious now, turning in his seat to tap at his watch impatiently and raise an eyebrow to question Burton as to the cause of the continuing delay. Leaning forward in his seat, Burton smoothed the troubled waters with a whispered explanation in Spanish which, judging by the lascivious belly laugh and furious nods of agreement this inspired in the pilot, I could only take as something extremely insulting to the female sex in general, and Linda Love in particular.

At last she appeared in the doorway of the house, flicking her golden curls behind her as she positioned the largest pair of dark glasses I had ever seen on the bridge of her exquisitely sculpted nose. Turning her face to the sun, she lingered on the porch for several seconds as if expecting such a grand entrance to be rewarded with a round of applause. Burton just muttered "Stupid bitch!" under his breath and motioned to the pilot to make his final preparations for take off.

In a body hugging outfit of horizontal stripes and with her face all but completely hidden behind those enormous glasses, she bore more than a passing resemblance to a giant bee as she strolled casually across the lawn towads us. Quite apt an image that, I concluded, all things considered: I'd certainly felt the full force of her sting over the past couple of days and the painful memory still lingered on. The very regrettable difference between her and the genuine article was that she had delivered her venom with her tongue and not, I'm extremely sorry to say, with her divinely rounded tail. Hmmm. . .; now *there* was a thought to while away the weary miles . . .

"About fucking time, too!" Burton snarled at her as she clambered on board.

"Screw you!" she bit back, pushing past him to park herself in the seat next to mine.

I turned my head tentatively towards her and offered a courteous smile of welcome. To my utter astonishment, she acknowledged this with a chirpy "Hi, Frank!" and beamed back.

Curiouser and curiouser, but any chance of enlarging upon this apparent thaw in our relationship was smothered at birth by the roar of the rotor blades above. We were standing on the tarmac at Malaga airport in a matter of minutes, and, our passports checked, we than transferred to a chartered Lear Jet for the short flight to Cannes.

Again Linda Love chose to sit beside me, leaning across once we were airborne to confuse me further by whispering: "Listen, Frank — I want to apologise for the hard time I've been giving you these past few days. I had my reasons, believe me, and one day I' explain them. Until then, please trust me; I'm on your side and want you to be on mine. So no hard feelings, huh? Friends?'

I accepted her hand and replied: "Sure . . . why not?" He attitude was certainly a change from the foul-mouthed bitchines she had shown over the past few days, but there was more tha that. She had hinted that her side was not Mikki Burton's side There might be something in that . . .

We were met at Nice Airport by a twelve-seater bus which spe us and our baggage to Cannes station where we boarded ou specially chartered train. All that Burton had previously told me about it could now be put down to the mutterings of a man whose riches had long since disqualified him from an appreciation of wha real luxury was; for here was splendour to match the opulence o the fabled Orient Express, a mobile Claridges or Georges Cinq dedicated entirely to the bizarre peccadilloes of the rock music fraternity, lacking only the uptight intrusions of hotel managers and the outraged complaints of other guests. Sixteen carriages long, its red and gold paintwork glittering in the Mediterranean sun, it had everything a touring rock band could possibly need: there was a rehearsal room, a games room, a central lounge with bar, movie and video facilities; the major suites towards the front of the train were decorated with quilted velvet and boasted their own bathrooms, twin double beds, hi-fi and , while the crew's quarters towards the back provided accommodation that compared favourably with any four star hotel; four of the carriages had been gutted to carry the equipment and luggage, and were provided with pheumatic hoists and extendable ramps as well. It was every tour manager's dream.

I was given a small compartment next to Burton's suite, equipped with a fold-down bed, a comfortable couch and a small hotplate on which I could brew my own tea or coffee. Strangely, Linda Love elected to share accommodation with Maggie Moran, an equally foul mouthed blues singer from Georgia, while Burton and Deva Ram occupied the principal suite. All Burton had to do summon me was rap on the dividing, wood-panelled wall, which e did with irritating frequency, treating me more like a bloody utler than a bodyguard.

The concert at the Palais des Festivals that evening was a isaster: not for the supporting acts who received as much pplause as they could possibly have expected, but because the vo encores demanded of Mikki Burton rang hollow by omparison. They seemed inspired more by disappointed nostalgia ıan by anything approaching genuine appreciation.

Mind you, he got what he deserved, for Burton had not 'eathered well. His band was made up of flabby session musicians ı their forties, doing enough to warrant their wage-packets but ot a semi-quaver more, going through the motions with world-'eary cynicism. Burton did his damndest, throwing himself round the stage with the kind of gyrations that had whipped udiences into a frenzy nearly two decades before, but it soon ecame obvious that he just couldn't do it anymore. After two umbers he was sweating profusely and gasping for breath, his oice crackling and losing its range as the set wore on.

The only saving grace was the laser beam light show he mployed to climax his act; an intricate pattern of pencil thin eams sweeping across him as he fell to the floor and stretched out n the shape of a crucifix. It all fell rather flat despite the lights. The audience didn't realise the show had finished for several econds, then there was some spasmodic clapping which was gradually taken up by the rest of the crowd and eventually swelled o a polite, if somewhat reluctant, demand for more of the same.

I was rather pleased, myself; seeing him humiliated like that. Burton was furious, of course, and blamed everyone but himself; the lighting was wrong, he couldn't hear himself through his monitor speakers, his back-up band were a 'bunch of fucking morons!' Snubbing the post-concert party, he went straight fron the stage to a waiting limousine, leaving me to collect his stage outfits and other paraphenalia from the dressing room before joining him for the ten minute drive back to the train.

With a bottle of bourbon which he'd snatched from the bar o the way through, he disappeared into his suite in the company o Deva Ram, kicking the door shut behind them. My duties over fo the night I retired to my room for the first decent bit of shut-eye i nearly two days.

Through the partition, I could hear him screaming at Dev Ram, slamming cupboard doors, throwing furniture about: drifted off to sleep with a satisfied smile on my lips . . .

***

Over breakfast the following morning, I persuaded Burton that the case would be more secure deposited in a bank in town, reinforcing my argument with the reminder that the train would be bringing us back to Cannes at the end of the tour, allowing us to retrieve it then. He grudgingly agreed, pointing out that the train would be under way in less than two hours and, if I wasn't back by then, it would just have to leave without me. Don't tempt me, I thought; don't tempt me!

Making the most of my hour of freedom, I got rid of the case at the first bank I saw then went looking for a phone. To my immense relief, Smedley informed me that the Chief was on the road from Scotland at that very moment and would be back at his desk the following morning. I didn't bother Smedley with the details of all that had happened since our last conversation, there being too much to tell and too many loose ends still to be tied. And anyway, I was looking forward to hammering Kaplan himself with it, so I promised to call back the following day.

By eleven o'clock, we were under way and speeding north through the dry French countryside towards Belgium. Half an hour into our journey, we were summoned to a briefing in the central lounge by the Tour Manager, a no-nonsense two hundred pounder from Detroit called Rick.

Burton didn't bother to attend, still smarting after last night's fiasco and attempting to re-establish his star status with this totally unnecessary display of petulance. He sent me in his place, charging me with the responsiblity of collecting all the relevant information for subsequent relay when he reverted to a more reasonable state of mind.

The animal act of this particular travelling circus arrived first; a band called Alabama Red who had opened the show the previous evening with half an hour of musical carnage, flying hair and buckskin fringes; spilled beer and an abundance of earthy Redneck humour. Not yet thirty miles into the tour, singer Ronnie La Rue had already fulfilled a life-long ambition by urinating out of a carriage window at another train passing the other way. The fact that most of it had blown back over him in the process had not, apparently, dampened his enjoyment of the experience.

Bobbie Montgomery and his film star wife, Monique Delorme looked more than passingly disgusted as Ronnie drolled loudly over the incident. He was completely out of place on a tour like this with his existentialist love songs, delivered in that slightly off key quiver of a voice that remains the exclusive and undisputed territory of the French. La Delorme was only there to comb her husband's chest and hitch a ride to Rome, where she would lay bare the city's finest salons like an elegant locust.

Errol James, formerly Arthur Tidmarsh from East Acton, was the next to arrive. He minced in, leaving apologies for his late arrival to his personal hairdresser, business adviser and extremely close friend, Maurice. The boy had talent alright, whatever the doubts about his hormonal balance. Like someone with a hang-up about the state of their underwear in anticipation of suddenly being taken to hospital, he changed his outfits five or six times a day and was never seen with the same colour hair more than once a month. He also had the essential qualification for all would-be superstars: the ability to smell a camera a mile away.

While Maurice mixed their extremely dry Martinis, Errol chanced an ill-advised smile in the direction of Clarence Davis, the enormous, ape-like bass player from Alabama Red. All he got in return was an irreverent and dramatically loud fart, followed by a raucous round of applause from the rest of the band.

A blast of cool air came through the doorway with Denver and

Honey, the husband and wife singing team who looked like they'd been fighting all the way from Tennessee. Not that Denver ever argued — he just listened loudly. Honey told him where to sit and apologised for his unpunctuality.

Maggie Moran never apologised for anything. She roared in, kicked Ronnie's feet out of the way, grabbed a bottle of vodka from behind the bar and settled herself in a heap on the floor. This was obviously going to be one of her better days. She had a chip on her shoulder the size of the Grand Canyon, hating herself for being fat, ugly, female and white. She took a greedy gulp from the bottle, belched, then offered it to Maurice. He pretended not to notice and turned, trembling in his seat, to gaze vacantly at the passing countryside.

So these were to be my travelling companions for the next month. They were a weird bunch, and light years removed in terms of lifestyle, personality and outlook from anyone I'd met before. Still, they seemed to accept my presence amongst them without any misgivings, so I saw no reason why I shouldn't return the compliment.

Rick handed each of us a tour folder, containing an itinerary of concert dates and usefuul information about the cities we'd be visiting along the way. We were to visit seven countries in all, completing a punishing schedule of twenty three concert dates, the 'days-off' being filled with receptions, press conferences, radio interviews and TV slots.

"OK — now it's Rule Book time!" Rick said after running through the concert dates. "There are no hotel rooms to smash up on this tour, just the train. So the word is — *don't*! The record company has put a lot of bread into this and the kind of places we'll be playing won't come anywhere near covering the costs. This tour could do you all a lot of good, so don't screw it up. You'll only be hurting youselves.

"Rule Two: no dope across frontiers. We've got contacts in every country who'll deliver whatever poisons you want to use, and what you do on the train is your own business. But border posts are going to be heavy and I'll come down like a ton of horse shit on anyone who puts the train or future projects at risk.

"And Ronnie . . . ?"

La Rue looked up with his customary guilty grin .

". . . despite anything you may have heard to the contrary, the age of consent over here is still well in excess of twelve. So keep your phrase books handy and ask to see birth certificates before — not after!"

"Aw, shit!" Ronnie La Rue replied. " 'Sposin' ah fall in LOVE? Ah'm talkin' 'bout real love, man, jus' like in '*True Teen Romance*'!"

Rick's advice to take a lot of cold showers caused Ronnie to grimace and bury his face in Clarence's chest. The giant bass player hooked a tender arm around his shoulders and planted a reassuring kiss on the top of his head. Everyone cracked up, including Bobby Montgomery who was instantly pulled up by his wife with a look that would have warped a steel girder.

"I think that just about wraps it up," Rick said in conclusion. "Any questions?"

Again, Ronnie La Rue's hand shot in the air.

"Yeah, right, man. Now ah ain't accusin' nobody, but I wanna report a theft!"

"Theft?"

"That's what I said, man — theft! 'Fore we left the States ah bought me a lil ol' book called '*How to do Europe on a Lid o' Grass a day*', an' now it's gone missin' from mah room. Ah wouldn't usually bitch 'bout a thing like that — but, well — that's what ah call ESSENTIAL information!"

We had a scheduled stop-over in Paris during the afternoon, so I took the opportunity to find a phone booth in the station and put through a call to London. Kaplan had returned, as Smedley had promised, and I was put straight through.

As soon as he came on the line, I exploded; the irritations of the last three days were suddenly into a tirade lasting several minutes.

Kaplan let me rant on, making no attempt to interrupt or calm ıe down until my offensive finally petered out in the face of his pparent indifference. Now it was his turn, his voice measured and ɛassuring as he said:

'Now listen, Rodgers, and listen very carefully. I can well ınderstand you being . . . well, none too pleased with me for ꞉eeping you out there another month, but I had my reasons, ɔelieve me.

'As your first reports came through, Sir George was all for ꞉ancelling the contract, there and then. He felt that Burton had ʌorked a flanker and he didn't want to be involved with anything he least bit suspicious. But I was intrigued. We had been hired to ɔerform a simple courier job, but it was fast becoming apparent ꞉hat there was a lot more to it than that . . ."

"You're telling me!" I interrupted unnecessarily.

"So when Burton's request came through to retain your services, I persuaded Sir George that the best policy would be to accept. It would give you the chance to find out what was really going on. You see, we've got a reputation to maintain, and if The Workshop was seen to be actively involved in anything the least bit illegal — as this is shaping up to be — then our credibility would vanish overnight.

"So I need you there, Frank. I need to know what's going on so I can place the matter in the hands of the proper authorities if need be . . . before it's too late!"

"I can see that, Chief," I assured him. "But it's put me in a hell of a position out here. I might have got rid of the briefcase, but now I've been given the job of looking after its new owner . . . which boils down to the same thing! They'll be coming after Burton sooner or later, and I'll be stuck right in the firing line . . ."

"I realise that, Frank — but what else can I do? You've obviously handled the situation very well so far, and I've every confidence that you'll continue to do so. And think what might be at stake here: from what you've just told me, it appears that the CIA are involved, British Intelligence, the KGB . . . we don't know 'how' or 'why', but this could well turn out to be a question of national security. We can't walk away from something like that now can we?"

I could, I thought: very easily. I didn't tell Kaplan that though. Instead, I sighed: "OK, Major. You're the boss. But if things get really hairy, you'll just have to pull me out. I've been lucky so far but, if your suspicions are correct, then we're already well out of our depth. Let the boy scouts in Intelligence handle it; they seem to enjoy this sort of thing!"

"You have my word on that, Frank. But stay with if for the time being, and keep me in touch. And . . . Frank?"

"Yes, Chief?"

"Well done!"

What could I say after that? It was as near to a compliment as Kaplan ever got, and I felt as if he'd just patted me on the back. In fact, it was an irate French lady, tapping me on the shoulder with her umbrella in her impatience to get to the phone.

It was time I was gone anyway. So I rang off, promising to check in as often as our busy schedule would allow. I returned to the train, mulling over what Kaplan had said. There was no way out now; I would just have to grit my teeth and see it through. The Chief's explanation had given me some sense of purpose, but it did nothing to alter the fact that it was going to be a very, very long month ahead.

***

Brussels, Amsterdam, Stockholm, Hamburg. . . it all passed by in a blur as I was plunged into the peculiar insanity of a rock n' roll tour. Time dragged its heels in a tedium of endless travel while I hung around Burton, waiting for him to find some trivial errand for me to run.

But there were moments of priceless hilarity along the way too: like Maggie Moran baring her flabby arse to an unresponsive audience in Sweden, or Clarence Davis describing a session with a large, gum-chewing lady of the press from Australia who, after ten minutes grunting and groaning on a dressing room table, propped herself up on one elbow to enquire if he's 'slimed' yet!

And there was that Sunday morning, leaving a drizzle drenched Vienna for the trek to Munich. Ronnie La Rue rushed onto the train with only seconds to spare, towing behind him a diminutive girl in her late teens, who, despite her size, sported the largest pair of breasts I had ever seen in my life. Very proud of them she was too . . as was Ronnie. He suggested I might take the opportunity to play with them awhile before the rest of his band could get their greedy paws on her, an offer which I politely declined.

Twenty miles west of Linz, the train was halted for an hour outside a tiny village while repairs were carried out to the line ahead. Eye-catching as 'The Sonic Special' was, the entire population of some sixty odd people and several dogs filed out of Morning Service and plodded across the narrow dividing field to examine the phenomenon. Within minutes, the random groups had gathered in a tight cluster by one of the carriages near the front. Intrigued, I went to investigate.

I can't remember when I've laughed so long or so loudly. There through an unshuttered window, the hairy buttocks of Ronnie L Rue rose and fell as he pumped furiously away at the little lad with the enormous boobs. Unaware that the train had stopped, h pressed on for a full five minutes before reaching a triumphant cheek clenching climax. Spontaneous applause broke out amongs the younger members of the assembled crowd as his backside sank slowly from sight for the last time.

Suddenly, he became aware of his audience. Grinning stupidly he adjusted the beat-up stetson, he'd worn throughout the entir performance, wound down his window and stuck his head out. Fo the next half hour, he told them jokes which nobody understoo but which everybody laughed at, had his photograph taken, wit his arms around many a little old lady's shoulder, and handed ou autographed pictures of him and the rest of the band. As I'v already said. . . priceless; absolutely priceless

Moments like that, however, were few and far between. As th tour settled into an endless rhythm of one night stands in vas concert halls where hopeful promoters saw their profits disappea in banks of empty seats, a deep malaise set in.

My relationship with Burton grew progressively worse as on disastrous performance followed another and I was forced to stan aside and watch him slide further and further down the ladder adding further to his troubles by drinking heavily and consumin vast quantities of the comprehensive catalogue of drugs whic Deva Ram always seemed to have available.

On the whole, my job was really very dull. As Burton's minder I was required to stay within spitting distance wherever he went running irritating little errands for him or sitting through interminable sound checks where the ageing idol would change his routine for the umpteenth time, much to the undisguised annoyance of the road crew, the lighting engineers, his back-up band and, I have to admit, my ear drums.

Once fully inflated, an ego may sag and collapse but it never isappears completely. Or so it seemed with Mikki Burton. I ouldn't help but feel sorry for the guy, as, night after night, the nce mighty legion of die-hard fans never materialised and the pplause grew thinner and began to smack of charity. He tried to ut a brave face on it, whatever he was feeling inside, and put his aith in the rock n' roll maxim that there was always another gig nd if the fans hadn't made it to Copenhagen or Hamburg or vhatever, then they were bound to pack out the theatre the ollowing night.

In between the concert dates and the endles travelling, Burton's nner circle — myself, Deva Ram and Linda Love when she could be bothered — were required to join him whenever the schedule demanded the obligatory TV appearance, press conference or record company reception. The press conferences were the worst; seen one and you've really seen them all. No matter what the language difference, I swear they asked him the same idiotic questions and received the same equally idiotic answers at every one.

But Burton loved the TV appearances. We were forced to hang around his dressing room, drinking courtesy booze out of styrofoam cups and watch him get larded up with make-up before he pranced on, displaying an appetite for a camera like a hungry fox for an unguarded chicken farm. You'd think the guy would have been sick of the whole phoney business after nearly twenty years of the same old thing all over the world, but not a bit of it; the lights, the sycophantic prattling of the interviewers and the potential size of his audience seemed to galvanise him into life, only to collapse again when his five minutes slot came to an end.

The thing that really bugged me was him needing me there at all. After all the hectic to-ings and fro-ings of Torremolinos, the routine of the tour came across as somewhat tepid, as tame as a vicarage tea party by comparison. The more lifeless it became, the more I was obliged to adopt the role of gentleman-in-waiting, Burton insisting on my ever present company.

As I've already made painfully clear, the tour was not really my idea of a good time. Even when the occasional rock n' roll perk came our way — free records, left over booze, that kind of thing — do you think I got the benefit of it? Not a chance, the other parasites higher up the pecking order always contriving to get there first.

The backstage party after the show at the Olympiahalle in Munich was following the predictable pattern with a crowd of particularly uninspiring hangers-on devouring everything in sight like a swarm of Gucci dressed locusts. The dressing room door was pushed open and in stepped a short, bearded and balding man in his early forties. I was half-heartedly downing a tumbler of Wild Turkey bourbon and trying to catch the eye of a plump but not unappealing faulein on the far side of the room, when I saw Burton leap from his seat and make a bee-line for the guy with the beard.

This was rather unusual in itself, as Burton never gave anyone the time of day, let alone blow his cool in an outward show of enthusiasm for a new face. Intrigued, I moved nearer to Burton and the beard, who was now frantically shaking his head up and down as Burton pummeled his back as if rushing to the aid of someone who had just swallowed a two bob bit.

Within seconds, Burton was bawling at a nearby waiter and demanding that food and drink be brought to the Royal Presence. Clearly the beard was a 'somebody' because, no sooner had the hapless waiter delivered a heavily laden tray of drinks and sandwiches, than the inner circle were summoned to meet him.

By now Burton had an avuncular arm wrapped around the beard's neck and was smiling broadly as he introduced Klaus Heinemann, renowned as one of the finest recording engineers in the world. I can't say I was that impressed with the guy, but appearances are obviously deceptive as Burton was clearly over the moon with the opportunity to renew his acquaintance, the pair now launching into meaningless music business gossip about who was 'laying down' what and where, who was on 'smack' or 'snow', and so on.

I hung around like a bad smell trying to fix an intelligent expression on my face and looking for a convenient exit line so I could return my attentions to the well endowed blonde in the corner, when Burton started clapping his hands together — a sure sign that he wanted to go out on the town.

In many ways, my position in the Burton entourage was a cross between a social worker looking after a delinquent child and a serf on a fuedal estate. He didn't so much talk to me as make strange bellowings and gesticulations, indecipherable at first exposure but which had become familiar as prolonged experience gave me the key to his code. Handclapping, accompanied by a sort of whooping cry, meant everyone directly connected with the great man were expected to present themselves in orderly muster for one of his mystery tours, usually ending up in a hideously expensive night club where the bouncers would look at us as if we were the relief cleaners reporting for the early shift.

Still, there was no way of avoiding it short of sending Burton into an apoplectic fit. With cries of "McCulloch's in town!', he herded us into the back of a waiting Mecedes and we drove off into the night in the direction of Am Tucherpark and The Hilton.

By the time we arrived at the hotel, I had gathered from the exchanges between Heinemann and Burton that 'McCulloch' was Andy McCulloch, a one-time protegé of Burton and The Rats who had made some recordings for Mammoth Records in the early seventies before going on to greater and grander things.

"I made him! I fuckin' made him!" Burton shouted enthusiasticaly to no-one in particular as we filed into the Hilton foyer, startling an obsequious night porter who smiled politely and agreed: *"Ja, mein herr!"*. The girl behind the desk offered a practised smile of indulgence, playing it safe on the assumption that this particular band of fools were probably rich ones before politely giving us directions to McCulloch's suite on the top floor.

As we rode up in the lift, Burton's former bravado seemed to have fled in fright and I began to feel myself part of a diplomatic legation on a visit to an enemy who had resoundingly beaten us in a long and bloody war. It was no skin off my nose, of course, but a Heinemman peppered his conversation with details c McCulloch's astronomical sales figures and albums that had 'gon platinum', I could see Burton shrink further and further into hi shell, like a very old, very tired turtle.

As we reached the door of McCulloch's suite, we could hear th sounds of hysterical girlish laughter above breaking glass an pulsating music. Burton smiled nervously at us as if pleading fo encouragement, then knocked on the door with the timidity of . schoolboy tapping at the headmaster's study.

Despite the noise, the door was quickly opened by a thickse heavy with all the charm of a Doberman Pinscher. It came as : complete surprise that he possessed the brain power to speak a all, but I managed to pick up a slurred and disinterested: "Yeah' Whaddyawant?"

Burton opened his mouth as if to speak but nothing came out, so I stepped into the breach to reply:" We want to see Andy McCulloch."

"Don't everybody...?" the ape sneered, enjoying his own joke He looked us up and down, his eyes lingering especially on Burton but without the slightest hint of recognition.

"Just tell your employer that Mikki Burton is here to see him — OK?" I tried again.

He looked us over yet again and shrugged." 'Spouse that'll be alright," he concluded, stepping aside to let us in.

I squeezed past him, the others followed me like a gaggle of lost ducks. We found ourselves in a short corridor which opened out into a vast, oval shaped room which seemed to be filled with dangerously young girls and medallion decorated men old enough to be their grandfathers. In the centre of the room I noticed the shattered remnants of a glass coffee table, the pieces of which were now being scrutinised by a saucer-eyed, elfin-like girl who couldn't have been more than fifteen.

While I studied a pair of scantily clad blondes gyrating frantically together on the floor in a far corner of the room. Burton nd Heinemann went looking for Andy McCulloch. A few noments later, I saw Burton's head poking around the door of a maller room off to my left, beckoning us to follow him inside. Heinemann and I started for the door to answer the summons, but Linda and Deva Ram decided they had already seen enough and eft, promising to see us later on board the train.

We joined Burton in the suite's master bedroom where McCulloch was holding court. After the noise and bright lights of he main room, it took me a moment to adjust to the relative quiet and subtle, subdued lighting. Directly opposite the door, beside wall-length window doors which led to a canopy covered balcony, was a loose arrangement of four steel and leather reclining chairs, each one of which must have cost the best part of my annual salary.

McCulloch was sitting with his back to the door, looking out across the balcony at the lights of the city below. Half turning round, he gestured towards the other chairs, indicating that we should sit down.

For a long time nobody spoke, McCulloch continuing to stare out of the window through heavily made-up eyes while Burton and Heinemann exchanged awkward, uncomfortable glances. At last, McCulloch turned in his chair to say, softly: "I hear you're making a come back, Mikki?"

Burton cleared his throat and chanced a knowing wink. "Yeah... well, you know how things are, Andy. The new album needs a push..."

His voice trailed off as McCulloch eased back further in his chair, stroking and caressing one of the arms as if it were the neck of a beautiful woman.

"Time was, Mikki" he resumed, "when your albums didn't need pushing."

Burton smiled and shrugged theatrically, but it was a hollow, empty gesture, his true emotions revealed by a sudden narrowing of his eyes. I'd already decided I didn't like McCulloch and was at a loss to under how anyone possibly could. And why Burton was putting himself through this torture was equally inexplicable. didn't dwell on it, though: to borrow a phrase which Burton tenc to use with irritating regularity... 'That's rock n' roll!'

Another deafening silence fell. McCulloch closed his eyes, th rhythmic tapping of his fingers on the arm of the chair the onl indication that he was still awake. Whatever dope McCulloch wa on, it certainly appeared to be heap powerful medicine; deepl bloodshot eyes, a voice which sounded like it came from anothe part of the room altogether and the constant stroking of his hands now on his face, now along his thighs as if he were applying a invisible lotion to the parts of his body not covered by his loose sil robe.

I was not a million miles away from sleep myself whe Heinemann chose to throw this glacial conversation into overdriv by suggesting: "Now might be a good time — ja? — for you two t make an album?"

I had no way of knowing whether the German had bee promoted into this by Burton, but I noticed him wince with eithe fear or embarrassment — or both — as the German spoke.

"Together?" McCulloch queried, making no effort to disguis the contempt in his voice.

"Ja, it could be good." Heinemann continued enthusiastically not picking up the atmosphere. "Your styles would complemen each other, I think. Maybe you would call it 'Ten Years On' o 'Together Again'... I leave it to you, naturally." Here he pausec and gave a thin, nervous laugh. "And I would hope you would ask me to mix it..."

"You, Klaus?" McCulloch retorted through a purposefully exaggerated sneer. "I wouldn't let you mix a pancake for me after the last album I did with you. When I put something down on tape, I want it to stay on, not wiped off the final mix because you didn't happen to like it! That's what makes me the star. That's why I'm the dog and you're the tail..."

Then turning back to Burton, he continued: "I'd like to help you out, Mikki, I really would. But I don't see how I can fit you in. I've

›t album comitments for the next three years, and a world tour ›ming up later this year. You know how it is, man? You've been ıere yourself..."

Burton knew how it was alright. Or, rather, how is had been. Sure, sure," he managed unconvincingly; "Another time ɜrhaps?"

"Yeah, why not? Some other time. Let's wait and see how this ɜw album of yours does — OK?"

Things were getting out of hand,, McCulloch was obviously ɛginning to enjoy himself and all at our lord and master's ‹pense. If he had come at Burton with a knife I could have done ›mething about it; that's what I'm getting paid for after all. But ıis was way out of my league and I could do no more but sit ıere in silence and witness Burton's humiliation, made no less ainful by the fact that he'd brought it on himself.

"Listen," McCulloch rejoined to round things off in style, "why ot have a drink with me before you go? For old times' sake, eh? ∖ little Dom Perignon, perhaps? Or why not fit in a bit of xercise? You used to be keen on that, I seem to remember..."

McCulloch's jargon has lost me, but then he pointed across the ıarkened room to a king size bed where two girls were sleepinng in ‹ach other's arms.

"If you're not up to it Mikki, perhaps your two friends..."

Finally Burton snapped, clenching his fists and jumping out of ıis chair to scream: "Don't you fuckin' patronise me, McCulloch! 'm a long way from finished yet... and don't you ever forget it!"

McCulloch closed his eyes and waved his hand in a mock ʹarewell. As we reached the door, I could hear him whispering: 'Bye, bye, Lazarus. Bye, bye...

Back into the old routine again, I found myself with less and less to do: there were no legions of autograph hunters to beat back from the stage door; no giggling groupies climbing through his compartant window at dead of night; and, despite his fears, no snipers with high-powered rifles perching in the gallery as he toiled through his tired old act. The plain fact was that nobody wa interested in Burton anymore.

And I saw very little of Linda Love. She seemed to be avoidin me yet, when we did run into one another, she was warm an friendly and always ready to swap small talk over the occasion drink. But she would not be drawn on the mysterious messag she'd delivered on the flight out to Cannes. Nor did she have muc to do with Mikki Burton. She was always around to run the od errand for him, advise him on a choice of stage costume o accompany him to receptions and parties but, on the train out o the public eye, she generally kept her distance. Attending only th occasional conceert, she would retire early to the compartment sh shared with Maggie Moran, never once spending the night i Burton's suite.

As the tour drew to its close, I had relegated memories o Curtis, Bryant and the Chinese puzzle of intrigue in Torremolino to a dim and distant past. Inactivity had softened me, taken awa my edge. Once more I began counting the days, looking forwar to Burton completing his business with the case and setting m free. With nothing to report, my calls to Kaplan became less an less frequent and , without his regular pep talks to keep me on th right track, I had lost any urge to discover the contents of the cas and delve deeper into Burton's affairs. But then, three days befor the scheduled end of the tour, we arrived in Rome and I foun myself back in the thick of it with a vengeance.

After that night's concert, the whole company adjourned to th 'Antica Pesa', a jet-set night club right out of a Martini ad, west o the river on Via Garabaldi.

The evening was not a success. Indeed it was a downright blood saster. For a start, we had to contend with a near suicidal laurice, inconsolable in the wake of Errol James' departure, ıortly after the show, in the company of three baby faced *aparazzi*. We had been sneered at from the instant we'd filed ırough the door. Service was painfully and purposefully slow, the nal bill only adding injury to insult with its resemblance to the alian National Debt.

Things finally boiled over into violence when Ronnie La Rue olitely asked a stunning, raven haired nymphet to dance, only to e hoisted off the floor by two gorillas acting on instructions from he girl's 'boyfriend'. Predictably, the rest of the band rushed to heir singer's defence, and it wasn't long before the tables were eing upturned and chairs thrown about in a cowboy-style bar-oom brawl.

I shepherded Burton to safety through a back entrance, flagging lown a passing cab and despatching him back to the train. Then I eturned to the club, pitching in as best I could. It was a hell of a ight, and I have to own up to enjoying it immensely, having at last omething to really get my teeth into. Rick managed to sort things out eventually, getting us all outside and clear of trouble before the police arrived. All, that is, except Deva Ram...

He was nowhere to be found. There was no sign of him back at he club and we all assumed that he had slipped out earlier and eturned to the train under his own steam. But there was no news of him there either. I was now faced with the chore of calming and reassuring Mikki Burton. He was completely distraught, inevitably blaming Ram's disappearance on me. Pointing out that I had been retained as *his* minder and not his guru's cut no ice whatsoever.

I really didn't know how much longer I could put up with Burton's prima donna histrionics. Now anybody would tell you that normally I'm a very patient man. 'You'd make a wonderful fisherman,' as my old mum used to put it, and up to a point she was right. As long as it doesn't cause me direct pain or hardship, I'm more than prepared to be tolerant of other people's peculiarities and peccadilloes.

Burton, however, was beginning to get up my nose. He w pushing me way too far, and when I get pushed I get angry an push back.

"Let me make one thing crystal bloody clear, *Mister* Burton," found myself shouting. "I've had it right up to here and beyon with your constant bitching and whining. I'm here as a bodyguar not a frigging whipping boy!"

I was really warming to my subject now and Burton could d nothing but stand and gape.

"What's more," I continued, "I couldn't give a tuppenny tos about your phoney guru. For all I know, he's buggered off wit someone else sicker and richer than you!"

Burton appeared poised between breaking down in a flood o tears or punching me on the jaw. In the end he did neither slumping dejectedly into a chair and looking like a cross between whipped spaniel and a deflated air-bed.

At this point we fell silent. That is, I fastened the zipper on m runaway mouth and Burton didn't seem inclined to reply. As m anger subsided, I experienced a rash moment of sympathy. He wa looking so lost and alone. However painful for the audience, it ha to be hurting him more. He knew he wasn't cutting the mustar anymore — everybody did — but he had been pushed onto thi tour by an investment conscious record company, desperate t recoup the money they'd advanced him in the fatter years b promoting him now as a born-again gravy-train. And there wa ego involved in it too; memories of the heady days when The Rat could sell out Madison Square for as many concerts as the deigned to give, flattered and feted wherever they went, anywhere in the world. Memories like that just don't go away.

Looking at him now, head bowed and shoulders hunched, he appeared a completely broken man. The true nature of the relationship between Burton and Deva Ram remained a mystery to me but, witnessing his reaction to the guru's disappearance, I began to look on it as none too healthy. I had never seen Ram impart any kind of spiritual advice, bogus or otherwise, and there ıd been times when I'd received the direct impression that ɪrton didn't even like him. Unlike the rest of his entourage, to ɦit yours truly and Linda Love, who ran small errands for the llen star as well as performing whatever duties her role as istress demanded, nothing seemed to be expected of Deva Ram her than constant attendance. The more I thought about it, the ranger the whole business became; the less sense it all made. If urton didn't like him, as I suspected, and if he wasn't a musician, money-lender or a poor man's Maharishi — then what the hell as he? It was clear that Burton needed Deva Ram and appeared ›st without him, but I remained completely at a loss to understand xactly why.

By now, Burton had begun to revive. He chanced a tepid smile. Yeah, listen, man . . . I've got some heavy things to deal with ght now, know what I mean? Like, there's a lot of pressure . . ."

His voice trailed off, and he began to fidget with a large silver ing on the index finger of his right hand. I didn't know quite what ɔ say, so I played the proverbial three wise monkeys and said othing. Another deafening silence separated us, Burton ontinuing to bite his lip and stare vacantly ahead.

"Listen," I said after a while, trying to make light of it. "He'll robably turn up soon. There could be a thousand and one xplanations where he's gone. He's probably finding it hard to get ı cab wearing that orange frock of his . . ."

Burton didn't appear to appreciate the joke, or even hear it for hat matter, so I continued: "Why not try to rest? Or have a drink n the bar. Anything to get your mind off it."

Still getting no reaction, I gave up and went looking for Linda. I racked her down in the bar where she was attending to Ronnie La Rue's badly bruised knuckles. Ronnie seemed to be enjoying himself, his face contorting into every kind of grimace as he continued his futile attempts to fondle her well rounded backside with his free hand.

"Not interrupting anything, am I?" I asked as I entered the bar.

"'Fraid not, man" Ronnie replied. "Ah'm workin' on it,

though. . ."

I looked at Linda and said: "I think Mikki's in a bad way. I don seem able to do anything with him. Perhaps you . . ."

"Of course," she complied, leaving Ronnie with a playful sla across his freshly bandaged knuckles as she joined me in th corridor.

"The asshole's probably just playing for sympathy," she sighe "He's just like a little kid at times like these."

"Oh, well — might as well get it over with. He needs his nann and nanny's not going to get any peace until he gets what he wants. . ."

Eventually, Linda and I settled him down with a bottle o bourbon and a couple of sleeping pills, but the lull in the hostiliti was only temporary. Just after dawn, I was woken by the sound o voices raised in violent argument filtering through the wall fro the adjoining compartment. Burton and the Tour Manager we on the point of exchanging blows by the time I broke into Burton suite, wedging myself between them and pushing Burton into chair.

Quite correctly, Rick was refusing to delay the departure of th train, pointing out that we were on a pre-arranged schedule an could be stalled there for days before getting further traffi clearance. Burton, however, was having none of that, insisting w stay put until they discovered what had happened to Deva Ram

But there was something else; something above and beyon concern for his friend that was driving Burton crazy. And whatever it was, it was scaring him shitless: I could see it in hi eyes, in the nervous restlessness of his every movement, in th undisguisable panic behind his voice. He wasn't letting on, though not then, anyway.

Finally, Rick stormed off with a parting "No way, Mikki! N fucking way!", leaving the two of us alone in Burton's suite.

"There's something else bugging you, isn't there?" I prompted "Something you haven't told me?"

His face was buried in his hands, but he looked up to snarl

Who asked you? Piss off and leave me alone! It's none of your bodding business!"

I stood my ground. "But I think it *is* my business! You hired me to protect you, remember? How the hell am I supposed to do that if you won't tell me what's going on?"

Again he bowed his head, running his fingers nervously through his hair. I hovered indecisively, the silence lasting for what seemed a long, long time. Then, quite suddenly, he got up from his chair and began fumbling around in the top drawer of the bureau, retrieving a crumpled sheet of paper which he thrust into my hand.

"Here! Read this! I found it on my bed when I got back tonight!"

I smoothed it out and read:

YOUR FOOLISHNESS HAS DESTROYED THE BOND OF FAITH BETWEEN US. OUR AGREEMENT IS THEREFORE CANCELLED. THE PRICE IS NOW ONE MILLION DOLLARS AND YOUR LIFE. THIS IS FINAL.

"So what's it mean?" I asked. "Who's it from?"

He opened his mouth as if to speak but immediately thought better of it, seeming to find a new resolve as he snatched the message out of my hand and tore it savagely into tiny pieces.

"Get out!" he screamed at me, stabbing at my chest and shoving me towards the door. "Get out and leave me alone!"

I grabbed at his hands and spun him round, hoisting him up by his collar and pushing him against the wall.

"Tell me, you stupid bastard!" I shouted, "Who sent that note? What the hell's going on here?"

His body went limp as he turned his head away to whimper: "I can't, I . . . I've told you too much already. You've read the note, you know what they'll do."

"Who?" I persisted. "Who are *they*?"

Still he refused to answer, eyes closed as he continued to shake his head, his voice now a hoarse whisper, choked with sobs.

"Well, it's your bloody funeral, mate!" I spat through clenched teeth, letting him go and watching his body slide slowly down the

wall. He was a hunched, pathetic figure huddled on the floor as
turned my back and walked away, closing the door gently behi
me.

***

We were about an hour out of Rome, passing through flat, ope
farmland when they showed their hand. Suddenly the train jolted
the rhythmic rattling of the tracks replaced by the grating squeal o
the brakes as we shuddered to a halt.

They were lined up either side, perhaps as many as thirt
altogether, their eyes hidden behind dark glasses, machine gun
and rifles cradled in their arms. Up ahead, the line was blocked b
a truck. My first thought was that it was a kidnap attempt by som
terrorist group, but somehow they didn't look right, and the
made no move to board the train.

I had been alone in the bar, doing my best to forget Mikk
Burton and his troubles, when the train pulled up. As soon as
realised what was happening, I raced along the corridor t
Burton's compartment. Before I was half-way there I knew who i
was who had stopped the train. I found him backed against the
wall by the window, peering cautiously out through a chink in the
closed curtains. He was trembling uncontrollably.

"What'll I do?" he whined as I burst through the door. "Help
me, Frank! For God's sake, help me!"

I prised him away from the window and shook him. "Pull
yourself together! You're no use to anyone like this . . . least of al

ourself!"

I steered him towards a chair then returned to the window, fting the curtain slightly to study the scene outside.

"Why didn't you tell me the Mafia were after you for hrissakes? Were you born stupid, or did you have to work at it? . . wait a minute . . . there's something happening out here . . ."

Slowly, and with military precision, they were lowering their eapons and filing off in the direction of the cars. I could hear the ngines starting and the crunch of their tyres on the dry, sun-baked arth, then watched as they backed away from the tracks and sped ff across the surrounding fields, disappearing behind an orange loud of dust.

"It's alright," I said with a sneer. "You can change your trousers ow. They've gone. And it looks like they've left you a calling ard . . ."

I left Burton and hurried outside, helping the bound and loodied Deva Ram back onto the train and into Burton's room.

He looked like he'd been through a combine harvester. Twice. His nose was broken, his lips cut, congealed blood coating every rack and crevice of his face. His body was covered with more ruises than a crate of bananas; weals made by a thin whip cut leep across his shoulders and back.

Waving the hysterical, horror struck Burton aside, I laid Deva Ram on the bed and loosened the ropes that bound his hands and feet. And then the guru broke his silence, screaming at Burton in a voice which owed more to the beaches of Santa Monica, I fancied, than to the hidden temples of Tibet: "They could've fucking killed me, man! Jesus Christ . . . I *told* you what would happen! You just don't fuck around with guys like that! And they don't like being double-crossed, man. Give 'em the film, for Chrissakes! It ain't worth this . . ."

"Shutup! Shutup!" Burton bellowed back, pushing me out of the way and grabbing Deva Ram by the throat. "Shut your stupid mouth, you asshole! Not here . . . not now . . .!"

I pulled him off, calming him down with a well delivered left

hook which sent him sprawling across the floor. The adrenalin w
pumping now; I was getting close . . .

I returned to the bed, seizing Deva Ram by the shoulders a
hoisting him upright. "What film?" I yelled, shaking him. "W
did they do this to you . . .?"

But it was already too late, Deva Ram had realised his slip a
had turned his head away, his mouth tight shut once again.

"What about you?" I called to Burton across the room. "Do
you think it's time you told me what all this is about?"

Nursing his jaw, he scrambled to his knees but said nothing.
turned from one to the other but neither would look me in the ey

"Alright, then!" I told them finally. "If that's the way you wa
to play it, you're on your own. From this moment on you can lo
after yourselves . . . I quit!"

*

I had been bluffing, of course. It was a gamble but one which
felt was well worth taking. Burton was running scared and ha
already proved he was way out of his depth, and displaying les
backbone than the average jellyfish. Sooner or later, I was sure h
would realise how vulnerable he was without me and com
begging for the protection he so obviously needed. I would the
make him tell me everything as a condition of my return to duty
mystery solved; Kaplan happy; Frank Rogers flying home t
collect his medal.

That was the theory, anyway. But as the hours became days
with still no sign of any initiative from Burton it began to look as i
I'd blown it. Kaplan intimated as much when I called in to repor
on our brush with the Mafia and Ram's revelation about the film.

"I think you've handled this very badly, Rogers," he said, the

›ne of his voice and the use of my surname indicating his .spleasure. "If this scheme of yours backfires, then we'll be no ırther forward and your time out there would have been ›mpletely wasted!"

"With respect, Major," I butted in defensively. "I'm here and ɔu're not. I know the man. He knows he's bitten off more than he an chew and it's terrifying the shit out of him . . . if you'll pardon ıe expression. He's due to make his deal with the film in a few ay's time. I'm convinced he'll come through by then . . ."

"Well, I hope you're right," Kaplan resumed. "Intelligence ave been screaming blue bloody murder since losing that chap of ıeirs . . what was his name again? . . ."

"Toby Hamilton," I reminded him.

"Yes, Hamilton. They agreed to let us run with the ball for a vhile as you were already on the spot, but they're getting mpatient. What am I supposed to tell them now? That you've lecided you've had enough? That you've walked away from it just vhen we'd started to get somewhere?"

"It won't come to that, Chief," I hastened to reassure him — ınd, perhaps, myself. "I'm certain of it."

There was a pause, and then: "Look, Rogers; I'm determined to ee this through to the bitter end. If the worst comes to the worst, you'll just have to go to Burton and apologise . . ."

"Aw, come on, Major — I can't do that!"

"Sorry, but that's the way it's got to be! I need you there when the crunch comes, and if there's no other way, then so be it. And Rogers? That is an order!"

*

It never came to that, but it was a very close run thing. So close, in fact, that I was actually trying to find Burton to make m humiliating peace when he tapped me on the shoulder with th suggestion that we disappear somewhere quiet to 'put our paper together'! This, I was relieved to discover, involved nothing mor sinister than retiring to his dressing room to mend some fences.

We were at the end of tour party, held backstage after the fina concert at the Paris Olympia. The performance he'd just put in t close the show had proved, yet again, his staggering prowess as has-been, so I assumed he had decided to give the party a miss an had already returned to the train in one of his moods. I stayed lon enough to pour some Dutch courage down my throat and was o the point of following him when he emerged from a concealin huddle of obviously tone-deaf well-wishers and made hi approach.

He was all smiles now, making friendly small talk as he escorted me to his dressing room, sat me down in a comfortable chair and handed me a very large slug of bourbon.

We sipped our drinks in silence. I saw no reason why I should make the first move. At last, he looked up and said: "The thing is, Frank, I want . . . this is really difficult for me, man, y'know? . . . what I want is to put all the crap behind us and get back to where we were, know what I mean? Patch things up so we can still be friends . . ."

"We can't *still* be something we never were in the first place," I pointed out. "What you're really trying to say is you're sorry for the bum's rush you've been giving me and you want me back as your minder until you can get rid of that film. Right?"

His eyes narrowed, but he was beaten and he knew it. He slumped down further in his chair, sighed pointedly and accepted my summary of the situation with a resigned shrug.

"Yeah, alright, man . . . if you want me to eat 'humble-pie', then consider it done. I'm sorry — OK? Now, are you coming back to work for me or what . . .?"

"Depends, "I replied, not showing my immense relief. "If you want me back, you'll have to start giving me some answers . . ."

"Like what?"

"Like why are you so scared? Is it just the Mafia, or are there hers after your blood too? What's on that film? What's . . ."

"Hold it, Frank! he interrupted, raising his hand. "Please. You on't realise what you're asking. I can't . . . I just can't!"

"Then it's no deal!" I told him." Just drop me off at Malaga irport on your way back tomorrow . . ."

"Alright! Alright!" He stood up and poured himself another rink, taking a deep pull at his glass before turning back to me to xplain: "There are some things that I can't tell you. Not yet, nyway. Perhaps when this is over I'll be able to tell you the whole ory, but there's no way I can do that here and now. Leave if you ave to, but I'm afraid that's how it is.

"But there are things you should know — in my interest as well s yours. So I'll tell you what I can and leave it to you to make your wn decisions after. OK?"

I nodded and told him to go ahead.

"Back in 1970, I bought a piece of film from Al Rossi in New York . . . and don't ask my 'why' or 'what's' on it, 'cos those are wo of the things I won't tell you. All you need to know is that nine was only part of a much longer film, the rest of the footage ut up and sold in the same way. One of the other buyers needed a ot of bread in a hurry a few years back and offered to sell me his bit of the film. When I saw it I knew . . ."

He checked himself, rubbing his glass thoughtfully between the palms of his hands before continuing: "And then, a couple of nonths ago, Rossi turned up in Torremolinos wanting to buy back hat last bit of film. He came straight out and offered me three nillion dollars for it! No haggling, nothing! Naturally, I jumped at t and made the deal."

"And that's what I've been carrying in the briefcase? That other piece of film?"

He nodded.

"So why are they after you now? What went wrong?"

His lips tightened and he hung his head. "I got greedy, Frank —

that's what. I got to thinking that if it was worth three million him, then it had to be worth more to someone else. I knew wh that someone was . . . and don't waste your breath asking 'whc because that's another thing I'm keeping to myself. So I made th other deal, this time for five million, and told Rossi to go play wi himself!"

I stared at him incredulously. "Did you seriously believe h would leave it at that? You must have been out of your mind!

"But I was, Frank. I was. I just couldn't think straight. All I sa were these dollar signs flashing in front of my eyes . . . know what mean? You see, man — I'm busted! Broke! I couldn't get m hands on more than twenty grand in an emergency . . ."

"You're breaking my heart!"

"It's no joke, man! Like, that might seem like a lot of bread t you, but it's peanuts to me. I've got an *image* to keep up; it expected of me! That kind of money might keep me alive for year or two . . . but what then? If you lose your job, you ca always do something else — sweep up in a supermarket, drive cab . . . anything! You'd be just another face in the crowd. But nc me; not Mikki Burton. You must see that. That's why I've had t go through with this godawful tour, and why I decided to dum Rossi and set up this other deal.

"I know I've been stupid, but what can I do? I'm making th trade in three day's time. Perhaps Rossi'll leave me alone afte that . . ."

"Are you crazy?" I sneered, "You're pissing in the wind if yo think that. You know as well as I do how these people operate They've made you an offer which included your life and, fron where I'm sitting, that looks like the best deal you're likely to get My advice would be to take it, and put the missing four millior down to experience!"

He shook his head. "Too late for that, Frank. The money's already on its way and I'm facing the same kind of threat from the other party if I don't come through with my end of the deal. So you see . . . I'm a loser, whichever way I play it. That's why I'm asking u to hang round for another couple of days. I don't know what 1 do after that, but I can worry about that when the time comes. fter all, I can stay lost for a long, long time on five million llars. Perhaps forever.

"But I'm right out in the open until then and that's why I need our help. Please, Frank . . . just give me those few more days. 'hat d'you say? Huh?"

My decision had already been made for me, of course, but there as no way I was going to tell Burton that. The jigsaw was ginning to slot into place, but I was still left scrabbling for the issing pieces. Whether he would end up volunteering the rest of e story or force me to beat it out of him remained to be seen, but was obvious he had told me as much as he was going to for the oment.

"And you'll fill in the gaps for me if I get you through this in one iece?" I checked before giving my answer.

"Maybe yes, maybe no . . ." he replied tantalisingly, . . ."I just on't know! One thing's certain, though — you'll never find out ith me six feet under, now will you?"

Still I didn't answer. He had dangled a carrot, and I could tell rom the expectant expression on his face that he considered it uicy enough to win me over. And that was exactly how I wanted im: the more co-operative his mood over the next two or three lays the better . . .

"Alright, Mikki," I conceded at last. "I accept. But I'm warning you now . . . don't make an enemy of me again. If you want me on your side, you better make damn sure you stay on mine!"

He smiled and leaned forward in his chair, stretching out his hand. We shook on the new agreement, but we were anything but friends: it was the beginning of the end . . .

Dusk was falling when we arrived back at Burton's villa. It had been a long and tiring day, the previous evening's party having continued in every compartment and corridor of the train on the journey from Paris to the South. Even Burton joined in, throwing it back and sharing the craziness as it he hadn't a care in the worl I knew differently, of course, but I had to admit it was his b performance of the whole tour. I was obliged to stay with hi throughout and forced to match him drink for drink, belch f belch. By the time we disembarked in Cannes, we had dru ourselves sober and had nothing to show for the experience sa niggling little headaches, destined to come of age as grouchy, bra numbing hangovers on the flight back to Spain.

It was just as well that I'd had the foresight to call Kaplan befo we left Paris while I was still relatively in control. Intrigued, h listened patiently as I recounted the details of Burton's story, b his only advice was to soldier on and, above all else, *find out wh was on the film*! Only then, he explained, could he decide wh course of action to take; whether to stop Burton's deal goin through or, regretfully to continue to turn a blind eye behind mask of official ignorance.

"Keep Burton alive . . . and keep him talking!" was the neare he came to giving me a direct order. With two more days to g before Burton could close the deal, and away from the securit given by the tour party, I knew that would be a lot easier said tha done . . . on both counts! Nevertheless, I left him with a chirpy an confident "Will do, Chief!!" and rang off.

At ten o'clock that evening Burton was still alive but, in n mood to do any talking: not to Linda, nor even Deva Ram — an definitely not to me! We had been back for half hour or so, all o which time we'd spent by the pool, sipping long drinks and listening to the sounds of the encroaching evening. Crickets chirruped spasmodically from the cover of the surrounding hills, now black in silhouette against the the last fiery glow of the setting sun; below us, we could see distant lights twinkling in the buildings lining the shorefront, or the occasional fishing boat putting out to sea. Trigger was stretched out adoringly at her returned master's feet, her docked tail wagging appreciatively at Burton's every move.

Thankfully, Deva Ram had already disappeared to an early bed, nd Linda soon announced that she was going to run a long, cool ath, and then retire herself. Burton and I were left alone.

"Fancy a swim, Frank?" he asked after a while, "I don't know bout you, but my head feels like it's still on the train!"

"No thanks," I replied, raising my glass. "I think I'll take mine lear, if it's all the same to you."

"Suit yourself," he grunted, disappearing into the house to merge, ten minutes later, wearing trunks and robe and carrying a owel draped across his arm. Recognising the uniform, Trigger vent bounding up to him, barking in joyous anticipation as she led he way back to the pool. Not waiting for her master, she campered off to the water's edge and threw herself in.

As she hit the water a vicious crackle ran round the pool. The log's howl lasted no more than a second before it was lost in a hrashing maelstrom of foam. The water seemed to posess a life of ts own, as if it wanted to throw the creature out again, and poor Trigger was being hideously convulsed in its grip, jaws open in a silent cry of pain, back arched, hair standing on end. At last all was still again apart from the occasional hissing crackle and the occasional tremble which ran down the floating corpse of the animal.

"Stay away!" I shouted across at the stunned Mikki Burton. "Don't go near that pool!"

He didn't seem to hear me, already down on his knees at the poolside, reaching out towards his dog's dead body.

I threw myself at him, dragging him away and pinning him to the ground. "Leave it, Mikki! Leave it! I've seen this before . . . the pool's live!"

"But . . . but my dog . . ." he protested, trying to push me off. 'Trigger . . . I've got to . . ."

"There's nothing you can do!" I screamed at him. "She's dead!"

He stopped fighting. The loss of his dog seemed to drain away the last of his spirits, and he began to sob uncontrollably. I left him and checked the perimeter of the pool, finding an exposed multi-core cable snaking into the pool from the cover of a cypress hedge that led towards an outhouse twenty yards away. Here it had be wired directly into a power switch. Seeing a pair of rubber glov amongst the litter of stored gardening implements, I reached out tentative hand and turned it off.

"That was meant for you, you realise," I said to Burton as returned to the pool.

He stared at the dog's body, still floating in the middle of th pool, now saturated and bloated with water. "I'll kill him for this! he spat venomously. "So help me . . . I'll kill him!"

"Who? Who are you going to kill, Mikki?"

"Rossi, of course . . ." he replied; " . . .who else?"

I grabbed him by the shoulders and spun him round, lookin him directly in the eye. "This wasn't Rossi!" I told him. "The could have killed you outside Rome if they'd wanted to. There' somebody else behind this! Who, Mikki? Who?"

He stared at me with glazed, expressionless eyes, opening hi mouth as if to speak then turning his head away to look back at th pool.

"Who is it?" I demanded, shaking him back to his senses "Don't fuck me around, Mikki . . . I've got to know!"

He shrugged me off and stepped back, unmistakeable violenc burning in his eyes. I covered up, fully expecting him to throw punch at me. But it never came: suddenly, all the fight seemed t leave him, his body appearing to physically shrink before my eye as he dropped his arms dejectedly and hung his head in defeat

"Alright," he mumbled through a weary sigh, turning towards the house; "Come with me . . ."

He retrieved the briefcase from the safe in his study, then led the way to a projection room, two flights above. The lights were turned on to reveal a large, circular room containing about twenty seats, tiered and laid out in rows like a mini-cinema, a bar set against one wall and a huge screen suspended from the ceiling at the far end.

He ushered me to a seat and unlocked the case, loading the film into the projector before lowering the lights. Then, grabbing a ttle of whisky and two glasses from the bar, he settled himself :o the seat next to mine and began: "It was early summer. 1969. e were in L.A., me and the rest of the guys in a house 'erlooking the city on Oriole Drive."

Los Angeles was the place to be at the time: the *only* place to :. A city of swimming pools, someone called it, and I guess that st about sums it up. It was like Disneyland, all day and everyday, ıow what I mean? You can't imagine what it was like; you've got) idea . . .

"We were treated like Gods, Frank: making our own rules, cut ff from the outside world, mixing only with our own kind. The nly reason for getting up in the morning was getting stoned and :tting laid. And the parties . . . endless parties, every single night, ıoving from one house to another. The faces were always the ıme: rock people, movie people, groupies, hangers-on . . . 'eaks.

"It was at Denny Winslow's place . . . remember him, do you?"

"Yes," I replied. "Yes, of course. He was one of the Winslow rothers; from The Surfers. I've still got a few of their albums ıcked away somewhere . . ."

"Yeah, that's him," Burton confirmed. "Anyway, he had this ouse out at Malibu, right on the beach. He asked us all over to neet this guy he called The Wizard. Now Denny used to collect reaks like other people collect beer mats, all kinds of crazies . . . rain damaged acid heads, religious nuts, reincarnated Mahatma Ghandis . . . you know the sort of thing. So we weren't that excited ıbout this Wizard of his but . . . what the hell? . . . a party's a party.

"A bunch of us got there early. There was no sign of The Wizard, but Denny insisted on playing some tapes he'd made of the guy playing his own material. It was lousy, but we couldn't tell Denny that. He was out of his head — as usual — and just kept raving on about what a genius this guy was, how he was the greatest thing to happen to music since the invention of the gramophone, crap like that.

"Around midnight, the place was getting really crowded and t party started spilling over onto the beach. And then The Wiza arrived with about twenty or thirty others, mostly chicks, hanging on his every word, doing whatever he told them. Th built some fires on the beach and sat around in a circle, joining the choruses of his songs, banging tambourines and beer can whatever they could get their hands on.

"They were all well loaded on acid, and I was no exception. was all getting very witchy and very weird, especially when th Wizard started dishing out orders to his 'disciples', telling 'em t fuck each other, or cut themselves so they could drink their ow blood, crazy stuff like that. And they all did it; whatever he saic just like they were hypnotised or something.

"And then it started getting out of hand."

He rose and returned to the projector, rolling the film. watched, fascinated: it was silent, poorly lit and jerky like a hom movie, but I could pick out some famous faces: Cathy Ellis th singer, movie star Shaw Maclean, Mike Sargeant the British po star turned Hollywood producer. And then there was a close-up o this diminutive figure, sitting cross-legged on the sand anc strumming a guitar, wild eyes peering at the camera through mane of bushy black hair.

"Stop the film! "I called out to Burton. "That's him isn't it? Th Wizard?"

Burton nodded. "Recognise him?"

Of course I did: who wouldn't? A face that was soon to be had been plastered over the front pages of every newspaper in the world; the essence of the American nightmare; the bogey man incarnate; . . . Charlie Manson.

Now it all began to fit into place. Just like everybody else at the time, I had pored over every gruesome detail of Sharon Tate's murder and the catalogue of evil that was revealed later at Manson's trial. And I remembered the rumours of other murders, and the films his gang had made of them; the so-called 'Manson Snuff Tapes'. This, I realised with mounting horror, was one of em.

Burton started the film again. The action seemed to have mped forward, now focusing on the naked flesh writhing about the sand. The detail was hazy as the camera panned from side to de, zooming in and out, never settling. Then it swept round to nger on the terrified face of a beautiful young girl, held to the round by three or four men while others stripped her of her othes. Jumping wildly from one revolting close-up to another, ie film condensed her rape to a matter of seconds before homing n on the attempt by one of her attackers to take her from behind. His failure provoked a furious attack, his fists pummelling iciously into her ribs and kidneys. Other hands tried to pull him ff but he was back on camera just seconds later, rolling her over nto her back, a knife raised above his head. . .

The blade came down once, twice . . . I don't know how many imes more as I had to look away, sickened and appalled. Finally, ie grabbed her by the hair and yanked her lifeless body upright, litting her throat. And it was at that instant he turned to face the amera.

The whirring of the projector died as Burton locked the image on freeze-frame. Although I had never seen that face before, I knew instantly who it was.

"That's Calvin, isn't it?" I checked with Burton, my voice now brittle and trembling.

"Yes; that's Calvin," he replied in a matter-of-fact way, returning to his seat. "We never knew who he was, you see? He was a nobody then, just another college kid who'd flipped out on too much acid. Not even Rossi knew. He cut up the film and sold that piece to Shaw Maclean, as he was one of the guys laying into that chick. When Shaw found out he had cancer he was desperate to raise some bread for this quack clinic in Mexico, so he gave his old buddy Mikki Burton a call and . . . well, you already know the rest."

"And the girl?" I asked. "Who was she?"

"Dunno," Burton shrugged. "Some chick, that's all . . . "

Suddenly very angry, my fists clenched involuntarily.

"Is that all you've got to say? *Some chick*? A girl was murdere for Chrissakes! Doesn't that mean anything to you?"

He turned to face me, composed and dispassionate. "I'll tell yo what it means to me, man . . . five million dollars, that's what!

"You callous bastard!" I spat.

"Maybe so; maybe so. But I didn't kill her, did I? Calvin did.

"But you were there! Didn't you see what was going o Couldn't you have stopped it?"

He shook his head, almost scornfully. "You don't understan Frank! We were all wasted, totally wiped out. When you're lik that, you just don't know what's real anymore. And anyway, I wa up at the house at the time, so I had no idea what was happenin It wasn't until afterwards, when I saw her body . . ."

"So what happened then? Surely you must have felt somethin seeing her like . . . like that?"

"Oh, yes . . ." he replied, suddenly subdued. "I felt somethin alright. You want to know what happened? I got an erection, man A fucking hard-on! And that was the last time . . ."

The door flew open and there was Linda Love, wrapped in robe and still wet from her bath.

"Mikki — I've just heard about Trigger, I . . .

She froze, her eyes locked on the image on the screen. Burto sprang from his seat to turn if off but it was already too late. He eyes dilated with shock and she clampled her hand across her mouth as if she were about to be sick, running from the room and slamming the door behind her.

Burton chased after her and I followed on a few moments later, keeping a respectful, and somewhat cowardly, distance. I reached the bottom of the stairs in time to see Linda bristling past, an overnight bag slung across her shoulder, her hair still dripping wet, the thin cotton dress she'd scrambled into clinging her body.

"Come back here, you bitch!" Burton screamed in pursuit. pushing past me to follow her outside. As he caught up with her she suddenly turned and swung her bag at him, knocking him to e ground. Before he could reach her again she was in her car and eeding away along the drive, tyres squealing and brake lights ashing as she roared through the gates and disappeared from ew.

"Good riddance!!" Burton bellowed into the night, punching e air with his fist and kicking out furiously at the loose stones overing the gravelled drive. "Who needs you . . . who fucking eeds you?!"

* * *

"Rogers? Is that you? My word, you're bright and early today. 've only just got into the office myself. You sound out of breath . . ."

"Yes, Chief. I've been running. Listen, I haven't much time. Burton was still asleep when I left but he'll be screaming for me as oon as he wakes up. I've sneaked out on the promise of an early morning jog, but he'll get suspicious if I'm away very much onger."

"You'd better get on with it, then," he suggested.

And get on with it I did: I told him the whole story and could ense by the involuntary grunts of horror coming over the line that e was no less appalled than I had been the previous evening.

"God, that's awful!" he said quietly as I concluded the tale. "I hadn't expected anything like that!"

"Nor did I, Chief; nor did I. The question is, what do we do now?"

There was a brief silence, then: "When is Burton making this deal?"

"Noon tomorrow. At least, that's what he's told me. I can't see any reason for him to lie."

"Where? At his villa?"

"As far as I know," I replied.

"And Calvin? Will he be there?"

I didn't know, but I thought that he would be, considering what was at stake. Kaplan agreed, but added: "No matter. There'll be no place left for him to hide after this particular balloon goes up!

"You can leave the arrangements to me now, Frank. But let me know if there's any change in Burton's plans in the meantime. I don't want half the Spanish police force turning up at noon tomorrow to find our bird has already flown!"

"And what about me?" I asked. "What do you want me to do?"

"Nothing — in a word. Your part in this is more or less over as far as I'm concerned."

"Meaning I can come home?" I ventured hopefully.

"Meaning, Frank, that I want you to play it very cool, do the job Burton's hired you for and make sure nothing goes wrong between now and then!

"I don't think Calvin will make another attempt on Burton's life; not at this stage of the game. As I see it, he's shot his bolt as far as that goes. Nor do I think Rossi will make any further move until he's sure which way Burton is going to jump. But, if I'm wrong, and it comes down to a choice of saving Burton or the film . . . for God's sake, save the film! Without that, we've got nothing. If Calvin gets his hands on it, then he's bound to destroy it and there goes the only evidence. And if Rossi gets the chance to sell it to the KGB . . . well, I shudder to think what would happen then. Any man willing to cough up five million dollars to cover his tracks would, surely, be capable of passing on classified information if the chips were down"

"Sorry to interrupt, Chief" I butted in, checking my watch, "but I'd better be making tracks . . ."

"Yes, yes, of course," he agreed, adding cheerfully: "You've done a fine piece of work here, Frank. I think you might have earned yourself a little holiday when you get back."

"Don't tell me . . ." I said. "Another week in Iceland — right?"

He didn't reply, ringing off with an ominous, and uncharacteristic, chuckle.

The temperature must have risen by a good ten degrees while I was phoning Kaplan, or so it felt as I jogged the mile and a half or so back to the villa from Benalmadena, all of it uphill. Sweating profusely, red faced and out of breath, I was met by José as I aggered up the short flight of steps to the house to be told that urton had already breakfasted and was waiting for me in his udy.

"Where the hell've you been, man?" he asked with undisguised ritation as I entered.

"Jogging . . ." I replied, somewhat superfluously, and coughing olently as I subsided into a chair.

"Done you good, has it?"

"T'rrific!" I spluttered back in a hacking wheeze. "Nothing like !"

"When you've fully recovered," he continued, "come over here nd look at this."

There was a newspaper spread across his desk. "Here," he said, abbing at a small article hidden away on one of the inside pages; What do you make of that?"

"Not a lot" I confessed in perfect honesty; "I don't read panish."

Not that I had to speak the lingo to recognise Calvin's name in he headline, nor to pick out his now familiar face from the cluster f local dignitaries who surrounded him in the accompanying icture. Burton explained that the article was about the opening eremony Calvin had performed the previous day at a new JGC lant near Algeciras. I already knew about that from Toby Iamilton but I didn't say anything to Burton.

And then he pointed to the last paragraph. "According to this," e informed me, "Calvin's chartered a yacht and plans to spend a hort holiday crusing around the southern coast. And it's due to lock at Malaga later today . . . "

"So he's coming to make the deal himself?" I checked.

"That's right, Frank. He insisted on it. That's why we've had to wait till now, giving him the opportunity to tie it in with the opening of this new factory of his."

"And the deal's going to be done here, is it? Noon tomorrow, as arranged?"

A frown creased his brow as he nodded and asked: "Are you

trying to pump me or something?"

"Certainly not. I am just trying to find out what th arrangements are, it's extremely difficult to protect somebody you have no idea what's going to happen next. It's for you ow good, Mikki".

"I suppose so," Burton conceded with a grunt, folding th newspaper neatly before dropping it into a waste bin beside h desk.

"What do you think, Frank? I mean what happened last nig Was Calvin behind it?"

I shrugged. "Looks that way, doesn't it? But who knows fo certain? If it was Calvin, trying to save himself five million dollar can you really blame him? You've got yourself involved in a dirt game, Mikki, and that's the way it's played.

"As I told you last night, I don't think it had anything to do wit Rossi. They wouldn't make you an offer, only to corpse you befor you've had the opportunity to take it. Of course, it could b somebody else; another element you haven't got around to tellin me about yet?"

I didn't mention Bryant, of course: the way I saw it, it was odds on that the girl in the film was his missing daughter, Linda Presuming he had some idea what was on the film, it would b logical to look no further than its present guardian for he murderer. Reason enough for a revenge killing, I would hav thought. Burton was at the party, after all, and all the othe famous faces were now dead . . .

"Mikki?" I said, "I saw a lot of people on that film last nigh that I recognised, and I've just realised you seem to be the onl one still alive. Tell me, how did the others die?"

"That's a hell of a question!" he replied, puzzled. "Why? You don't think . . ."

"That's someone's been bumping off everyone who happened to be at the party that night? Maybe not; perhaps it's just a coincidence. A lot of things can happen in fourteen years, I suppose. But I'd still like to know . . . "

He thought a while, then said: "Well, you know what happened the rest of the Rats: John and Freddy died in the same car crash; oz took too many pills one night and never woke up. Shaw aclean died of cancer; Denny Winslow fell off his boat and awned . . . too stoned to swim, probably; Cathy Ellis O.D.'d; lanson's in jail, of course . . . who else?"

"Mike Sargeant? What happened to him?"

"Search me! I never really knew him that well, but as far as I now he's still making rotten movies in Hollywood."

"Forget it, Mikki," I concluded. "It was just a hunch, that's all. robably nothing in it . . ."

"No," he agreed. "Probably not . . ."

The thought made him uncomfortable, though. I could tell. It 'as understandable enough: if there was someone else, someone e didn't know about, systematically eliminating everyone who 'as at the party, then Burton's name would be getting pretty near he top by now. Even if he managed to keep out of reach of Rossi nd Calvin, there would always be the fear of the unknown; the aceless autograph hunter with a gun hidden in his jacket, the riendly dealer rattling a bottle of strange coloured pills . . .

"So" I said changing the subject, much to Burton's relief. 'What's on for today. You said you wanted me to go to Malaga?"

"Yes, Frank. Just check the bullring over for me, will you? Security-wise, I mean."

That sounded pretty pointless to me, and I told him so. There would be upwards of ten thousand people there for the concert that evening, and any one of them could be carrying a gun.

"Well, do it anyway!" he snapped. "That's what you're being paid for. Make sure no-one can get into the backstage area without the proper passes, that's the main thing. We've got to go to some godawful civic reception in the town hall afterwards, but you don't have to worry about that; the police'll be handling the arrangements there."

"So when do you wt me to go?" I asked.

"What are you still standing here for?" he replied.

PART FOUR:
THROUGH A GLASS DARKLY

FOR NOW WE SEE THROUGH A GLASS DARKLY,
BUT THEN FACE TO FACE

Corinthians: 2

ırton told me to take one of his cars for the journey into Malaga. ›elected the least ostentatious of the four, an open-topped Alfa ›meo, the vintage Bentley and the magnificently preserved uesenberg seeming not quite apt somehow. Unfortunately, his ımborghini was jacked up and minus two of its wheels, denying e the opportunity to fulfill one of life's little ambitions by taking ıat.

I drove slowly towards Malaga, enjoying the sun and wind on y face, the panorama of palm trees and distant hills, and the nmediate response of the highly tuned engine as I overtook the ccasional lumbering lorry to escape the choking fumes of its xhaust. And I must own up to feeling a certain self-congratulory nugness; only a day to go, my mission practically accomplished,, ıe guilty about to be brought to book. No matter how tricky the ıeeting with Calvin, and possibly Curtis, was likely to be, I was onvinced that the worst was already behind me and was ncouraged to whistle a cheerful tune as I drove, beating out an ccompanying rhythm with my fingers on the steering wheel. If I'd ›een more alert, I might have noticed the car following me, a amiliar face peering through the windscreen to keep a check on ny every move.

The bullring was deserted. A huge stage had been erected at he southernmost end, the equipment for that evening's concert already set up, the lights positioned on scaffolding above and on ›ither side of the stage. All this had been done the previous day, he road crew having flown out with the equipment directly after the Paris show to leave themselves enough time for some well deserved rest and relaxation before returning to the bullring for Burton's sound check around two o'clock that afternoon.

There was really nothing for me to do, but I went through the notions nevertheless. I had checked the backstage area and was tanding in the middle of the ring, looking for a shady corner vhere I could snatch forty winks, when I heard a sound behind ne. One of the main gates into the ring had burst open, and as I spun round a fighting bull plunged into the arena.

At first it looked almost as surprised as I must have done, b once its eye adjusted to the light it began to trot rapidly round t ring. Then it saw me and paused, snorting and pawing at the dus ground.

I remained where I was, my brain working over-time. Th nearest gap in the barrier was over thirty yards away, and I kne that the bull was a great deal faster than me. I was up to it to mak the first move. As long as it kept snorting and scraping the groun I figured I would be able to move gradually towards the exit, an without taking my eyes from it I began to sidle sideways. The bu looked young and was clearly fresh. It swished its tail from on side to the other and every time it snorted tossed its head so that i great black horns flashed in the sun: I couldn't help but imagin what it would be like to have one of them buried deep in my guts and the thought sent a shiver down my spine.

Suddenly, the snorting and pawing stopped. The beast's blood shot eyes seemed to cloud for an instant, it shuffled a couple c steps to the side and then began to lumber towards me, gatherin speed with every step. I hadn't realised just how big Spanis fighting bulls were at close quarters: muscles rippled along ever inch of its sleek black body; the spread of its horns seemed to b three, maybe four feet across; the ground beneath my fee trembled as it pounded across the arena.

Under the circumstances, I remained remarkably calm — that's to say I managed to stay just this side of passing out with fear There was very little I could do, but wait until the bull was almos upon me, then throw myself to one side, rolling over in the dust as it lumbered past.

It turned, tossing its head back and bellowing angrily, its hind quarters swaying from side to side as it collected itself for another charge. I scrambled to my feet and sprinted towards the shelter of the barricade but then, still ten yards short, I tripped and measured my length on the sand. The bull was now at top speed, his head already lowered, his horns prepared to hook me off the ground.

A shot rang out. The bull seemed more surprised than hurt, ılling up only feet away, a confused expression came into its eyes ; blood spurted from the gaping hole between them. Another ıot, this time bringing the animal to its knees, its head jerking up efore it let loose an agonised roar. Finally it rolled over onto its de, red foam beginning to froth around its mouth as it entered ıe final convulsions before death.

"Better get out of here, buddy!" a voice said.

He was standing over me, the gun now dangling by his side and linting in the sun. I shaded my eyes and squinted up at him.

"Bryant! What the hell . . ."

"Come on!" he interrupted harshly, grabbing me by the arm nd hoisting me upright. "We can talk outside. Follow me!"

He was already hurrying across the ring. I caught up with him at he mouth of the exit tunnel, spinning him round and shouting: 'Wait, you bastard! I'm not going anywhere with you!"

"Listen bud," he replied, shrugging me off. "I've just saved your life, haven't I! All I want is to . . ."

"What? Finish the job yourself? Carry on where you left off at the airport . . .?"

"I wasn't trying to kill you!" he broke in, shaking his head. "I was trying to *stop* you! Jesus Christ . . . are you that dumb? I don't waste bullets, bud. I hit what I aim at. Your proof is lying right there in the sand!"

He had a point: stopping a charging bull in its tracks at twenty paces had nothing whatsoever to do with beginner's luck. This one was a skilled marksman.

"Now . . ." he resumed; "Are you going to walk, or do I have to carry you out?"

I submitted with a shrug. "Where are we going?"

He didn't reply, turning away from me again to march briskly off down the tunnel.

Without slackening his pace, he led me to a car parked in the street outside, climbed into the driving seat and leant across to open the passenger door so I could slip in beside him.

"Hello, Frank." A familiar voice came from the back se

"Linda?! What on earth are you doing here?"

"Let's drive, shall we?" Bryant suggested, not giving Linda t time to offer an explanation. "It's too public here for my liking.

I turned to look at her again as we drove off. She respond with a thin, nervous smile then looked away, peering through h window. Bryant drove towards the outskirts of town then came a halt in a secluded side street, carefully selecting his spot so th he could check on the approach of unwanted visitors from eith end.

He killed the engine and turned in his seat to face me. "So yo saw the film last night, I hear?"

"Yes," I replied. Then, lowering my voice, I added: "The girl . she was your daughter, wasn't she?"

He did not need to reply. The pain on his face was answ enough.

"And now you know who killed her," I continued. "Or did yo know all along?"

"No; not for sure," Linda explained. "We had our suspicion though. We knew Mikki bought the film from Shaw Maclear although he never said anything about it to me. And then, a coupl of months ago, Al Rossi turned up at the house and I realise something was going on. Mikki started acting very strangely, eve less of a human being than normal, locking himself away in hi study with Deva Ram, hardly saying a word to me. One night while he was out, I went through the drawers of his desk an discovered a collection of magazine and newspaper clippings, a about Calvin. We put two and two together and, last night, we go proof . . ."

"You keep saying 'we'," I interrupted. "Have I misse something along the way, or am I just being dumb?"

"Sorry, Frank," she replied. "I should have explained. My rea name's not Linda Love. It's Bryant. Jennifer Bryant. The girl in the film was my sister, Linda . . ."

"So you took her name and became Burton's mistress to find

t who killed her? Jesus, how could you? I mean, it could have en him, couldn't it? How could you share the bed of a man who ght have murdered your own sister?"

She leaned forward and cradled her chin on arms folded across e back of my seat.

"But it wasn't like that, Frank," she said softly. "I was never his istress' as you put it. The question never arose. He can't you e. He's impotent . . ."

So that was what he was trying to tell me last night, just as Linda irst into the room. "And that was the last time . . ." he had gun to say, and now Linda had finished the sentence for him. So w I knew: it explained a lot.

"I worked for him, that's all," she continued. "I came out here try to get close to him; met him in a night club and then, a short hile after, he offered me a job. Secretary, housekeeper, maid. nd he needed someone to be seen with, y'know? For the sake of ppearances. To keep his secret safe. That was part of the deal. hat's what he paid me for . . .!"

"He paid you?" I asked, shocked and disapproving.

"Of course. Why not?" she shrugged in reply. "It was my job. ou get paid for what you do, don't you?"

I still couldn't quite put the two together. It was so... well, dd. Such a relationship was beyond my experience, beyond my nderstanding: to live like that, to pretend to be the lover of a nan you already knew to be involved, if only by association, in he savage murder of your own flesh and blood? And accept noney for it too? Perhaps I'm old fashioned, but we would never do anything like that in Bermondsey...

"So how long has this been going on?" I asked, "The two of ou, working together like this?"

"We started after Jennifer's mother died," Bryant took over. "It seemed the only thing to do, somehow. I'd lost a daughter, a on . . . and, finally, a wife. What would you have done if you had een me? Walk away from it? Not me, buddy. My whole life had een spent upholding the law; doing what's right. And if wanting

to see justice done to the bastard responsible for the lives of thr
of my family isn't right, then I don't know what else in the wor
is!"

"So why didn't you tell me this before?" I asked. "At th
airport? Or my flat?"

"Would you have listened?" he replied then, raising his voic
"Are you listening now?"

I turned away without answering, chastened and somewha
ashamed.

Linda took up the story. "Tom — that was my brother — told u
about the film before he died. He'd gone to look for Linda i
L.A., heard about the film, then followed it to New York. We sti
didn't know the girl on the film *was* Linda, but everything seeme
to point to it. We knew she hung out with that crowd from he
letters home and from what her room-mate had told us. We didn
want to believe it . . . but we just had to know.

"That's why Tom went to New York. He never saw the film, bu
he got enough information about it to tell us who had been at tha
beach party and who was doing the bidding when the Mafia cut th
film up and sold it."

"So why didn't you go to the police? After what happened to
Tom?"

Bryant laughed bitterly. "We tried that but no-one wanted to
know. All we got was blank faces and a referral to Missing
Persons. Call it politics, if you like. You see, they'd already
hooked the big fish, Manson, and that's as far as they wanted it to
go. All the others, the ones that crawled back into the woodwork
after the Tate murders, hangers-on like Burton and Maclean and
all the rest . . . well, let's just say that, between them, they pay an
awful lot of taxes . . . if you know what I mean?

"So you can see why we had to do it ourselves. We took up
where my son had left off, trying to track down that final piece of
film. Any one of them could have had it, but we didn't know who.
We finally traced it to Maclean, but he was already dead by then . .

"Just like all the others . . . "I suddenly found myself saying.

Bryant didn't answer.

"You're not suggesting we had anything to do with that?" Linda apped at me, genuinely horrified.

"Leave it, Jenny! We want him as a friend, not an enemy!" ien, turning to me, he said: "My daughter seems to think you n help us. That's why we followed you here today, and why 're telling you all this."

"Help? How? What do you think I can do?"

"Get the film for us, Frank," Linda replied. "You can do it. ikki trusts you and . . ."

I shook my head. "No way! Absolutely no way! And that's not rough any misguided loyalty to Mikki Burton, I can assure you. I n't tell you how, but soon Calvin will get his just deserts. and at's good enough for me. I might be with you in spirit, but don't k me to join in your personal vendetta. That I *won't* do!"

"But, Frank! You saw the film. You saw what he did to her. urely after that . . ."

Bryant raised a hand to silence his daughter. "And that's your nal word?" he asked, looking into my eyes.

"I'm sorry, but yes; yes, it is. It has to be."

Silence fell. There was nothing more to be said. Bryant started ie engine and drove off back towards the bullring.

"What will you do now?" I asked as he drew up alongside.

He shrugged. "I don't know. If you were in our shoes, what ould you do?"

I couldn't answer, realising at once how crass and insensitive my question had been. I could have offered the glib, logical counsel to et justice be done, but what room could there be left for logic after the pain and heartbreak that Calvin had put them through? And I realised that they had come too far to stop now. Calvin deserved everything he had coming to him, there could be no denying that, but the policy of an eye-for-an-eye seldom had anything to do with what I understand as 'justice'. Not in my experience; not in the final analysis. Calvin should count himself lucky if the police catch up with him first...

As I opened my door, I turned to Bryant to ask: "Was it you w let that bull loose? To win me over by making a great show saving my life?"

He shook his head. "Hell, no. I don't know who it was. I did s a guy leaving as I was coming in, though. Seemed to be in a l hurry . . ."

"Can you describe him? No . . . don't bother; I'll tell yo American, six one, six two or thereabouts, well cut hair, da glasses, possibly wearing a suit?"

"That's the guy! Who is he?"

"His name's Randall Curtis," I told him. "Works for Calvi And if you see him again, my advice would be to stay well clea He's a professional killer and they don't come any meaner . . . tak it from me!"

"So what about you?" Linda asked. "What are you going to c now?"

"Hang around and wait for Burton to show up, I suppose. Don worry, I won't tell him anything about this."

"And after?" she persisted. "When it's over?"

"Go back to London, tidy up the mess your father mde of m flat — and forget everything you've told me today. That's wha you wanted, isn't it?"

She smiled, reaching out to take my hand. "Look after yoursel Frank. You're one of the good guys, you know that? I'm sorry fo all the shit I gave you, but you can see now why I had to do it. had to keep you out on the street so my father could get at th case. It was . . . "

"It's O.K.," I assured her, squeezing her hand. "I understand If you're ever in London, and all that . . . er . . . your father's go my address!"

"Time we were going Jenny," Bryant interrupted with a father' practised timing, turning the key in the ignition.

"And I must be going to," I said as I stepped out of the car "Good luck . . . to both of you!"

They drove off and I crossed the street towards the bullring, just time to see some workmen loading the bull's carcass into the ck of a lorry.

***

The afternoon dragged on endlessly. With nothing to do, I sat i the stands and watched Burton bitch his way through his soun check, constantly complaining about the feedback from h microphone, the inability to hear himself through his monito speakers (a definite advantage, I would have thought), the bran of bourbon in his dressing room. I didn't tell him about m meeting with Bryant and Linda, of course, nor about m *contretemps* with the bull. There would have been little point: fo some season, probably for old time's sake, Curtis had tried t cancel my contract and had failed. End of story. Burton was to uptight to listen to my troubles anyway, anxious to get this concer behind him and get onto the really important business schedule for noon the following day.

What made it worse was that he no longer had Deva Ram ther to hold his hand. The guru had cried off the concert an subsequent reception by sloping off after only half an hour claiming he was ill. He didn't look any worse than usual but i wasn't worth worrying about, except for the effect it had o Burton's nerves.

An hour or so before showtime, in the last minutes before the turnstiles were unlocked, I set off on my customary pre-concer security check. After a month-long tour, following the same routine night after night, I could have done it in my sleep: brief the backstage security guards on exactly who was to be allowed in and who not, which passes gave access to which particular areas, and so on; check under the stage and in the dressing rooms; issue last nute instructions to the bouncers lined up in front of the stage to)tect Burton from his delirious fans, realising as I did so that :y would have been far better deployed at the other end, forcing ck the hordes of disappointed punters streaming towards the sh desk to demand their money back, halfway through the show.

also had to check the locks on the laser mixing desk, the box of :ks which controlled the direction and intensity of the beams :d to climax Burton's act. Joe, the lighting engineer, had set the els and co-ordinates the night before, working from a cross nted on the stage to indicate the exact spot where Burton would l and assume his crucifixion pose. All that was left for Joe to do s to flick a single switch on his lighting console at the propriate moment, and the lasers would run through their pre- t programme automatically.

"Aren't they dangerous?" I had asked him, early on in the tour.

"These?" he scoffed. "Nah . . . wouldn't give a headache to a dgerigar. I suppose they could be, at full power, but they're rfectly harmless at the normal level.

"That's why I padlock the cover on the desk after I've set the ogramme . . . and why you have to check it after me! If anyone ppened to brush past the desk and nudge one of those density ntrols to 'high' . . . whoooosh! . . . no more Mikki Burton!"

I spent most of Burton's act in the hospitality bar backstage. My mples were still throbbing from the ghastly noise he'd made at e run-through that afternoon, and I was determined not to go rough it again, even if it was for the last time. So I waited until e last possible moment before making my way to the side of the age, ready for Burton's exit at the end of his show. I took up a osition alongside Joe, bent over his console and furiously flicking vitches to squeeze the maximum effect out of the banks of lights e had at his fingertips.

"How's it been?" I shouted above the noise.

"What?" he replied, screwing up his face and cupping a hand to is ear.

"The show?" I tried again. "How's it gone tonight?"

He shook his head and stuck out a disapproving lower li "Lousy as ever!" he retorted. "The punters seem to be enjoying though . . ."

"What? I didn't hear that?"

"I said the audience are . . . oh, forget it, Frank — I'll catch yc later, OK?"

I nodded an acknowledgement and he redirected his attention the mixing desk, with Burton winding himself up for the big finis it was almost time to flick the switch for the lasers.

We didn't realise what was happening at first. Nobody did; th band kept on playing, the audience went wild and hoote enthusiastically, thinking it was all part of the act. But we coul smell the burning flesh; we could see the smoke as Burton clothes began to smoulder then burst into flames; the horror on h face, his mouth open but in too much agony to cry out.

"Turn it off! I screamed at Joe; "For Christ's sake . . . TURN I OFF!!"

But he didn't hear me. He was staring blankly ahead, unable t comprehend what was going on. I pushed him out of the way an pulled the master switch on the lighting console, plunging the stag into darkness.

The audience were still going crazy, shouting '*Bravo! Bravo!* . . MORE! MORE! MORE!'. But as I ran onto the stage to smothe the flames with a tarpaulin, followed by three of the road crev who helped me carry Burton's lifeless body into the wings, th cheering faltered then died away altogether. The entire aren became gripped in an eerie, breathless silence. There was a singl scream, and then another, and another, swelling to a single unified wail of anguish and terror as the rush for the exit tunnel began in earnest, the crowd swept this way and that in waves o irrational panic, shouting, pushing, punching, kicking. Hundred of people knocked to the ground and trampled on. Chaos reigned.

"What went wrong?" I yelled at Joe, taking him by the shoulders in an attempt to shake him back to his senses. He wa rigid with shock. I unhooked the ring of keys from his belt and shed him aside, then unlocked the series of padlocks which tened the security cover to the laser mixing desk. I wrenched it en and could see at a glance that every one of the density ntrols had been switched to maximum power.

And then I saw Curtis, hurrying away across the backstage area make his escape through the now unguarded gates. I reached e street in time to see him scramble into a car and roar away at ll throttle, heading west. I gave chase on foot, encouraged by the ght of him held up at a busy intersection about two hundred rds ahead. I noticed a taxi inching out of a nearby side street and an in front to bring it to a halt, wrenching open the driver's door say the line that every cabbie longs to hear: "Follow that car!"

"Señor?" he replied, gaping at me in total bewilderment.

There was no time for further debate, so I pulled him from his b and pushed him to the ground, jumped into the empty seat and celerated away with my foot pressed flat on the floor.

The intersection was clear by now so I made a quick decision d swung to the left. I had guessed right and soon I picked up his il lights speeding away along la Farola towards the Malaga ocks.

He had left the car straddled across the narrow entrance to the uayside, forcing me to abandon the cab and sprint after him. lthough he appeared to be in much better physical shape, I soon egan to gain ground and closed the gap between us to no more han twenty yards.

And then he stopped running, swinging round to face me, his and already reaching inside his jacket for his gun. Now I could ee what had been slowing him down: a familiar looking briefcase, ucked beneath his arm. I threw myself to the ground, his first ullet whistling over my head and ricochetting off the concrete urface of the quayside a few feet behind me. His second thudded nto where my head would have been had I not rolled behind the aterpillar-tracked wheels of a mobile crane.

With a parting shot to keep me at bay, he turned and ran off gain, constantly checking over his shoulder, the gun still waving

ominously in his hand. I realised there was no chance of catch
him now and, without a gun of my own to back me up, any furt
attempt to chase after him in the open would be inviting cer
death. So I kept on his tail as best I could, staying in the shad
and making the most of whatever cover I could find.

I was crouched behind a pile of empty packingg cases and s
some thirty yards away, but there was enough light coming fr
the deck of the luxury cruiser for me to recognise the figure
Calvin hovering impatiently at the top of the gangplank, urgi
him to hurry on board. He snatched the case fr
Curtis's hand and disappeared into one of the cabins while t
gunman retired to the after-deck, steadying his gun arm across t
stern-rail as the yacht slipped its moorings and edged away fr
the quay towards the harbour entrance.

I swore under my breath, as I crouched helpless, watching t
yacht pull inexorably away, water churning in its wake as it clear
the quay and headed for the open sea.

There were three explosions: the first amidships, blowing t
bridge and saloon to pieces; the second ripping a gaping hole in t
yacht's side as the engines blew apart. A billowing ball of flan
engulfed the whole boat and she began to list steeply to port.
could see a couple of her crew running frantically about her dec
both of them blazing and screaming in agony, making ghast
silhouettes against the brilliant orange flames.

And then the fuel tanks caught, a mighty explosion hurtli
debris a hundred feet into the air. There was nothing left, t
wreckage of Calvin's yacht raining down as fiery splinters to igni
the patches of oil which floated on the surface of the sea, t
violated waters foaming around the mangled remains of the hull i
eruptive fury, sucking it under in a matter of seconds. There wou
be no survivors.

It had all gone terribly, terribly wrong: Burton dead, Calvin an
Curtis blown to bits along with the tape . . . and then again –
maybe not! I suddenly remembered that Burton had not returne
the film to the briefcase the previous evening, putting the

›arately in the safe in his study. It was a long shot, but it was just ssible it could still be there.

This was no place to be, anyway: already I could hear the distant ıil of police sirens closing in. The last thing I needed then was a ›anish police interrogation. The keys were still in Curtis' car so I ok that: it was faster than the taxi, which would probably have en reported stolen by now, in any case.

Ignoring speed limits and every other traffice law in the book, I ade it back to the villa in twenty minutes flat. I was relieved to ıd the gates open, and I was able to make my approach without sturbing Deva Ram or José. There would be enough wailing and east beating over Burton's death in the hours to come, and I was no mood for any lengthy inquests there and then.

A dim light was burning in the study, a thin sliver showing ıderneath the door. I pushed it open and stepped inside.

"José? What are you doing here?" I asked in surprise, seeing ıe shadowy outline of the manservant sitting behind Burton's esk, his face hidden by the glare of the lamp in front of him.

There was no answer; no flicker of movement whatsoever. I rossed the room and mounted the dais, reaching out to take him y the shoulder . . .

He fell forward, his forehead cracking against the desk. Even in ıe half-light cast by the reading lamp I could see the bullet hole in is neck, the blood co-agulated and dried on his collar.

"Poor sod . . ." I breathed, easing him back to an upright osition in the chair. My eyes swivelled instinctively to the safe nd it came as no surprise to see the heavy steel door hanging pen. I left José and knelt down in front of it not really knowing vhat I expected to find, but desperate for any kind of evidence in he wake of the missing film.

"Is this what you're looking for?" a voice said behind me, a gun arrel pressing into the soft flesh below my ear. Slowly, I turned ny head and looked up: there, dangling between the thumb and orefinger of Deva Ram's spare hand, was a reel of film.

*

"Get up!" he ordered, taking a step back but keeping the g levelled at my head, then "Sit down!" nodding towards an emp chair standing against the wall.

"...one arm, one leg, one nod of the head..." I mumbled as I to my seat.

"What was that?" he snapped.

"Nothing," I replied. "Nothing at all."

He was out of his orange robes now and dressed in an everyd business suit, the collar and tie sitting uncomfortably around neck. He was not very good at this sort of thing, I conclude judging by the way the gun was shaking in his hand. That cou work to my advantage: but, then again, it also made him very, ve dangerous . . .

"Did you have to kill José?" I asked, not taking my eyes fro the gun.

"Me? You've got it wrong there, man. I didn't kill him . . .

"Well, who did then? You've got the film. And the gun. Th gets you elected as far as I'm concerned!"

"No, no, man," he replied. "I tell you . . . I had nothing to d with it. He was like that when I got back from the bullring. When checked the safe, the film was still there but the briefcase ha gone. Whoever took the case must've snuffed him . . ."

"Curtis took it," I explained.

"Who?"

"Randall Curtis. Works for Calvin. Or, to be more precise, *di* work for Calvin. They're both dead. So is Mikki . . ."

He seemed to sway, the news obviously taking him complete by surprise.

He was startled, understandably.

"Mikki? Dead? How . . .? . . . who did it . . .?"

I shrugged. "Curtis, I think, but I can't be sure. This is all such sodding mess. I'm not sure of anything anymore."

Headlights swept across the dimly lit room as a car crunched to halt outside. Deva Ram moved cautiously across to the windo and peered out.

'hey're here," he announced. "Outside! Quickly . . . move!"
:ollowed his instructions and led the way into the hall. Not
ıg his eyes from me, Deva Ram unlatched the door and held it
ı. In bustled Al Rossi, closely followed by two stereotyped
s who shared the lumbering gait of an oran-utang and had
; to match. Under any other circumstances I would have
hed; under these I didn't dare.

s that it?" Rossi sneered contemptuously at Deva Ram,
ıting to the film in his hand.

he erstwhile guru nodded, his face grey with fear, his voice
ıing to have fled in fright.

've got your money here. "Rossi continued, tapping the
:he case by his side. "One hundred thousand dollars . . as
nged!"

eath, apparently, was getting cheaper by the day. Of course, I
d have ruined everyone's day by telling Rossi that his intended
m was already dead, but I realised that 'everyone' was certain
nclude yours truly so I decided against it.

Who's this?" Rossi asked, pointing at me.

Er . . . that's Mikki's minder," Deva Ram explained in a
rse whisper. "He's just told me that Mikki's dead . . ."

Is he?" the Mafia boss laughed. "That's lucky, isn't it?
:cially for you, I would have thought."

)eva Ram studied the floor. But said nothing. His moment of
ırning was a brief one however, interrupted by Rossi in his
ıatience to close the deal. He snatched the film from Ram's
ıd, unrolling about two feet of it and holding it up to the light.

'Can't see a fuckin' thing here..." he cursed under his breath.
en, turning back to Deva Ram, he snapped: "You gotta
jection room in this place?"

'This way", Deva Ram replied meekly, leading the way to the
rd floor. I followed on behind, sandwiched between Rossi's two
owbacks.

'Know how to work this thing?" Rossi asked me as we entered
: room, stabbing a finger at the projector. He handed me the

film before I could offer a reply then turned away, settling hin in a back row seat and indicating that Deva Ram should take seat beside him.

To my immeasurable relief, a quick inspection showed that projector was simplicity itself to operate, so I fed the film thro the rollers and connected it and other spool, shouting, "Pop anyone?" in an attempt to relieve the tension.

Rossi turned in his seat and sneered: "Shut it, creep! Jus' the film, will ya?", then motioned to one of the guards to join by the projector. I doused the lights and the film began..

It was one of my favourites: the one where the coloured m goes out for the day, leaving Tom to do the housework while J runs riot in the fridge . . .

Rossi had obviously seen it before. His hands were alre around Deva Ram's throat as he screamed: "What the fuck's tl You tryin' to make a monkey outta me, or what ?!?"

Right on cue, the two real monkeys rushed to their keeper's hoisting the unfortunate Deva Ram out of his seat, and hold him while Rossi punched him repeatedly in the stoma Mercifully they had forgotten about their projectionist, and as cartoon continued to flicker I took my opportunity to dodge ou the room and dash down the stairs.

Three shots rang out as I reached my car. They were clos followed by Deva Ram crashing through the third floor windo clutching his chest. He bounced off Rossi's car and lay still on drive. That was one guru who would never see California aga

***

t was only after I'd scrambled into my car that I realised I uld have taken the precaution of throwing away their keys. rsing myself for my stupidity, I started back towards their car, y to glimpse their shadows through the annexe windows as they ried down the stairs. I knew I'd never make it in time, so I inted back to my car and screamed away along the drive, ough the gates and turned east towards Torremolinos.

riving by instinct, I kept my eyes fixed on the rear view rror, only occasionally diverting my attention to the road ahead. the time they came into view I was already on Montemar and ng like a bat out of hell for the centre of town, snaking in and t of the heavy evening traffic and watching their headlights bob d weave behind me as they tried to catch up.

As we approached the outskirts, the traffic conditions became mediately more congested and chaotic and this appeared to rk in my favour, leaving them further and further behind. Not it it mattered anymore; I already knew I was in the clear. All I d to do was to keep them at bay for another mile or so and ey'd be left whistlin' Dixie. You see, I knew where I was going d they didn't. Now it was my turn to dish out the surprises...

Coming into town, I turned north along Palm de Mallorca then unding my horn to clear a path through the wall of pedestrians oking the pavement, I swerved off into a side street and bounced a short flight of steps to crash straight through the main doors the central police station.

Rossi screeched to a halt in the middle of the road behind me it that was as far as he got, the sight of all those brown uniforms id black helmets suddenly milling around my car proving iough to despatch him on his way again with a tyre squealing turn speed.

There must have beeen about twenty of them, all with drawn, all in a state of shock, not one of them appearing willi take the initiative of a first move. So I wound down my winc stuck my head out and smiled.

"Good evening, gentlemen," I said. "My name's Frank Roge and I'd be much obliged if you'd arrest me...!"

* * *

I spent four nights in the cells, and was more than happy tc so; a model prisoner, I beamed 'Gracias!' at the guard every t he locked me away. I couldn't get out but I was equally confic that nobody would get in. It was certainly the safest place to The guards weren't handing out song sheets so I was unable to in the spasmodic bouts of community singing as the stea swelling band of inebriates formed themselves into sway hiccoughing glee clubs. Nor could I share their enthusiasm for inevitable fist fights which erupted with monotonous regularit simply sat down in a corner and tried to remain inconspicuous, arms folded firmly across my chest to obscure the lettering on 'Official British Hooligan' sweat shirt. At times like those doesn't pay to advertise.

A couple of hours after my call to Kaplan, I was moved to a on my own. Whether this augured well or badly for my long te prospects I was unable to decide, but the immediate improvem 'hey allowed me just one phone call, early in the morning of the t day. Kaplan accepted the charges and groaned his way ough my necessarily brief resume of the story so far, ringing off h the ominously vague promise that he 'would see what he ıld do'. He must have got on my case pretty quickly though, as I s never formally charged with anything more serious than turbing the peace.

I was fully expecting some pretty heavy interrogation; bright nts shining in my eyes, electrodes dangling down the front of my users, that kind of thing. They could have hardly missed Deva .m splattered all over the driveway when they went to Burton's la to collect my personal effects, and there was also the ıbarrassment of a dead rock n roll star at the bullring in Malaga. ıe fact that I was both his house guest and his employee should ve raised an eyebrow or two but, if it did, they were certainly eping it a secret from me.

They just left me alone. At first I had been unceremoniously ımped in a communal cell which became more and more amped for space as the night drifted into the early hours the quality of the company was certainly welcome.

Still, it was better than nothing, and certainly beat the hell out of ıother night, of fledgling Mario Lanzas and slow-motion re-runs f the 'Thriller in Manilla'. And it gave me time to think; time I eeded. 'For every door that shuts, son,' my old mum used to ɛgularly remind me, 'another one is sure to open'. She must have ot it wrong somewhere, as the exact opposite had been happening ɔ me. No sooner had I solved the riddle of Burton's case than I ɔund myself enmeshed in a web of confusion and intrigue which vould require the combined talents of Hercule Poirot, Phillip Aarlowe and, not forgetting the mystery of the dead dog in the wimming pool, probably Rin-Tin-Tin as well to untangle.

It bore down on me, oppressed me; a maze of blind alleys and lead ends. Bryant, Calvin, Linda Love: I seemed to know less ıbout them now than I did before I met them. Who fixed the lasers o fry Mikki Burton? Who planted the bomb? Was it already on the yacht or in the briefcase that Curtis carried on board? W switched the film and, perhaps most important of all, where hell was it now?

For three long days, and four even longer nights, I paced arou my tiny cell and tried to puzzle it out, sleeping fitfully, my mi churning continuously, denying me rest. But salvation arrived the morning of the fourth day when, just after what passed breakfast, I was taken upstairs to meet a pin striped suit all the w from Madrid.

He introduced himself as Norman Pettybridge, an Unc Secretary at the British Embassy, and broke the news that I w about to be deported.

"T'rrific!" I grinned in reply, my response taking him somewh by surprise.

"This is no matter for levity, Rogers," he pointed out with d diplomatic gravity. "You seem . . . well, almost pleased . .

"I am, mate!" I confirmed. "Which way's the plane . . ."

With the dingy back room echoing to the swelling strains *Land of Hope and Glory*, I hurriedly collected my passport a the tatty collection of dirty clothes that were all I had. Wh Pettybridge 'sorted out the form' with the Guardia Commandar or whatever he called himself, I began to conjure up visions steak and kidney pie and foaming pints of Young's Best. I'd h more than enough paella to last me a lifetime, and a bellyfull Spain.

It soon became apparent, however, that Rogers, Frank, was n returning home as the all-conquering hero, having done sterlin stuff for Queen and Country. Far from it; the way Pettybridge an the Commandant were going on, you'd think they were bringing i Ronald Biggs or Lord Lucan. I was made to sign countless form in triplicate naturally, before a thoroughly unpleasant Spanis bobby handcuffed himself to me.

So much for doing your bit, I thought, as I saw a distinctly rope looking paddy wagon draw up in front of the police station. O well; it was nice to know that I was being sent home in style. Whe the formalities were duly completed, Pettybridge, myself and surly Spanish copper climbed into the back of the police van 1 set off for the airport.

Ve must have looked an odd trio; Pettybridge dressed to the ies in his inadvisedly heavy pin striped suit, me looking like a gitive from a chain gang, and the guard who kept giving me his ke-one-wrong-move-and-you're-a-dead-man look.

A nice, quiet ride to the airport was more than I could have ped for.

Sure enough no sooner were we on the road to Malaga than I came aware of Pettybridge clearing his throat prior to delivering messsage of earth shattering import.

"Look here, Rogers — this has been a major cock-up all und!" he said after a pregnant pause.

"Don't worry," I assured him. "I won't hold it against you."

Pettybridge did his best to look furious, but I can't say it othered me.

"This is not," he spluttered eventually, "the time nor place for ny of your barrow boy comedy routines!"

By now I was getting the distinct feeling that Norman and I eren't going to see eye to eye. I had locked antlers with too many f his type when I was in the Army not to realise that we had about s much in common as Mahatma Ghandi and Attila the Hun. robably less, come to think of it. Norman Pettybridge was a erfect specimen of the kind of bigoted minor public school bore who took themselves and their jobs far too seriously.

"We've got egg all over our faces on this one, Rogers. I'm xpecting you to put us straight on one of two matters so we can ort out this dog's dinner you've left behind."

He paused for a moment to adjust his tie. "Quite frankly," he continued, "we've got more than enough to do as it is, what with he usual round of shoplifters, drunks and hooligans. That's without having to explain away murders, crashed cars and all the rest of the hoo-hah you've created while you've been on Spanish soil. We're not exactly in the best odour with the Spanish

Government at the moment, what with Gibraltar, the Falkla
and so on."

I really think he expected me to sympathise with him, spill
beans and then join him for a trip to the tuck shop where we wo
all have a jolly good feed.

"I can only repeat what I've said already," I replied. "I was se
over here as a courier and was then asked to do a little 'mindi
for a singer called Mikki Burton . . ."

"Not very successfully it would seem," he interrupted smug

I shrugged. "You can't win 'em all, Norman old son. As far
I'm concerned, I've done my job and there's not a single bloo
thing either you or the Spanish authorities can pin on me. Not th
you'd want to, of course, us being such chums and all . .

Pettybridge looked as if he had had enough, which was fine
me. I was not going to tell him anything anyway. Leaning across
my guard I started to make semaphore signals to indicate that
was in sore need of a cigarette. This procedure took far long
than I'd hoped as my friend from the Guardia was none too brigh
Eventually, he produed a battered packet of *Celtas* and dredge
out a particularly filthy looking item, which he proferred betwee
thumb and forefinger.

Beggars can't be choosers, so I stuck the thing in my mouth,
it, and promptly went into a paroxysm of violent coughing.
hadn't had a cigarette for days and the smoke hit my lungs like th
exhaust fumes of a London bus. While the Spaniard roared wit
laughter, just about breaking my wrist in the process, Pettybridg
fanned himself frantically like an irritable old woman at a coloni
tea party.

It was in this state of disarray that we arrived at Malaga Airport
and as we pulled up to the terminal I began to wonder whether
would be let off the leash before we entered the building. I coul
see the Tour Operators' coaches lined up in the airport car par
and the steady stream of tourists who were pouring into th
terminal. There was absolutely no mistaking where this lot had al
been on holiday: each group seemed equally laden with stuffe

ıkeys, sombreros, leather drinking bottles and all the other aphenalia of a fortnight in Torremolinos.

n a moment we were outside and in the midst of the throng. tybridge was doing his level best to maintain his diplomatic *ıg froid*, but he only succeeded in looking like a misplaced bank nager. I was still braceleted to the policeman and was naturally racting a few odd looks. As I went into my Hunchback of Notre ıme number, complete with Charles Laughton' rolling eyes, ttybridge swung round on the heels of his well polished black ɔgues and snapped; "For Christ's sake Rogers, try to brace up. ɔu're not on Brighton pier now and I'm going to make damn sure u superiors learn of your infantile behaviour."

I somehow didn't think Kaplan would be too bothered, and I ıs in no mood to be browbeaten by the likes of Pettybridge.

"Please, please don't tell anybody," I begged sarcastically. "It's e missus you see - if I lose my job I won't be able to pay for her ɔeration."

"Oh, do shut up and pull yourself together!' Pettybridge said in ıs best Captain of the 1st XI voice.

We were now well into the terminal and Pettybridge was arching his squad of misfits towards Passport Control. They emed to be expecting us and produced another sheaf of forms to ː signed and countersigned. At last, when the signing was ɔmpleted, Pettybridge gave the guard the nod which he ɔmpletely failed to pick up until I had given him a few bars of 'lease Release Me' and the passport officer had given him an arful of abuse. When the penny finally dropped, he did his athetic best to look like John Wayne bringing in another esperado as he undid my handcuffs.

Without further ado I strode through Passport Control not othering to look back and see whether Pettybridge had emembered to wave his little white hankie. The chances were he ıad forgotten to bring it with him.

*

By tea time that afternoon I was being de-briefed in Kapla office over a glass of his finest malt.

"Bit of a bloody mess, all in all," he decided in conclusi "Damn shame we couldn't have collared Calvin as planned. Stil suppose justice was done in the end . . ."

"How did you swing my deportation order?" I asked, natura curious.

"That was easy enough," he replied with a smile. "Th couldn't get rid of you fast enough! The whole affair's been p under wraps, and that's the way they want it to stay. Not exac good for trade, publicity like that. Not in a place li Torremolinos . . ."

"No; wouldn't be . . . " I agreed.

He topped up my glass, then observed: "There are still to many loose ends for my liking, Frank. You were there; is it a clearer to you, now that you've had time to think about it?

"Not really, Chief," I replied in all honesty. "All the time I w in jail, I kept churning over everything that had happene especially on that last day, but ended up facing the same bri wall, time and time again.

"For example: who killed Mikki Burton? Was it Curtis, a seems likely . . . or could it have been Bryant? They were both a the bullring earlier that day, after all. And Deva Ram: was h 'persuaded' to co-operate with Rossi after being kidnapped i Rome, or was that just a put-up job to cover his tracks? Who kille José? Who switched the films? Did Bryant have anything to d with those other deaths . . . Winslow, Cathy Ellis, the rest of th Rats and God knows who else? If so, is Linda Love as innocent a she claims, or is she just a good actress? And, perhaps mos puzzling of all, who planted the bomb that killed Calvin?

"Sorry, Chief; I'm as much in the dark about all those question

ʻou are. The list just goes on and on . . ."

Perhaps this might help," he said, passing over the current e of the *International Herald Tribune* and indicating a small cle at the foot of the front page, with the headline 'CALVIN 'STERY'

A spokesman for the FBI said today that they had obtained ·ortant evidence relating to the case, in the form of nymously delivered film. He refused to specify the nature of film, but did say that it was proving 'very helpful'.'

"Bryant?" I ventured, looking up.

"That's who my money would be on," the Chief agreed. "And it uld seem to answer a lot of those other questions too. But nehow, Frank, I don't think we'll ever know — not for sure"

I tended to agree, and told him so. Time was getting on and ere seemed nothing more to be said, so I finished my drink and epared to take my leave. Halfway through the door, he stopped and said: "That little holiday I promised you . . ."

"Yes, Chief?" I responded eagerly, glad that he'd brought it up d I hadn't needed to.

"What's today?"

"Wednesday," I told him.

"Good, good! Take the rest of the week off and report back ere at nine o'clock sharp Monday morning. I'll have something se for you by then!"

"Cheers, Chief" I sighed, totally underwhelmed by his enerosity; "You're all heart . . ."

Driving back to my flat, I suddenly remembered what a god wful mess was waiting to celebrate my return, and I gave an nvoluntary groan at the thought of spending the rest of my little holiday' on my hands and knees clearing it up. Some omecoming! Not for me the little woman waiting with a smile and omething tasty on the kitchen table. Fat chance.

The more I thought about it, the more depressed I became, so I lecided to gird my loins for the labours ahead with a pre-emptive visit to the *Duke of York*. As I walked into my local, I recognised a few of the regulars, good nine to five men all, risking life limb working in the hazardous environment of a building soc or an insurance office. They had me down as a diving equipn salesman, and I was happy to punctuate their fantasy with tal bathyspheres and derring-do in the North Sea. If I ever told th what I really did for a living, they doubtless wouldn't believe m didn't myself half the time.

By the time I started on my fourth pint of Young's Best, world had taken on a far kindlier aspect. The bull battered ch shop of my flat was still, if not a million miles away, then at lea hundred yards removed across The Green, and finding my back in the old routine I had begun to feel halfway human aga

Looking round at the trouble free faces of my bar-proppi companions, I couldn't help but feel I might be better off do something more relaxing than sorting out other people's di work. If I'd stayed much longer, I would probably have fou myself promising to join the Rotary Club and take up somethi acceptable like matchbox collecting. So I left the pub before could get around to taking my resolutions seriously, knowing o too well they would all go out of the window as soon as my fo day's leave was over.

Quite honestly, I was absolutely knackered, and it's at times li those, when my defences are really down, that I seriously consid taking up semi-detached living, saving up for a set of Tony Jack golf clubs or an annual holiday in Spain. No; anywhere but Spai I am what I am and that's all that I am. Not for the first time, realised that I had turned into the kind of man my dear old n used to warn me about and, equally, that there was not a dam thing I could do about it.

Picking up the month's accumulation of mail on my way into t house, my attention was immediately drawn to an enormous bu envelope with 'METROPOLITANN POLICE' printed in t bottom right hand corner.

"This is it, Ginger old son..." I told myself as I ran my fing along the flap to open it;"... it'll be handlebars and cycle clips f

›u from now on!”

The letter inside contained no more than five or six lines, but owed all the artistry of creative writing at its very best. For not ıly did it inform me that the blood test I'd been given at Ealing ck had proved negative and that no further charges would be rought against me, it also managed to deliver a subtle warning ıat I'd be best advised to think twice before doing it again...

“T'riffic,” I sighed, my shoulders sagging with relief; “Asbo-ıtely bloody terrific!”

The spell was broken by the familiar croak of my landlady's oice, echoing down the hall.

“You're back then?” she observed through lips clamped tightly round a cigarette, screwing up her face as the smoke drifted into er eyes.

“Right first time, Mrs. P... “I smiled in return, already moving owards the stairs to escape the inevitably lengthy têtê-à-têtê that vould result if I allowed our relationship to develop any further I was nearing the top of the stairs when she called after me, telling me something about a ‘young lady’ who had come to visit me a few hours earlier. Whoever she was, she was obviously no longer there so I immediately lost interest.

Remembering what was laying in wait for me on the other side, I approached the door to my flat with trepidation, turning the keys in the lock and pushing it ajar, my eyes half closed to cushion the shock.

I got a shock alright, but certainly not the one I had been expecting. My first thoughts were that my flat had been let to someone else in my absence, but then I realised that all my personal belongings were still there: books back on their shelves, records replaced in their racks, Mum's picture back on the mantlepiece; the furniture had been righted, the table tops freshly polished, the carpet swept, the drawers replaced and repacked.

I hurried to the kitchen and found the same storey there; everything neat and tidy as a new pin. Ditto the bedroom but, returning to the sitting room, I turned in the doorway for another look and found the explanation I'd been seeking scrawled lipstick on the mirror above my bed.

I stared at it in astonishment for several seconds, then felt face cracking into a grin as I read the simple, two words messag '. . . LOVE, LINDA . . .'!

THE END

HOLIDAY GUIDE

TORREMOLINOS

MESSENGER BOOKS (Passport Series)

A typical Torremolinos setting for those seeking refreshment

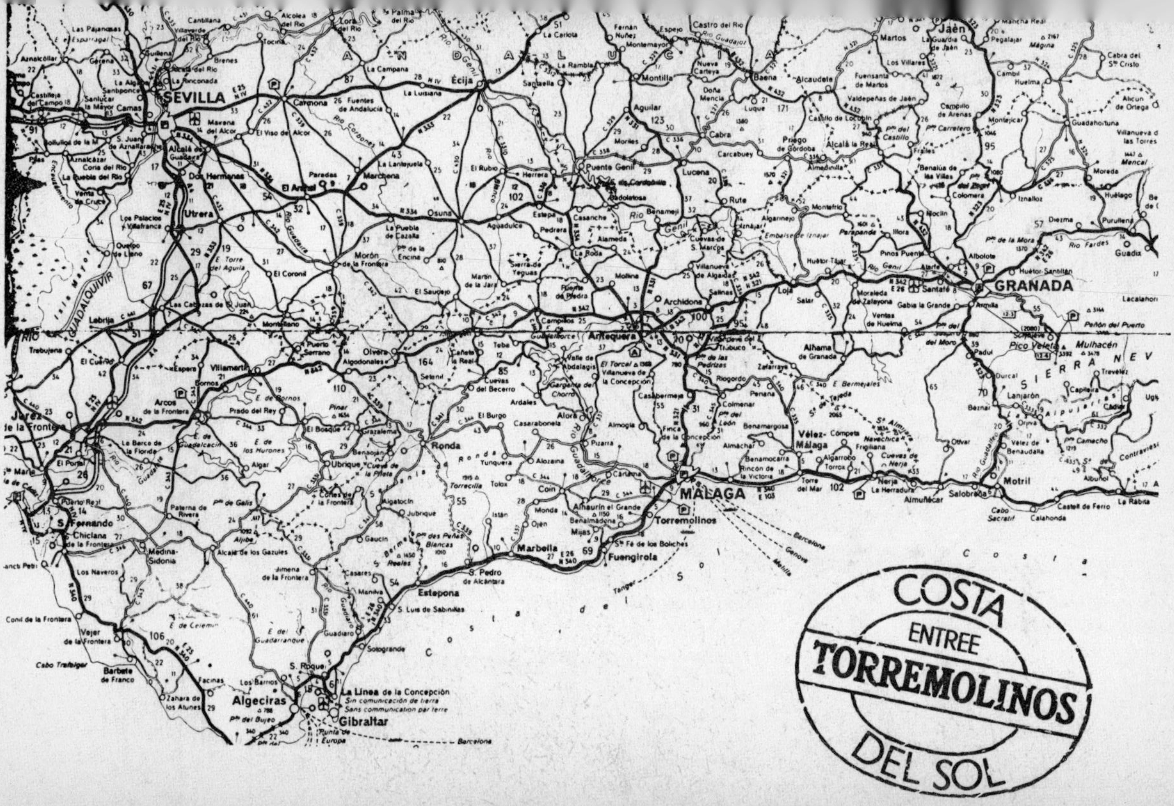

COSTA
ENTREE
TORREMOLINOS
DEL SOL
Costa del Sol
SEVILLA
GRANADA
MALAGA
Torremolinos
Fuengirola
Marbella
Estepona
Algeciras
Gibraltar
La Linea de la Concepción
Sin comunicación de tierra
Sans communication par terre
Ronda
Antequera
Jerez de la Frontera
Cádiz
Córdoba
Motril
Nerja
Vélez-Málaga
Écija
Osuna
Utrera
Carmona
Lucena
Loja
Jaén
Guadix
Mulhacén
Pico Veleta
SIERRA NEV
Tanger
Barcelona
Genova
Melilla
GUADALQUIVIR

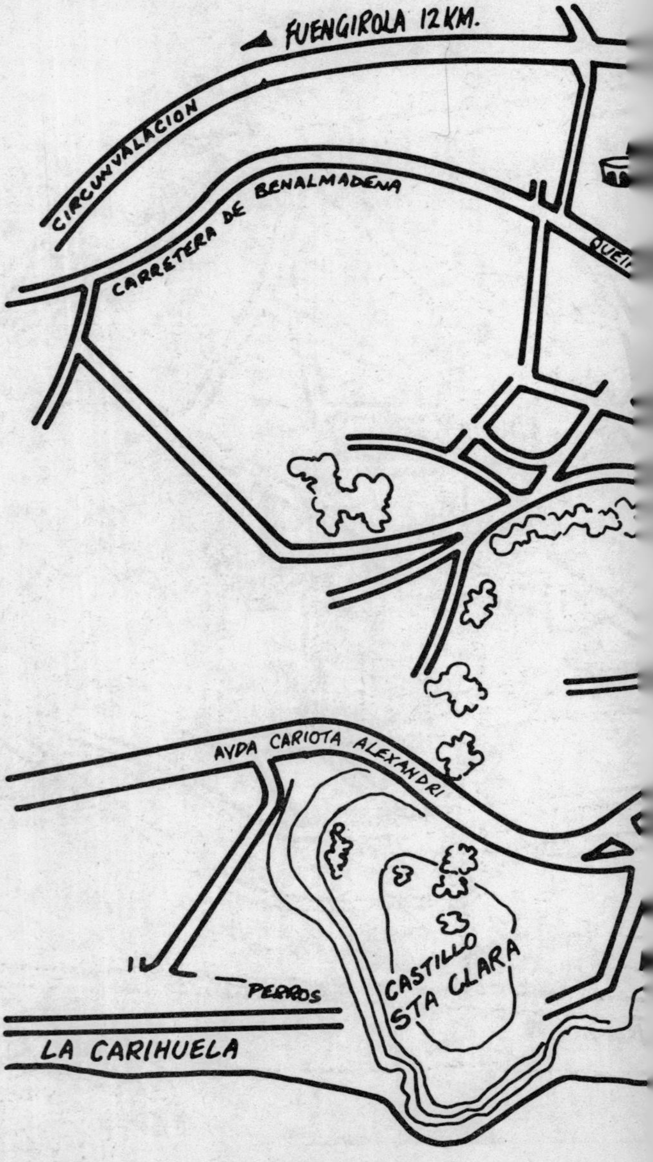
FUENGIROLA 12 KM.
CIRCUNVALACION
CARRETERA DE BENALMADENA
AVDA CARIOTA ALEXANDRI
PERROS
CASTILLO
STA CLARA
LA CARIHUELA

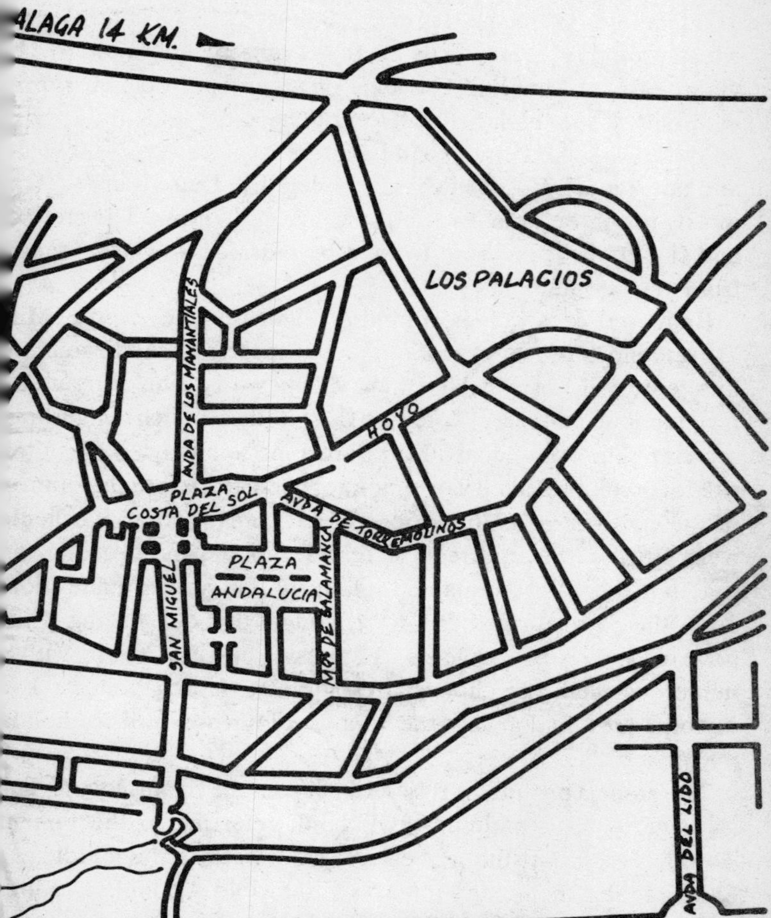

COSTA
ENTREE
TORREMOLINOS
DEL SOL

Torremolinos

Torremolinos is on the Costa del Sol — The Sunshine Coast which stretches from Tarifa in the Straits of Gibralter to C: Gata, east of Almeria. This part of Spain is protected from extremes of the inland climate by the Serrania de Ronda and Sierra Nevada and enjoys mild winters — (12 deg. C - 54 deg. and hot summers — (26 deg. C - 79 deg. F). There is enough ra mostly in winter, to allow subtropical crops to grow. The grey sa and shingle beaches were formed by moraine — glacial depo: from the mountains.

Built on a rocky promontory beneath the Sierra Mij Torremolinos is a cosmopolitan tourist resort. At the beginning this century it was a small fishing village with a single street an few humble cottages. Tradition has it that a rich Englishm: searching the entire coast from Barcelona to Huelva for a suitab site for a villa, selected Torremolinos. Shortly before the outbre of the civil war in 1936, a lodge was founded and all its client were English. Several modest restaurants appeared at the sa time but the village remained relatively remote and undevelop until the '50s. It is hard to envisage the old fishing villa nowadays as one explores the busy, bustling town with numerous high-rise hotels, restaurants, bars, 'boites', live discotheques, and always the happy, colourful crowds of holida makers.

The name Torremolinos is derived from the Spanish word Tor — tower — and molino — windmill, referring to the Piment Tower, which can still be seen and dates back to the middle age Some of the street names refer back to the old windmills — Moli del Batan, Molinillo, Molino de Manojas.

Torremolinos is only 14 km. from Malaga, the capital of t province, where the airport is. It is a good centre from which visit many beautiful and interesting places inland, Granada a Ronda being particularly noteworthy.

cursions

rther details and booking where necessary can be arranged ough hotels and travel couriers. For information about coach cursions, contact Calle de la Cruz 26, Edificio Sylvia 1, Tel 385 4.

alaga

ie capital of the province, citadel and cathedral town with rdens, parks, museums — including the Fine Arts Museum ıich has paintings done by Picasso as a child.

ijas

charming and very typical Andalusian inland town, with white ›uses, wrought iron balconies, narrow twisting streets and a ıique, square bullring. There is a small museum with a collection miniatures, and fine views from various points. A 'donkey taxi' rvice is available as an alternative to walking.

Iarbella

arts of this town have interesting relics of the many invasions to hich Spain has been subjected: Phoenician, Arab, Carthaginian, reek, Roman and Vandal. There is a ruined Muslim castle. As sewhere on this coast, the old part of the town is engulfed by a vely new town with shops, nightclubs, cafes, restaurants and a ullring.

enalmadena

1 km. This is an impressive resort with some parts still retaining riginal Andalusian features. There is a bullring and the museum ontains a priceless collection of pre-Colombian works of art and Roman and Muslim artefacts.

ivoli — Arroyo de la Miel

ituated between Torremolinos and Benalmadena, Tivoli is a plendid amusement park covering 20 acres, with entertainment of all sorts:— rides, restaurants, clubs, vintage car track, pen arcades, fountains and gardens with an open-air theatre for li shows. The name of the village — Arroyo de la Miel, means t stream of honey. There is also a Hipermarket and a street mark of Friday mornings.

Nerja

51 km from Malaga on the N340 road to Armena. here is a 3,0 year old cave where, once a year, classical ballet is performed, well as Spanish ballet. Other caves (cuevas) can be visite beautifully displayed and lit to highlight the weird shapes ar images of the stalagmites and stalactites and the subterrane lakes.

Ronda

A magnificent town perched on an immense rock on a plateau hig in the hills north west of Torremolinos. The road climbs towar the town through the mountains, bordered by ravines ar precipices, staggeringly beautiful, and it is well worth a day car-hire to visit this town. Ronda is known as the cradle bullfighting: Francisco Romero, the 'father of modern bullfigh ing' was born there and the present bullring, inaugurated in 178 is one of the oldest in Spain, with the most tradition and characte The town is built on two sides of a steep gorge, linked by a bridg and has many ancient and historic buildings, as well as a networ of charming, narrow streets and squares and peaceful garden The old town lies behind walls that remain from the Mooris occupation which lasted until 1485. Noteworthy are:— Mondra gon Palace, Collegiate Church, House of the Moorish King Palace of Marquess of Salvatierra, Moorish Baths. It is a town t stroll around and savour; there are many souvenir shops an antique shops and excellent eating places.

Granada

A city of enormous charm and versatility which should be visite ɔre than once. There are many coach tours to chose from. Of rticular attraction are:—

ɪe Alhambra — or red castle, which must be one of the most ·autiful and remarkable fortresses ever built, and **The Generalife** · the summer palace of the Kings of Granada, with cool, terraced ater-gardens and walks and pavilions. The Sierra Nevada, owcapped, massive and impressive, lies to the south, with skiing season.

euta — Tetuan (North Africa)

ɔr the more intrepid tourist there are excursions from Torremoli- ɔs to Tetuan, to see the exotic life of an old Moroccan town. The ɪy starts early with a coach ride down to Algeciras, from where it possible to get good views of Gibraltar, across the bay. A ferry osses the Straits of Gibraltar to Ceuta. Moroccan food is served ıd there is a walk through the Casbah — the market — past ıake-charmers and carpet sellers. On the return journey, the ɔaches stop in Ceuta, so that tourists may make good use of the uty-free shops where prices are extremely attractive.

eaches

here are good beaches all along the coast and the swimming is ıfe. Paddle boats, sailing boats and wind surfers can be hired, and ɪere are wind-surfing schools for the beginner, with a practice- oard set up on the beach. Sun beds and beach umbrellas can be ired for the day on all beaches for only a few pesetas. First time isitors to the Mediterranean should be warned of the very real angers of over-enthusiastic sunbathing. It is advisable to stay out f the sun between 12 noon and 4 p.m. during the first few days, as ɪe sun's rays are strongest then. Fair skins should be protected ɪith an oil, bearing a high sun-barrier rating. A hat is advised, vhen walking around in the sun: (an enormus range of styles can e bought in the town,) and dark glasses help to prevent ɪeadaches from the unaccustomed glare of the sun.

Carihuela Fishing Village

Between Torremolinos centre and Benalmadena Costa, down the water front, there is the Carihuela fishing village. Along t beach there is a promenade full of fish bars and restaurants, typi Spanish bars, souvenir shops, stalls, and even English pubs. T food is varied and excellent. Among the many good restuarar are:—

El Cangrejo, (the crab)
Casa Paco
El Roquero
Casa Guaquin

Fuengirola

This is a popular resort between Torremolinos and Marbella. has the longest promenade on the coast and a good shoppir centre. There are restaurants here to cater for every taste fro Indonesian to Fillipian to English. The Shakespeare is a popul: English restaurant, for those who are feeling homesick.

Kontike Expedition

This starts with a coach drive through the beautiful Andalucia countryside to the picturesque mountain village of Alora. Here, typical Spanish breakfast is served with coffee and churros (a typ of doughnut) followed by a small tumbler of brandy! The coac then climbs higher into the mountains to a beautiful lake, wher passengers board catamarans for a riotous boat trip. This i concluded with a meal of spare-ribs, salad, sardines, countr bread, baked potatoes, and dessert. Unlimited wine is served an the day concludes with a sangria party.

Donkey ride

A coach ride down the coast past Marbella and then inland to th pretty village of Istan. Here, after a light refreshment at an ol farmhouse, it is possible to mount donkeys and trek up througl the hills along the banks of a river. A wonderfully relaxed way o

e Torremolinos beaches are a big attraction

seeing more of the countryside, followed by an Andalucian-
lunch.

Jose Banus Marina — Marbella
For those who enjoy smart boats and a millionaire atmosph
this marina is worth a visit. Here can be seen boats that are m
like floating hotels, with their own helicopter pads on deck and
a few famous faces and names — a film star's pleasure groun
surrounded by boutiques and bars and restaurants, where
prices reflect the affluence of the boat-owners!

Casinos
Nueva Andalucia next to Puerto Banus, Marbella.
Torrequebrada, in Benalmadena.

Fortuna Night-club
One of the best international clubs on the Costa del Sol. Flame
dancing, international cabaret and entertainment into the sm
hours.

Sporting facilities
When the attraction of lying on the beach has worn off, there
many opportunities for partaking in every sort of sport. Ap
from the various boats that can be hired, there is also **water-skii
skin diving and fishing. Underwater fishing,** especially on the co
of Granada, offers fine opportunities to catch eel, grouper a
dorado, especially among the rocks. It is also possible to fish
sword-fish, not far from land and abundant.
There are numerous **tennis clubs** up and down the coast, and ma
of the hotels have their own courts.
Riding is very popular and there are a number of riding scho
with expert teachers.
Hunting. Apply through the tourist office in Malaga: Larios 5, T
21 34 45. Near the coast, among other game, is the famous 'ca
hispanica' (wild mountain goat.)

. A very popular sport on the Costa del Sol, with an ever :asing number of courses and clubs.

;

re are several places in the region that are famous for their ling' waters. In Carratraca, in the province of Malaga, the :rs are known for their help in the treatment of rheumatic sses, and in Tolox, also in the province of Malaga, the waters used to help respiratory ailments. In Granada there is the jaron spar with seven springs, used for many different plaints, and Alhama de Granada, which is good for rheumat- In Marbella there is a clinic specialising in geriatric and venation treatments which claims spectacular results in restor- strength and Youth!

:re is an excellent and extremely cheap bus service that covers Costa del Sol from one end to the other, as well as the many ursion tours by chartered coach.

rist Information

remolinos. Oficina de Turismo
Nogalera — Tel. 38 15 78.

llfighting

s best to have some idea of what you are in for and what it is all out. First timers are advised that it can be an upsetting perience.

Bullfighting on horseback was considered an honourable pass- ne among Spanish knights, from the Middle Ages until 18th ntury. Then the Bourbons, who had no love of such a ood-thirsty sport, arrived on the throne and it became a sport of lower classes, with the bullfighter on foot.

e fight is divided into three distinct acts (tercios), each marked trumpet calls.

e President enters his box. The band plays a paso-doble for the

Paseo — the Grand Entry — led by two mounted attendan 17th Century costume. These are followed by the toreros, or contestants: the three matadores (from matar — to kill), eac his 'costume of lights', leading his cuadrilla — team.

Act 1: entry of bull and assessment by matador.

The Cape: (capea). Peones — foot-followers — attract the b attention with the cape while the matador watches. He then ta over and plays the bull with his cape, demonstrating his skill courage and assessing the bull's speed, agility and intelliger

The Pikes: (pica). Picadores, on padded horses, thrust pikes the bull's withers. This slows it down and shows its skill.

Act 2: the banderillas.

To rouse the bull further, banderilleros plant pairs of beribbo darts in his withers, skillfully avoiding his horns.

Act 3: The kill

La faena de muleta — this is the deft work with the muleta, small red cape bound to a stick. The matador salutes the preside dedicates (brindar) the bull to a particular person or to the cro throws off his hat and faces the bull. With his sword in his ri hand and his muleta in his left, he plays the bull, displaying all grace, skill and courage.

The Estocada — the sword thrust. The matador advances on bull, his sword straight out before him and thrusts it down betwe the shoulder blades into the heart.

Trophies: a particularly brilliant performance by the matador be greeted by rapturous applause from the crowd and he will th be awarded one or both ears and occasionally the tail also

Other types of fight that are worth watching are:—

Capeas:— popular festivals at which young amateurs match th skill against bulls in village squares.

Novilladas:— 3 year old bulls, novillos, are fought by apprent toreadores, novilleros.

Rejoneador:— a fight where the matador is mounted.

pping:
: value of the peseta fluctuates from day to day. In Spring 1984, ough guide for easy calculation gives you 100 pesetas — 50 ice. 1,000 pesetas — £5. This is very approximate — in fact you getting slightly over 200 pesetas to the pound. Do not be npted to buy pesetas in the British airport on departure — you a better rate at the exchange banks in Spain.

nk hours: Monday - Friday: 9 a.m. - 2 p.m. Saturday: 9 a.m. - 1 n.

op hours: these vary enormously, tourist gift-shops tending to y open even during siesta in busy resorts. A rough guide would : 9 a.m. - 1 p.m.: 4 p.m. - 8 p.m. Saturday 9 a.m. - 2 p.m.

stage To U.K. Postcards, air mail, 26 pesetas. Letters, air mail, pesetas.

hat to bring back from Spain:

lass
ottery and earthenware, ceramics, damascene ware, terracotta,
oes,
ft leather clothes,
ather goods of all kinds, including embossed leather
igree jewellery
ce
nbroidery
opper ewers
arquetry
sparto grasswork
rpets
lmond products — marzipan, sugar almonds etc.
live oil
hawls
rought iron

willow baskets

There are so many shops in the town that it is possible to spe days browsing. Good bargains can be found in the local str markets which are held on different days. Times can be obtain from hotel reception.

The most popular shopping area is Calle San Miguel, and t arcades leading off it.

Food and drink

There are literally hundreds of restaurants and cafes in Torremc nos, offering an international choice of food. Many places prouc advertise English Breakfasts, and it is possible to visit Irish taver and Scottish bars. However, the local food is delicious, especia the sea food, and should be sampled. Prawns, shrimps, musse squid, sword-fish, mullet, and many more, all are served in variety of ways. Typical Spanish dishes include:—

Paella — famous Spanish risotto — a delicious concoction saffron rice with prawns, shrimps, mussels, squid, chicken, rabb peas, peppers etc.

Gazpacho — fresh vegetables served in a chilled, spicy sou

Shrimp 'al-pil-pil': shrimps in garlic and oil.

Goosefish soup.

Sopa de ajo — a thick soup of finely chopped garlic, with paprik breadcrumbs and eggs.

Huevos a la flamenca — baked eggs, asparagus, red peppers ar peas over a sausage and ham base.

Tortilla española, — Spanish potato omelet.

Fabada asturiana — a hearty stew of beans, ham, pork, sausag onions, garlic, saffron etc.

Cocas — Spanish-style pizza.

Tumbet — Potatoes, aubergines, peppers and tomato sauce. A good summer dish.

Espignada:— pie filled with eels and highly seasoned vegetable ical fruits include:— oranges, lemons, grapefruits, melons, pes, medlars. Dried fruit:— raisins, dates and figs. Almonds walnuts are locally grown.

ere is enormous variety of wine and champagne and spirits to t all pockets and all tastes. The wine of Malaga is universally nous and was known in the time of the Phoenicians and Romans its sweet flavour and bouquet. Local wines sold for less than 50 nce a bottle in supermarkets are excellent value. Most bars ve imaginative cocktails with 'house' names. Sangria is a pular drink: a mix of red wine, orange and lemon juice, brandy, neral water, slices of fruit and plenty of ice.

e duty-free shop in Malaga airport is well stocked with every rt of drink as well as tobacco and perfume and gifts.

eful Vocabulary

s, no	si, no
od morning	buenos dias
od afternoon	buenas tardes
odbye	hasta luego, hasta pronto, adios
ease	por favor
ank you	gracias
ank you very much	muchas gracias
cuse me	perdone
don't understand	no entiendo
hen?	¿cuando
hat time?	¿a que hora?
day	hoy
morrow	mañana
morrow morning	mañana por la mañana
morrow afternoon	mañana por la tarde
ow much? (cost)	¿cuanto? ¿vale?
o expensive	demasiado caro
uch	mucho

little	poco
more	màs
less	menos
big	grande
small	pequeño
all	todo
where is?	¿donde esta?
may one visit?	¿se pueda visitar?
on the right	a la derecha
on the left	a la izquierda
road works	obras
danger, dangerous	peligrosa
beware, take care	cuidado
open	abierto
closed	cerrado
no entry, prohibited	prohibido
entrance	entrada
exit	salida
apply to	dirigirse a
wait	esperar
beautiful	bello, hermosa
storey	piso
stairs, steps	escalera